To Rosa

Cheers !

A MONTH IN THE LIFE OF JACKSON GRIMES

By

Dickon Levinge

With my best wishes!

Best

[handwritten signature]

Published by New Generation Publishing in 2019

Copyright © Dickon Levinge 2019
www.dickonlevinge.com

First Edition

ISBN: 978-1-78955-692-6

www.newgeneration-publishing.com

New Generation Publishing

*Dedicated, with thanks, to the many reprobates &
renegades, fantasists & egotists, boulevardiers &
bullshitters I have encountered over the years.*

*There's a little bit of all of you in Jackson Grimes – and an
awful lot of Jackson Grimes in some of you.*

Prologue

'I'm not going to mention the Violinist by name. Not for fear of legal ramifications. Not to protect the innocent, the guilty, the living or the dead. And certainly not because it has been forgotten. I'm sure many of you will recall this vile, wretched creature's epithet from the countless newspaper columns, video-clips and click-bait stories during his moment of infamy.

'His name will not appear for two reasons. Firstly, it does not deserve any more recognition than it has already received. This selfish, arrogant, vile monster has already been afforded more attention than was ever deserved.

'Secondly, because this is not his story. This is the story of those whose lives were so drastically and suddenly altered by him and his impetuous, furious act of childish idiocy.

'All because he couldn't hit the right fucking note...'

Chapter 1

"I'm checking in," Jackson growled, leaning across the desk.

"Certainly, sir. May I have your booking reference?"

"I don't have one."

"Perhaps it's under your name."

"No, I mean I haven't booked."

"I see, sir. Well, that shouldn't be a problem. How long are you planning on staying with us?"

"The rest of my life."

The concierge's lively fingers paused and hovered over the keyboard. He flicked a nervous glance up to the grizzled, grey-haired man, who stared back at him with red-veined eyes.

"Or the end of the month, whichever comes first," Jackson added with a disarmingly warm grin.

The concierge returned a thin, reticent smile and, looking back to the screen, recommenced his rapid-fire typing. "And is it just you?"

"Christ, I hope so," Jackson sighed.

"Very good. I can offer you an executive room on the third floor–"

"No, no, no. Let me stop you there," Jackson interrupted, squinting at the name tag, "George. I'm not one of your fly-by-night tourists who's just rocked up on some shit-box, budget airline with an 'I Heart London' T-shirt and a fist full of Groupon vouchers. This is my town, George. I used to own this city. And I may have been away for a while but I've been coming to this fine establishment since the days when you were crapping in your nappies and drinking your milk straight from the tit. Now, I want a suite on the first floor, right up those stairs," he pointed towards the wide, sweeping staircase behind him. "Oooh!" he added, slapping the marble counter as if having had a minor epiphany, "The one Mick Jagger stays in."

George took a deep, controlled breath and forced another smile. "Your address, sir?"

"Right here."

"Yes, but where do you usually reside?"

"Well, I've been in Venice for the last few months. Paris before that."

"And what was your most recent address?"

"The Gritti Palace. So, George. You have a lot to live up to. Good luck."

George, feeling his overworked facial muscles beginning to ache, hit one final button and printed out a two-page form.

"Perhaps it would be easier if you were to just fill this out yourself, sir."

"Do you know, George, I think it would."

***

While George struggled with his new guest, half a mile north Sandra tentatively pushed her front door open to about half a foot and, as had recently become part of her routine, cautiously peered into her flat. Squinting, she strained her eyes to try and see to the far end of the long, windowless corridor. "Hugo?" she nervously called, "You there, sweetie?"

No reply.

Gripping the handle tightly – which, given her petite stature, was at about chest level – she pushed the door a little further open. Then took a first, brave step, again calling, "Hugo? Where are you, hun?"

Still nothing. Sandra took another step and, almost relaxing, placed a collection of Harrods and Harvey Nichols shopping bags on the hardwood floor. She paused to listen. Still silence.

Sandra pursed her lips and exhaled, both from the stifling heat and relief, as she stepped into her home and closed the door behind her. As soon as the lock clicked, she stopped. Froze. Listened. A low-base grunt. Slowly, she turned to face the corridor. She picked up the bags and took a few, cautious steps forward. Then she heard it again.

A loud, deep and excited, "Woof!" came from Hugo, an

2

enormous, a fawn Great Dane, all legs and smiles, as he erupted from the kitchen at the far end of the fifty-foot corridor and, gaining speed with every bound, hurled himself towards her. Sandra dropped the remaining bags and, as had recently become part of her routine, raised her hands, palms forward, while positioning herself in a, supposedly, solid and firm stance. Right foot in front of her, left behind, knees bent and ready for impact.

"Hugo, NO!" Sandra commanded, but Hugo was in the air before she'd even started saying his name. By the time she'd reached 'no' she was lying on her back and staring up at the ceiling. "Jesus, Hugo!"

Hugo, his happy tail thrashing her knees, came into her field of vision. Then obscured it completely as he gave her face a loving, sloppy lick, accompanied by another excited, "Woof", that could only have been his way of saying *"Welcome home!"*

As he turned to move away Sandra sat up and, knowing exactly what was about to follow, ordered, "Hugo, don't you *dare*!"

But it was too late. Hugo had cocked his leg and was, as had recently become part of his routine, urinating onto one of Sandra's fabulous, Jimmy Choo stilettos – dislodged from the impact, lying on its side and ripe for the pissing.

Defeated, Sandra lay back down and, again, stared up at the ceiling. Then she arched her head back to face the door and, while thinking of someone she knew to be somewhere beyond, screamed, "Bastard!"

***

"Max, you miserable old bastard, how the hell are you?"

Agog, Max nearly allowed the phone to slip from his hand. "Bloody hell," he finally replied, "Where in God's name have you been?"

"Oh, who cares where I've been? It's where I'm going that counts. Listen, I've just checked in to Claridge's–"

"Claridge's?" Max interrupted, as any responsible accountant would.

"Yes, Claridge's. Keep up, old boy. Hang on. TAXI!"

Max sighed, sat back down in his creaking, leather chair and switched on the speaker-phone. He patiently listened to the doors open and slam, followed by Jackson barking,

"Chelsea, mate. Quick as you like."

Max closed his eyes and took ten deep, measured breaths.

"Max, you still there?"

Max opened his eyes and affected a warm smile. "Yes, I'm still here," he calmly replied.

"Excellent. Let's do breakfast."

"Well, it's nearly noon."

"Is it? Sorry. My watch is still on continental time."

"Which would make it nearly one." Already, Max could feel his facade begin to crack and, as usual, he wondered if it would break towards frustration or amusement.

"Yeah, all right. No need to be picky. Look. The hotel isn't going to be ready for another couple of hours but I've heard of this fantastic new bistro up near the King's Road. It's called The New Chelsea Bistro. I'm hoping the menu is going to show a little more imagination than the name. Come and join me, yes? Lots to catch up on."

"Well, you're not wrong there, but–"

"Fantastic! I'll see you in a jiffy." The line went dead.

Max sat still for a moment, still wondering which way his emotions would swing. Then he felt the corners of his mouth curve into a bright, warm grin.

***

Half an hour later Max arrived at The New Chelsea Bistro. He went straight to the outdoor smoking area and scanned the seated crowd for that all-too-familiar, grey-streaked mop and heavy-set frame. The bulk almost disguised by an immaculately tailored, black Armani, double-breasted suit donned by a man who had clearly ignored any and all

4

sartorial changes since the early 1990s. Yet worn with such carefree confidence that it still looked fashionable.

As Max predicted, Jackson sat alone at a large, round table with an assortment of plates and glasses spread out before him.

Jackson looked up with a glowing smile and boomed, "Max, old boy! How are you? You have to try this Eggs Benedict." As if it were a a magic wand he waved his fork over his plate and enthused, "The hollandaise sauce is spectacular. It tastes like... It tastes like... Angels' pussy juice. No other way to describe it." He put down the fork, stood to greet Max with a tight, warm bear hug and, with a mischievous grin, bellowed, "Angels' fucking pussy juice, old boy!"

Max gave an unimpressed nod and casually replied, "Angels don't produce pussy juice, Jackson. They are made without genitalia." As they sat, Max flashed an apologetic smile to a nearby octogenarian couple, which entirely failed to quell their disapproving scowls.

"Really?" Jackson remarked, "Well, that hardly seems fair. Still. You've must try it. Goes perfectly with a Bloody Mary. The ones here aren't bad." Jackson leaned forward and quietly added, "Not as good as mine, of course, but still. Not bad." He waved over a waiter. "Two more of your fabulous Bloody Marys, please."

"No, I'm fine," Max protested.

"Bring them anyway. He might change his mind."

"I really won't."

"Does that mean you won't be wanting the champagne, sir?"

"What Godforsaken, twisted train of logic could possibly lead you to that conclusion?" Jackson asked, wide-eyed and dumbfounded.

"Very well, sir. Two Bloody Marys and a bottle of Veuve Clicquot."

"The most chilled bottle you can find, please. Christ, it's hot." As the waiter left Jackson returned his attention to Max.

"When did it get so hot in this town? And this late in the year, too?"

"Another Indian summer. They say it's going to be the new norm. Where the hell have you been?"

"Venice."

"Venice? Why?"

"What do you mean, why? What kind of a question is that? You go to Venice because it's Venice. Cheers." Jackson raised and then downed the end of his first Bloody Mary. As he put the glass down he frowned, cocking his head slightly and looking past Max with a squint of curiosity.

"When did you get back?"

"This morning."

"And you went straight to Claridge's?"

"Of course."

"Of course. And what, pray tell, am I doing here?"

"Having breakfast with your oldest and dearest friend. What else?" Jackson purposefully condescended.

"Lunch," Max corrected, pointing at his watch, "And I'm not having any. I have an actual, grown up business lunch appointment, for which I am already late. And you know what I mean. Out with it." Max leaned sideways into his Jackson's, now distracted, field of vision when the waiter returned with the fresh Bloody Marys and the bottle of champagne.

Jackson grabbed one of the dark red glasses before it touched the table. He took a long, deep sip, set the heavy glass onto he table and returned his attention to Max saying, "Truth be told, Maxwell, old boy, I'm in a spot of bother."

"Are you?" Max flatly responded.

"I am. Financially, that is."

"You can't be."

"I'm afraid I can be. I appear, in recent months, to have over-extended myself. Somewhat."

"And yet the first thing you did when you got back into town was to book a room in one of London's most expensive hotels."

"It's not a room. It's a suite."

"Seriously?"

"And not just any suite." Jackson leaned forward with a wide-eyed, childish grin and whispered, "It's the one Mick Jagger stays in."

"Mick Jagger – what is wrong with you?"

"Quite. And, if I'm perfectly honest, it was Venice that really wiped me out."

"Seriously?"

"Very seriously. It seems the Gritti Palace's rates have dramatically, and in my opinion quite scandalously, increased since my previous stay and, well, the bill rather took me off guard. Long story but, suffice it to say, I find I need access to the rest of my personal funds."

"The Gritti Palace? How long were you there for? And, the *rest* of your funds? Really?"

Jackson's reply came in the form of another long, thirsty sip, draining the glass, and a cocked eyebrow.

"Jesus," Max sighed.

"Indeed. So, you see my problem."

"Oh, I see your problem, all right."

"Well, good. I'm glad that's settled, then."

"What are you talking about? Nothing is settled. How can you think that anything has just been settled?"

"But, surely, as my lawyer and accountant, now that I've done the prudent and responsible thing by alerting you to my predicament, you're able to, well, you know, do your thing?"

"Do my thing?" Max's initial pleasure at seeing his friend was beginning to wane. "What, exactly, do you think my 'thing' is? I mean, first of all, I'm not your lawyer. I'm not even *a* lawyer. Secondly, I'm not actually an accountant. I am a personal wealth manager."

"Ha!"

"And, thirdly, the words 'prudent' and 'responsible' have no business, whatsoever, being anywhere near your lexicon."

"Oh, bravo. That was good. I have missed your broadsword-like wit." As Jackson spoke he removed the champagne from the ice bucket and, with one fluid movement, wrapped a white napkin around the body and moved to pour Max a glass. Max politely waved it off. Jackson poured one for himself, sat back and, again, looked past Max. He smiled, a twinkle in his eye, and raised his glass.

Max turned to see a woman, conservatively but stylishly dressed in white linen and a wide-brimmed hat, sitting alone with a book and a cup of coffee.

He looked back to Jackson jibed, "She's too young for you, *old* boy."

"The world is too young for me, Max."

Max responded with an amused half-smile, then his demeanour became serious and he asked, "Have you called your wife yet?"

Max watched for the flinch. The reach for the packet of Lucky Strikes. The ostentatious light of the Zippo and the first, deep drag. Then the hard stare back, which he knew would be the only reply.

"You should," Max quietly chided, then checked his watch. "Look, I really am late. Are you really sure about this?"

Jackson replied with a long, unflinching stare and a determined nod.

"Okay, then," Max sighed with a distinct tone of disapproval, "I'll make the arrangements when I get back to the office. But how you've managed to burn through–"

"Never mind that. And thank you. Max, Old Boy, you're a star. Stellar, fucking, legend. That's what you are."

Max stood.

"But…"

Max rolled his eyes and reluctantly replied, "Go on."

Jackson also stood and, leaning in close, quietly asked, "You don't have any readies on you, do you? You know. Just for tips."

"Oh, for the love of God." Max reached into his pocket and removed a money clip. Before he had a chance to peel off a few notes, the clip was snatched from his hand.

8

"That is mighty generous of you. I tell you what," Jackson magnanimously insisted, "Breakfast's on me."

Max couldn't help but give a smile as, while suffering another, intense bear hug, he replied, "I didn't have any breakfast, Jackson," After escaping the embrace with a hard, pat on Jackson's back, Max turned and walked away with a smile, calling over his shoulder, "Phone me later."

"I shall." Jackson called back, and he felt a warm, comfortable sensation in his being as he watched Max buttoning up the double-breast of a slim-cut, blue blazer whilst marching towards a row of growling black cabs.

Jackson threw another cigarette into his mouth and was about to light it when, from the corner of his eye, he caught another glimpse of the reading woman. The slight movement of her silent chuckle as she flicked over another page caught his attention. Her wry, crooked smile, half-hidden under the shadow of her hat's brim, piqued his interest.

Instead of sitting, he snapped the Zippo shut and returned the cigarette into the soft pack. He picked up the bottle of champagne, along with two flutes, which he cradled upside down by their bases. Holding his chest out and his stomach in, he swept forth.

"Hello," Jackson declared while placing the glasses on the table, as if greeting an old friend who'd been expecting him for a casual drink, "My companion has abandoned me along with this perfectly chilled bottle of champagne. Perhaps you might allow me to share it with you?"

Without waiting for a reply, he poured – while she stared at him with an unimpressed, suspicious glare. Narrowly peering across the open book and from below the wide-brim of her hat.

Jackson sat, beamed at her, raised his glass and sang, "Cheers."

Finally, she closed the book, leaned back and, in a soft, clipped cadence enquired, "Do we know each other?"

"Oh, no. But we should."

"Really." Her voice dropped an octave. "And why would

9

you think that?"

"Well," Jackson replied with bright eyes and a wicked grin, "Everybody should know me." He held his glass aloft with one hand while theatrically splaying the other, palm outward, as he exuberantly announced, "I'm Jackson Grimes."

She stared back at him and, for a moment, maintained a reserved, guarded facade. Then her eyes softened and she regarded Jackson with a squint of amused curiosity. She removed her hat revealing a high, finely lined forehead.

"Julia," she imparted as she leaned forward and reached for the champagne – when the violin crashed into her face. Splintering into countless, jagged shards of bloodied wood and twisted wire.

"Jesus Christ!" Jackson screamed. He found himself on his feet, backing away from Julia while she stared back at him – open-mouthed. Utterly confused. Shaking. Desperately trying to catch her breath so she could scream.

"Help!" Jackson shouted, looking around. Others sitting nearby simply stared, dumbfounded. He turned to one of them. "Well, fucking call someone!" he bellowed – forgetting that he, too, had a phone. He looked around. He looked up.

High above them, Jackson saw him. Thin-faced and pale with lank hair falling over hooded eyes, the man stared down from a fifth-floor window. Jackson felt his jaw clench as he noticed the bow in his hand. The Violinist stepped back, out of sight, and the window closed.

"You!" Jackson shouted, pointing up at the window, "Fucking you!" He took another step backwards, into the road.

It felt like he'd been given a hard shove from behind and Jackson fell to the ground. He rolled onto his back and looked up at the black taxi that had knocked him down. He could hear tyres screeching. Horns blazing. Gawkers shouting. Then it all faded away as smooth, comfortable blackness took over.

Finally, Julia screamed.

Chapter 2

"Don't worry. It's not yours."

The nurse was referring to the dried blood spatter across his white shirt that hung on the chair next to his bed, which Jackson had been staring at since he'd regained consciousness.

"Doesn't make it any easier to get out, though. Does it?" Jackson snarled.

The nurse glared at him, then jotted some notes on his chart and curtly replied, "You can go, now. Just a few cuts and bruises. You were lucky."

"What about her?" Jackson mumbled.

"Is she a friend of yours?"

"Not really. We'd just met."

The nurse gave him a cold half-smile and answered, "Quick as you can, please. We need the bed." She snapped the curtain shut.

Once she'd gone Jackson laid back down, scowled up at the ceiling and muttered, "And I need a drink."

***

Recently, I have begun to feel the innate, simmering anger I have, for a lifetime, revelled in with such pride and comfort, begin to morph into a dark, unwelcome and, at times, quite frightening sense of bitterness. Not all of the time. But there are moments. Bouts. And during these spells, where I would once laugh, I now sneer. Where I would once jest, I now jibe. Where I would once quip, I now wilfully, spitefully provoke. These are the times I fear I may be becoming cruel...

"Now, there's something you don't see too often these days."

Jackson, startled from his vague, addled attempt at concentration, turned to face the aged owner of the croaky, reedy voice. "Come again?" he grumbled, regarding the scrawny old man with a weary eye.

They sat as neighbours on grubby stools at the long bar, each with black pints before them. Shaking off his momentary annoyance at the interruption, Jackson reminded himself of one of the basic British pub rules: if you're alone at the bar, you're open to any and all conversation with any and all strangers. If you want to drink alone, go to a booth or a table. Or, better yet, go home.

"Pen an' paper," the old man toothlessly laughed in a smoky, cockney accent as he stabbed a wrinkled, yellowed finger down at Jackson's fine notepaper and Mont Blanc fountain pen. "Proper pen, an' all, hey? Not even a biro. Where's your iPad? Or your iPhone? Or, I don't know, your whatever 'i' they've come up with this week, hey?" He laughed again, his amused cackle fighting through a harsh, persistent cough which he soothed with a long draw from a white-topped stout.

Jackson smiled, deciding he liked this old fella. He pocketed his pen and paper, reached for his own drink and replied, "Well, I'm an old-fashioned sort of chap. An analogue man trapped in a digital world, you might say," Jackson uttered the statement in the clear, well-rehearsed cadence of a favourite slogan.

"Yeah. You and me both, mate." The two laughed together and Jackson looked around the proper, old-fashioned boozer. A thread-bare, faded carpet. The ceiling still yellow since they days before the smoking ban. Clapped out furniture – the upholstery stained and ragged, the varnish worn down to bare wood.

"This your local, then?" Jackson asked, slipping down from the stool and casually resting one elbow on the bar.

"Nah," the old man replied, "Across the street from the hospital. Come in here every week for a cheeky pint after me chemo." He pointed to his throat. "Got the cancer," he explained and, with a shaking hand, held up his Guinness. "Supposed to supplement the iron what's taken by the drugs. That's what I keep telling m'self, anyway," he added in a

12

conspiratorial whisper, then chuckled and sucked down the rest of his pint.

"Allow me to get you another," Jackson enthusiastically proffered, beckoning a red-faced, broad-shouldered barmaid.

"Nah, I should only have the one."

"Please," Jackson insisted.

"Ah, go on, then, mate. Twist me arm."

"Two pints of Guinness and large whisky, please, Nora." Jackson addressed Nora as if he'd been a regular for decades as opposed to a passer-by on his second drink. Nora's responding smile mirrored the sentiment.

"On the chasers, hey?" the old man grinned, "Wish I could still do that." Then he frowned and pointed to Jackson's shirt. "You been in the wars, then?"

Jackson glanced down at the dried bloodstains. He felt his smile disappear and his jaw clench. Then he flicked his eyes up at Nora as she brought his whisky while the pints settled. He nodded to her with an appreciative smile as he picked up the glass. Swirling the warm, amber liquid, he stared down into the dark spirit. Pretending he was going to nurse it as a libation but knowing full well he'd down it like a shot the moment his beer arrived. "No. Not me," he finally replied with a low mumble. Then he turned back to face the old man with a warm smile and added, "Someone else."

As he spoke, Jackson's peripheral vision caught the movement of Nora topping up the Guinness and, downing his whisky, he turned to face her. At that moment a large, Lycra-clad man with a shaved head and a thick, shapeless beard barged between him and the arriving pints, knocking Jackson's drinking arm. Jackson skilfully managed to finish the whisky, with only a drop spilling onto his chin, and glared at the intruder.

"Sorry, mate. Didn't see you there," the cyclist rasped. With a hard stare, Jackson watched the interloper push forward, lean across the bar and, dropping his cycling helmet on the counter, wave a ten pound note towards Nora. "Pint of lager, love," he cawed as Nora moved around him and delivered Jackson's pints.

"On the tab again?" she asked Jackson, irritation in her timbre.

"Please," Jackson softly replied. He gave her a reassuring smile and, flashing a glance at the cyclist, a friendly wink. She smiled back, rolled her eyes and moved on.

Jackson returned his attention to the old man, handing him a pint.

"Ah. Bless you, sir," the old man effused.

"You're more than welcome, my friend. Might I ask, what is your name?"

"It's Frank."

"What a pleasure it is to meet you, Frank. I'm Jackson. Now, we were discussing the various irritations and, indeed, irritants of the modern world. Were we not?"

"I suppose we were," Frank cackled.

"Well. Allow me to share with you one of my greatest vexations," and, with staccato syllables, he loudly vented, "Complete strangers calling me 'mate'."

"Oh, I'm sorry. It's just the way I speak."

"No, no, no. I don't mean you, Frank. You are my mate. We're having a drink together." He raised his pint. They clinked glasses, took long sips and, his voice gaining both volume and projection, Jackson continued, "No, I mean this casual way that people throw the word around to every odd and sod they meet on the street. It's so… it's so…" He looked up at the ceiling, holding his pint low and dramatically rolling his free hand as if conducting a musical search for the right word. At the same time, he repositioned himself to face the other side of the bar, so the cyclist was now directly behind him but closer, and concluded, "It's so fucking insincere. Don't you think, Frank?"

Flashing a nervous glance at the cyclist who had, he noticed, given Jackson a less than friendly look, Frank apprehensively replied, "Er, yeah. Yeah, I suppose. Sometimes."

"Sometimes. Exactly. I'd agree with you there, Frank.

Some… Times… Occasionally." Jackson gulped down half of his Guinness and, feeling his blood quicken, gleefully went on, "And on those occasions, it's almost always in the same context. Which is when some twat has physically inconvenienced you. And it's almost always in conjunction with another overused, rarely heartfelt word. 'Sorry'."

Frank gave a weak smile and nodded, then looked past Jackson towards the cyclist who, slumped across the bar, now glared at Jackson's nearing back.

"Interestingly enough," Jackson continued, his volume increasing as he inched backwards, "You mostly get it with bicyclists. These self-satisfied, holier-than-thou Lycra-louts, looking like ridiculously large packets of shrink-wrapped sausages, who peddle past at a rate of knots, usually at zebra or level crossings. Then, as they come close to knocking you over, they shout," Jackson affected a rasping inflection, "'Sorry, mate'!" He downed the rest of his pint, placed the glass on the counter, leaned back against the bar and, in the same mocking voice, repeated, "'Sorry, mate!' And, do you know what I want to say to these people, Frank?"

Frank remained silent. With wide, frightened eyes he stared up at the cyclist who now stood tall behind Jackson, glaring down at him.

"I want to call them back," Jackson effused, "and I want to say, No. No, you are not fucking sorry. And you are not my fucking mate. You are, in fact, a doubly disingenuous, selfish, arrogant…" He turned to meet the cyclist eye to eye and, with a well pleased grin, joyfully crescendoed, "…Fuck-wit!"

***

Finding himself in the Accident and Emergency department of St Thomas' Hospital twice before dinner time was not how Jackson had planned his day. Nevertheless, there he sat. Pressing a blood and beer sodden bar towel to the back of his gushing head.

The cyclist's right hook had, fortunately, failed to connect with Jackson, saving his face from any damage. Jackson had, in his own mind, skilfully avoided the punch with a swift, sideways duck that only a former high-school boxer could have achieved. In reality, as was plain to all who witnessed the altercation, he had narrowly escaped the punch in the style of a middle-aged drunk. Not so much ducking sideways as toppling backwards, tripping over a stool and tumbling head-first onto a table of glassware. A shard of which imbedded itself in the back of his skull.

"Right. We're ready for you, now," said the nurse. Then he gave Jackson a quizzical frown, double-checked the paperwork and flatly added, "Again."

Minutes later, Jackson sat in a sterile, curtained-off cubicle. The doctor, who looked to be in his early twenties but had the stance and confidence of a man in his late forties, loomed over him from behind.

"You were in here earlier, weren't you?"

"Yes. Ow!"

"Sorry. Just one more quick pinch and you shouldn't feel anything more," the doctor replied in the deep, authoritarian tone that only trained medics can muster. For a fleeting moment Jackson wondered if that was, actually, part of their training. An elocution module prior to their first residency called Politely Patronising Pronunciation.

"Ow! Goddamnit, that was neither quick nor a pinch!" Jackson griped, "What are you doing back there?"

"Just cleaning things up for you. Couple of stitches should do it," the doctor replied with some extra molasses added to his vocal texture, "Yes, you were part of that awful accident this afternoon. Terrible."

"Tell me about it," Jackson mumbled, slightly annoyed that the doctor had been correct and, true to his word, the pain was now dissipating. Giving way to a pleasant numbness and leaving him with nothing more to complain about. "Did you treat the girl?" he hesitatingly asked.

"A friend of yours?"

"Yes. Well. Sort of." In a moment of concentrated silence Jackson waited for an answer.

Finally, the doctor replied, "All done. Keep it dry for a few days. The stitches are dissolvable so that should be that." The doctor stressed the finality of the exchange by removing his latex gloves with two, sharp snaps.

Jackson stood, turned to face him and asked, "And my friend?"

"You mean your 'sort of' friend," the doctor condescendingly corrected, before abruptly yanking open the curtain and, with an imperious smile, stepping aside for Jackson to pass.

Cursing the doctor under his breath, Jackson stormed towards the nearest exit sign. Three minutes later, cursing the architect under his breath, he turned yet another corner into yet another dead end. He had yet to visit a hospital, and he had visited many, in which he had not found himself utterly lost as he attempted to leave. Getting in was rarely a problem. It was usually on a stretcher and he seldom remembered the details. Getting out, however, was, every time, another challenge entirely.

He about faced and marched back to the last crossing of identical, windowless corridors he had encountered.

"Are you lost?" asked a passing orderly.

"Nope," Jackson confidently lied, "Just heading for the exit."

"Oh, it's back where you came from."

"I can assure you it isn't."

"It is. You've just got to go up a floor."

"But I was in A and E. That's the ground floor."

"Yes, in the North Wing. But you've managed to get to the South Wing. You really have got yourself lost, haven't you?"

"It would seem so." Jackson bit the inside of his cheek, feeling his temper beginning to swell.

"On this side, the exit's on the first floor. It's a quirk of the architecture."

"Oh, is it?" Jackson grumbled.

"Just turn around and you'll find a lift. Go to the first floor. Then follow the blue line painted on the floor. You can't miss it." Jackson considered pointing out the danger of the orderly's last statement but, instead, he smiled, politely thanked him and moved on.

How could you have missed that lift? Jackson wondered while waiting for the massive, scratched, dented doors to open. *Probably too big to notice*, he decided. The neglected elevator's mechanical rumbling ended and the double-doors slowly, painfully opened with squeals of protest. Jackson stepped aside for two more orderlies, deftly managing a gurney, to exit. As he boarded he noticed that the person on the stretcher was motionless and covered with a sheet from head to toe. He shivered. *Behold your future.*

Jackson turned his attention to the control panel. Sure enough – first floor and exit. Just as he was about to press the button, he paused. He found himself staring at another destination. Sixth floor – ICU and recovery. Curious, he thought. He wondered if she'd be in there. He found himself tempted to go and see. After a moment of deliberation he decided it was an absurd idea. Irrational, misguided and foolish. He shook the moment off, took control of his impulse and resolved to go home.

Then he pressed the button for the sixth floor, watched the doors close and, taking a deep breath, cursed his own idiocy.

***

Julia's face was still. Quiet. The white, starched sheets were crisp and undisturbed but for the shallow rise and fall of her chest. Rhythmic and in time with her breathing, which was slow and silent.

A white, padded bandage covered her right eye and most of her forehead. As Jackson watched, he could see a small, moist bloodstain ever so slightly grow. Then she took a

18

slightly deeper, involuntary intake of breath and a small, almost mischievous smile curled the corners of her dry lips. The sedative was beginning to wear off, Jackson guessed, and Julia's mind was moving from the blackness of unconsciousness to the surreal world of dreamland. He wondered how she would react to the next stage. The arduous return to wakefulness. For some reason, one he could not quite fathom, he worried for her. He felt for her.

Jackson turned and was about to leave when he noticed a book, the one she had been reading, sitting on her bedside table. He wondered how it had got there. Surely, not the staff. Someone must have visited and left it for her. A husband, perhaps. Or a lover. Jackson, much to his surprise, felt a pang of jealousy. Then he looked closer at the book. He saw that the sides of the pages had an ugly, brown tinge go them. Her dried bloodstains. Not a husband or a lover then, he decided. No husband or lover could be that careless. Then he noticed the title of the book. *Venice*, by Jan Morris. He gave a single, quiet laugh and shook his head.

"What are you doing here!" Not a question, but a shrill demand.

Jackson turned to face an elderly matron glaring up at him.

"This is not an area for visitors," she hissed.

"You're quite right," Jackson replied, affecting his most charming smile which, he knew, would be utterly useless, "Actually, I'm a little lost. Looking for the way out."

"The way out? This is the sixth floor. How could the way out be on the sixth floor?"

"Good point," Jackson admitted. Then, after a moment's thought, dryly suggested, "A quirk of the architecture?"

"Out," the matron hissed. Jackson nodded and, with an overly courteous bow, made his way back to the lift.

***

In spite of the time nearing midnight, George was still manning the front desk when Jackson finally returned. He succeeded in remaining utterly unfazed, even managing a courteous smile as Jackson, bruised, dishevelled and bloodied, lurched his way towards him.

"George," Jackson dryly croaked, "Please. Tell me my suite is ready."

"Certainly, sir, and your luggage is in the bedroom," George cheerily replied, handing Jackson the keycard, "First floor, as you requested. Suite 101."

"Of course it is."

Jackson lumbered up the stairs, into the room and, without turning on the lights, stumbled towards the bed... onto which he heavily, gleefully collapsed, passing out as he fell.

Chapter 3

"You cook like a man." The words reverberated in Sandra's mind as she ran the blade deep into the red, tender meat. Slicing clean through and, with a few long, smooth strokes, halving the joint.

Every time she started work on a new menu, Jackson's first words to her, like an earworm, echoed back from the past and looped in her mind's ear. She could even hear the smile. Then, charming and charismatic. Now, through the grubby filter of history and experience, smug and swaggering.

"Excuse me, Mr Grimes?" she remembered replying, protesting far too much. Entirely too sweetly and with a shamefully coy grin. She cringed as she recalled that, she was pretty sure, she'd even fluttered her eyelids.

"Oh, please. Take it as a complement."

"I should take it to my supervisor."

"I am your supervisor."

"In that case, perhaps I should take it to your supervisor."

"Don't have one. It's my gaff, sweetheart."

"Sweetheart?" she had mimicked, raising an eyebrow and tilting her head, playfully rebuking her new, famous employer.

Sweetheart, Sandra bitterly remembered. Patronising son-of-a-bitch. She should have sued them there and then. Yet she couldn't help smiling while, as she began to slice the meat into thick, moist slices, she remembered.

"And what, exactly, do you mean by 'like a man'?"

"I mean, with passionate, reckless abandon. Just look at this wonderful workstation." She'd looked down at her designated kitchen area. This was her first day working for London's latest rising star, Jackson Grimes, in his new flagship West End eatery. She'd been told that he rarely ventured into the kitchen to see the chefs (or, as he insisted on calling them, cooks) preferring to stay front of house. Consorting with and playing to the customers. Particularly the wealthy and influential, with whom he was known to sit and carouse. Seducing them into purchasing, and helping them consume, copious volumes of convoluted cocktails and overpriced champagne.

The only time he did venture into the kitchen was to supervise special requests, or when new cooks had arrived and he had another form of seduction on his mind.

"It's a complete mess," Jackson had pointed out, sounding more impressed than displeased. After all, the kitchen wasn't his problem. He had a head chef, or chief cook, or something-or-other, whose name he could never remember, knocking about the place. "And yet there, in the centre, is a beautiful, perfect dish. Sweet, succulent and garnished to perfection." He'd ostentatiously waved his hand over the lamb cutlets Sandra had just left to rest, then turned to her and, with locked eye-contact and an impressed smile, added, "You've got talent." Sandra had felt her heart beat a little faster. A complement from Grimes. It was, she'd been told, unheard of. But she remained, she thought, cool. Aloof. That's how she was playing this one, she'd decided as he added, "A meal worthy of the finest restaurant in London."

"Just as well that it is in the finest restaurant in London, Mr Grimes," she'd quipped.

"Bravo, my dear." Jackson had replied.

Bravo-my-dear-fuck-you-sunshine, Sandra now thought as she furiously sliced through the meat, remembering how he gave that irksome, supercilious little bow that he always thought was so charming. As, at the time and to her shame, had she.

"My dear? What happened to sweetheart?" On 'sweetheart', she'd touched his elbow with the tips of her fingers.

And that was it. The flirtation had begun. Flirtation which lead to dinner, which lead to the bedroom, where they stayed for an entire bank holiday weekend. They may as well have moved in together. A month later, they did. And Jackson, now 'Jackie', made Sandra his Chief Cook.

Within a year they were engaged, business partners and,

in Sandra's world, one of London's most influential power couples. Top ten, at least.

She smiled as she recalled those heady days. Those long days. Those exciting days. Hard work morphing into harder play with no recognisable boundaries.

Those dangerous days, Max used to try to warn them over fabulous Sunday Brunches, along with Deborah.

"People need boundaries", Deborah and Max would exhort.

Deborah and Max had been married long before Sandra and Deborah even met. Otherwise, Deborah liked to say, Sandra would have been the maid of honour, just as Deborah was to be at Sandra and Jackson's wedding. It was Deborah who'd put Sandra forward for the job at Jackson's Bistro. It was Deborah and Max who brought them together.

It's all Deb's and Max's fault, Sandra suddenly found herself thinking, with a flash of anger as she finished the last slice, flipped it over and starting to carve it onto strips. Each downward cut more furious than the last. She eyed the massive pan, in which the oil began to bubble. It smoked a little and, right on cue, Hugo loped in. With a small grunt he sat, nose twitching, ears forward and eyes pleading, staring at the pan. Sandra threw him a glare, which then flashed past the hopeful dog to the peddle bin that, as of an hour ago, contained her soiled, brand-new Walter Steiger block heels.

"Not a chance, Hugo," she hissed, to which Hugo replied with a low, apologetic whimper as he lay down and lowered his jaw onto his extended paws. Sandra flashed him another look, this time catching his big, soft eyes and felt herself smile. "Jesus," she sighed, rebuking herself as she scraped the first batch of diced lamb into the hot pan, keeping back a couple of cubes which she threw to Hugo.

Hugo swallowed the meat with barely a chew and sat up, his expression of remorse now replaced with the sort of blind optimism reserved only for canines.

Sandra cut off a larger strip from the next slice to be diced and was just about to throw it to Hugo when her mobile phone vibrated. She looked at the screen. Deborah. *Speak of the fucking devil*, she thought.

"Speak of the devil," she answered, with a high voice and a wide smile, "I was just thinking about you. Were your ears burning?" She listened. She felt her face chill, her eyes widen and her smile vanish. "What?" she heard herself ask in a pitch at least two octaves lower than her greeting.

As she listened to Deborah, Hugo tentatively approached, his nose ever nearer to the strip of meat dangling from Sandra's hand, level with both her hip and his shoulder. She flashed him an angry glare, then threw the meat back onto the chopping board and yelled into the telephone, "He's fucking where?"

Chapter 4

"Jesus Christ, that's loud!" Jackson bellowed. Bleary-eyed, he turned on the bedside light and glared over at the old-fashioned telephone. A relic from the 1950s. Its shrill bell, he judged by the bleeding of his ears, had been purloined from an institutional fire alarm. "Jesus Christ, that's loud!" he repeated, this time with a rebuking, accusatory roar into the Bakelite mouthpiece. "Who the fuck is this!" As he yelled, Jackson noticed his mobile phone resting at the bottom of a jug of water beside his bed.

Interesting, he thought. He'd been tempted to dispose of that obnoxious device in just such a manner on many occasions.

A vague memory, more of a nebulous echo, floated across his mind. The constant, irritating vibration. Tap, tap, tapping on the glass-topped bedside table. Eyeing the mechanical vermin through a haze of semi-consciousness as, with each pulse, it skipped a little further along the surface.

Reaching out. Grabbing it. Feeling it shake in his fist, as if fighting for it's life, as he dropped it in the jug with a satisfying plop. Drowning the little pest forever. Then embracing the quiet calm. Falling back into the tranquility of soft, safe sleep.

"Mr Grimes?"

"What? I mean, yes. Who is this?"

"It's George, Mr Grimes. At the front desk."

"George. What time it is?"

"It's half-past six, sir."

"Good God, man! Why are you calling me at such an ungodly hour? Is there a fire? Did I ask for a wake-up call?"

"In the evening, Mr Grimes. It's half-past six in the evening."

"Oh. Well. What can I do for you, George?"

"Mr Grimes, there are two men down here to see you. Two police men?" The last line was slightly hushed, as if he'd partially covered the mouthpiece to hide an embarrassed whisper.

"And you told them I was here?"

"Well, yes."

"Jesus! What did you do that for? What do they want? What did I do?"

"Nothing. I mean, nothing that they're here for. They say you were supposed to make a statement about yesterday's accident?"

Jackson closed his eyes. He wasn't in the mood for this. Then again, he'd never be in the mood for this. He suspected he probably wasn't sober enough for this. Then again, he knew he'd never be sober enough for this.

"Mr Grimes?"

"Yes, George, I'm still here. Tell the officers I'll be right down. I'll meet them in the lobby. And do offer them a tea or a coffee, if they want one. Bobbies like that sort of thing, I'm led to believe." He hung up, stood and, with a whirling sensation immediately getting the better of him, sat down again.

Realising he was naked, Jackson looked around for his clothes. His suitcase, still unopened, lay in the corner. The garments he'd been wearing yesterday were balled up and stuffed under the bed. He could see the dried bloodstains on the creased shirt. Not the best look under the circumstances, he felt.

Jackson took a moment to think. During that moment he noticed an open bottle of red wine and a used empty glass on the coffee table. The remains of a midnight snack, he vaguely recalled. He filled the glass, knocked it back, refilled it and, after rising more carefully than before, padded his way into the bathroom.

Jackson placed his wine glass onto the black marble sink surround, leaned forward and examined his face in the concave side of the shaving mirror. Bleary, bloodshot eyes magnified and bulging towards him. Lines of laughter, tears, wisdom and misery enlarged into a puffed-out, fleshy landscape of weather-worn crevices and sun-bleached rifts. All cracked and eroded over misspent decades.

"Christ, you look like shit," Jackson sighed, before stretching back his dry, flaking lips to examine the crooked, broken teeth and blackened tongue beyond.

Rubbing three days' worth of greying stubble, he stepped back and locked eye contact with this aged stranger staring back at him, and he growled, "Everybody hates you."

The words came out as a familiar, well-rehearsed maxim. A daily mantra of despair. Jackson clenched his teeth and followed the statement with a squinted glower.

Then he frowned. His gaze caught something over the grey-haired shoulder of the beast in the mirror. There, on the inside hook of the bathroom door, hung the answer to his sartorial conundrum. He looked back to his mirrored self and the pair shared a wicked, conspiratorial smile along with a dry, impish cackle.

***

George stared, his eyes wide with embarrassment and his jaw clenched with disapproval, at Jackson descending the main stairway into the lobby. "Mr Grimes," he protested

"I know, George, I know," Jackson yawned, taking care not to spill any wine from the brim-filled glass as he pulled tight the cord of the white, Claridge's emblazoned bathrobe, "But I haven't had a chance to unpack, yet, and the clothes I was wearing are, to put it mildly, not in the best of nick. And, to be fair, you don't appear to have provided me with any slippers to match this wonderful bathrobe. Which is why I'm forced to look so ridiculous wearing it with these black loafers."

Before George could respond, Jackson looked past him at the two uniformed policemen and bellowed, "Gentlemen!" He approached the officers, both of whom regarded him with dour looks that, he assumed, reflected their professional demeanour. "I do apologise for keeping you waiting. Has

George offered you any refreshments?"

"We're fine, thank you," replied the first, with a polite nod.

"We're not here for refreshments, Mr Grimes," his colleague added with a clipped tone and a stiff neck, "Just to take a statement and then we'll be off."

"Very well, then," Jackson relied in a low, disappointed tone, concluding he didn't like this second officer as much as the first, "Shall we?" He gestured to a nearby seat.

"You're a hard man to pin down, Mr Grimes," the second officer, who Jackson decided was Bad Cop, griped as he sat.

"Yes," continued Good Cop, in a less judgemental tone, "We've been trying your mobile phone all day."

"I don't have a mobile phone."

"Since when?" Bad Cop probed, notebook and pen at the ready.

"Oh, I'd say…" Jackson consulted his Rolex Mariner and brightly replied, "Since about eleven-thirty," he sipped his wine, responded to Bad Cop's chiding glare with a wide grin, then continued to Good Cop, "Maybe a little closer to noon. How did you track me down, anyway?"

"It's our job to track people down, Mr Grimes!" Bad Cop rasped through clenched teeth, before being interrupted by his more diplomatic partner.

"Through your emergency contact at the hospital."

"Ah," Jackson sighed, "so I see." He looked past Good Cop and, rising from his seat, called out, "Max, old boy, what a pleasant surprise."

"A pleasant surprise?" Max replied as he blustered in, hurried and unsettled, "Jackson, what the hell has happened? Are you okay?"

"Yes, yes, I'm fine. Nothing going on that requires a lawyer. At least I hope not. Do I require a lawyer?" he asked Good Cop, suddenly worried.

"No," The officer turned to Max, "He doesn't require a lawyer."

"I'm not a lawyer," Max barked as he sat.

"Really?" Jackson retorted with a puzzled frown. "When

did you stop being a lawyer?"

"I've never been a lawyer! Not everybody with a law degree is a lawyer! Now, what the hell is going on?"

"If I might proceed," interrupted Good Cop, suddenly not appearing so good, Jackson noticed, "Mr Grimes witnessed an accident yesterday lunchtime. During which he also, I understand, suffered minor injury?"

"Oh, absolutely," Jackson affirmed with utmost seriousness, "And, possibly, not so minor. I might have to sue. If I can find a decent lawyer, that is. Since I've just found out that, apparently, I don't have one."

"Stick to the point, Jackson," Max prompted.

"Yes, that would be helpful," Good Cop agreed, while his increasingly tetchy partner frustratedly jotted, "If we could just get a brief statement from you."

"By all means," Jackson said, leaning back and spreading his palms, "Shall I begin?"

"Please."

"Well," Jackson took a sip of wine and cleared his throat, "It was a fresh, sun-kissed morning in Chelsea when I found myself sitting outside a charming bistro just off the King's Road."

Max closed his eyes and, tucking his chin into his chest and tried to make himself as small as possible.

"Al Fresco," Jackson continued, "I had just consumed, accompanied by a wonderfully spiced bloody Mary and a perfectly chilled glass of Veuve Clicquot, an Eggs Benedict. Which, as I think my friend here will attest, could only be describe as utterly delectable. It was the hollandaise sauce, you see. The only way I could really describe it was that it... Well... it tasted like angels'–"

"Jackson!" Max finally interjected, "Please. These officers are terribly busy. Perhaps you just get to the point?"

Jackson gave Max a knowing, mischievous grin, then continued, "Certainly. It was after my friend and, apparently, former lawyer here, had left that I approached and introduced myself to a creature of rare beauty. And just as she smiled, the sweetest of smiles, well," he raised his hand and, after a moment's hesitation, slapped it onto the table, "That's when it hit."

"By 'it', you mean the violin striking the lady?"

Jackson nodded. "The violin," he confirmed.

"And did you see him?"

"See who?"

"The suspect, Mr Grimes. The violinist."

"Oh, him? Absolutely! Standing up there, staring out of the window and then scurrying back into the shadows like the rodent he resembled."

"So, you think you'd recognise him again?"

"Oh, most certainly. Greasy haired, rat-faced, skinny streak of piss. I'd recognise him anywhere."

"Would you be willing to come into the station, sign a statement and look at some photographs?"

"Just tell me where and when and I'll be there."

"Savile Row Police Station, nine o'clock tomorrow?"

"Nine o'clock. In the morning?" Jackson winced, "Could we make it a little later?"

"Nine. He'll be there," Max flatly stated, bringing the discussion to a close.

***

A few moments later, Jackson and Max stood at the bottom of the steps watching the officers, as Jackson, much to Max's embarrassment, had put it, "Plod their way home".

"Christ, Jackson," Max groaned, "Less than two days back in town and you're already causing trouble."

"I didn't cause anything, thank you very much."

"Well, you're not exactly helping, are you? I mean, look at you. What are you doing?"

"Well, right now, I'm going to go upstairs, get dressed and then go to the Fumoir Bar, where I shall attempt to teach Frankie how to make a half-decent whisky sour. Why don't you go on ahead and I'll join you in, say, twenty minutes?

Give you a chance to catch up," Jackson raised his glass, "So I don't feel so guilty about drinking more than you."

"No. And you've never felt guilty about anything in your life. And, just to be clear, no."

"Max," Jackson grinned, leaning forward and placing his hand on Max's shoulder, "Come on. When was the last time you and I sat down for a good, old-fashioned boozing session?"

"It was a little under a year ago on our birthday and my head still hurts. So no, thank you. I'm going home."

"Why?"

"Why? Because I have a wife, Jackson. A wife I happen to love, and who loves me, and I'd like to keep it that way."

"Oh, please. She'll understand. One drink." Jackson gave Max's shoulder a gentle squeeze, an affectionate shake and hit him with another, puppy-dog smile. "These times are precious, old boy. They don't happen as often as they used to. And, who knows? One day, perhaps sooner rather than later, they may cease altogether."

Max rolled his eyes. "Jesus Christ, Jackson. That's a little cryptic, even for you." He checked his watch and sighed. "Okay. Twenty minutes, then one drink. One. And that's it. Understand?"

"Absolutely," Jackson sang, then turned to ascend the stairs. Max checked his watch, took out his phone and, while dialling Deborah, made his way towards the bar.

As Jackson padded his way up the stairs he happened to glance down at the cuff of his bathrobe, on which he noticed a small red wine stain. He tutted, gave it a rub, and then smiled with an impulsive, wicked thought. At the top of the stairs he turned to face the lobby below and called out, "Ahoy, George."

George, attending to an elderly American couple, each wearing a baseball cap declaring 'Fifty Years' Time Served', looked up to Jackson. To his horror, Jackson removed the robe and threw it down, bellowing, "Bit of a stain on this one, I'm afraid. Could you be a star and send up another? And

31

some slippers, please. There's a good chap."

From the entrance of the bar, Max watched with a wide grin as Jackson, naked, pale and flabby, turned towards his room, leaving George and his American guests agog.

***

"Well, Frankie. Now that you have mastered the whisky sour, let's move onto the Manhattan, shall we?" Jackson, once again wearing a black Armani suit, stood tall and confident behind the bar. He gestured to a row of five lowball glasses - each squat, heavy and filled with a golden elixir topped with an orange garnish.

Frankie, a dramatically beautiful woman in her late thirties, standing well over six foot and wearing a wide belt pulled tight to exaggerate her hourglass figure, smiled patiently and replied, "Well, thank you for that, Mr Grimes," in a husky, Southern United States accent, "But I really don't see why it took you three rounds to explain it to me."

"Well, you kept putting egg white in it. Egg white has no business in a whisky sour. That is a Boston sour." Jackson turned to face the elderly American couple, who sat with Max on the red velveted stools on the customer side of the small, mahogany bar, lent towards the elderly gentleman and whispered, "And we wouldn't want anything do with Boston, now. Would we, Phil?"

"God-damn, Celtic sons-of-bitches!" Phil spat in a thick, New York accent, while reaching for one of the drinks.

"Damn right, Phil," Jackson goaded, his usually clipped, rolling inflections casually drifting towards the mid-Atlantic, "You say it like it is."

"Aw, Jackie. Don't encourage him."

Jackson gave a slight shiver as the elderly lady called him 'Jackie', but smiled back saying, "So sorry, Babs." Then he raised his glass and loudly proclaimed, "And a happy, joyful anniversary to you both. Fifty years, hey? You guys have been married as long as I've been alive. Almost to the day."

32

"Like the hats say," Phil chortled, "A life sentence." Babs rolled her eyes and gave her husband a sharp dig in the side.

Jackson raised his glass and, leading the others, again toasted, "To a life sentence."

"A life sentence!" The group cheered. They drank and Jackson slammed down his now half empty glass. "Now," he moved on, "Manhattans. Yes?"

"No, Mr Grimes," Frankie smiled, "I think mixology class is through for tonight."

"Oh, please," Jackson gushed, "Call be Jackson."

"Jackson," Frankie repeated, smiling sweetly and looking him in the eye.

"Yes, Frankie," Jackson replied, mirroring her smile and stance.

Frankie leaned forward, as if to kiss his cheek, then whispered into his ear, "Get the hell out from behind my bar or you will never, ever be served in here again." She stepped back and with another wide, sweet grin added, "Comprende amigo?"

Jackson raised his hands in surrender. "Of course, Frankie. Your bar, your rules."

"Damn right, baby."

"Damn right, baby," Max repeated with a silly, tipsy laugh and whispered to Jackson, "She sounds like you when we first met."

Jackson raised his glass to Babs and Phil, drained it and he moved to join Max on the customer side of the bar. "Perhaps we should move to a table," he quietly suggested.

"Damn right, baby!" Max grinned, then broke into a minor fit of silly giggles.

"And may we have two large Hanyu 2000s?" Jackson asked Frankie as he and Max moved towards the corner table, "I've yet to try any of these Japanese whiskies and I hear that's a good one to start on."

"That it is," Frankie concurred, turning to the glass backlit shelves of golden whiskies behind the bar and retrieving the Hanyu from the top.

"Why is this bar full of Americans?" Max asked as he sat.

"Why shouldn't it be?" Jackson retorted, "This is the Fumoir Bar in Claridge's of London. The finest bar in the best hotel in the greatest, most cosmopolitan city in the world. This evening, it's full of Americans. Tomorrow, it could be full of Canadians. Or Australians, or Chinese, or Indians, or any breed of European you care to mention. That's what makes it so wonderful."

Max noted how, as Jackson expounded his love for the city and, indeed, the bar in which they sat, shone through. He smiled, feeling a warmth towards his friend.

Jackson quietened and the two relaxed in the corner table with their Japanese whiskeys. Jackson, with a wistful smile of nostalgia, looked around the familiar, tiny space. Red velvet and dark wood. A long, plush sofa running the length of the wood-panelled wall. Small, round tables with low, round seats. Crystal, art-deco light fixtures over a row of four black and white photographs, each of a twentieth century icon smoking with hungry, decadent relish. Jackson focused on the one nearest – a boyish Mick Jagger exhaling a white plume for a youthful Keith Richards to inhale.

"God, I would kill for a cigar right now," Jackson lamented. "I mean, how can they expect us to sit here, in the Fumoir Bar, sipping fine whisky, and not smoke an equally fine cigar? How can that even be allowed?"

"For once, Jackson, you will get no argument from me," Max replied, raising his Hanyu and taking a shallow sip.

Jackson leaned back, grinned and, with a dangerous twinkle in his eye, asked, "You remember it, Max?"

"Remember what?" Max apprehensively replied.

"Remember what? This," Jackson waved his hand around the general area, "Here. Us."

"Jackson, what are you talking about?"

"I'm talking about you and me, old boy. Here. On that day of all days, when it all changed. The first of July." Jackson leaned forward and ominously whispered, "Two-thousand and seven."

Max took a moment to recall, then smiled and, in unison, they both laughed – remembering how, at eleven o'clock in the morning on that date they met there, each furnished with a box of their favourite cigars. Equipped, armed and ready to take on the last day of liberty before that travesty of state intervention became law…

***

…"You mark my words, Max. This is just the beginning!" Jackson warned as he cut the paper seal on his box of twenty-five Cohiba Esplendidos. They sat in the same seat that they would twelve years later. Jackson a little thinner, a little less grey, but still wearing the same Armani suit. Max, the man with the portrait in his attic, looking exactly as he would a decade later – and, indeed, exactly as he had ten years previously. Strong jawed, disgustingly handsome and bearing the physique of an athlete in his prime. In spite of the fact that, to the best of Jackson's knowledge, Max had never even crossed the threshold of a gym.

"I think you're being a little paranoid, Jackson," Max attempted to reason as he lit his cigar, "I mean," he puffed, "They do have a point. Can you imagine working in here? Look at this place. You can hardly see the bar and it's only about eight feet away. Perhaps there really is a health and safety issue. You know. Passive smoking, and all that?"

"Oh, passive smoking. Passive fucking smoking. What a load of horse shit that is, and you know it."

"And remind me, again, why aren't we at your fine establishment today?"

"Because we have a strict no smoking policy."

"So, you deplore the smoking ban, yet your own restaurant is entirely no smoking."

"Of course it is. You can't have people trying to enjoy a fine dining experience while they're enveloped in the noxious exhaust fumes expelled the likes of us as we indulge in our vile habits. And, certainly not at the prices I charge."

"And you don't see a certain inconsistency, there?"

"Certainly not. I am just as capable of hypocrisy as the next man, old boy. But, in my defence, Jackson's is a place for first rate food, superb, overpriced wine and extravagant cocktails. All of which require the palate to remain unsullied by such pollutants as these," he took a particularly heavy drag and exhaled the smoke towards Max, shrouding them both in a blue-grey, wispy cloud, "This, on the other hand, is a place for enjoying insanely overpriced whiskies and puffing on exquisite cigars. That is, until tonight, when the fascists take over."

"Fascists."

"Damn right. Jackson's? My place, my rules. Not the government's. Here? Claridge's place, Claridge's rules. Not the government's. That's the way it should work, anyway. And this is just the beginning, Max. You mark my words." Jackson leaned forward, elbows on the table, and adopted his most conspiratorial demeanour. "Over the last decade or so, what have we seen? An anti-smoking propaganda campaign that even Edward fucking Bernays could have been proud of. Well, they've won the first battle. So, what do you think will be next?"

"I don't know, Jackson. Do tell."

"Booze, Max. That's what they're going to try and take away from us next," he defiantly held his glass aloft, "Bloody booze."

"I sincerely doubt that," Max replied with a patronising chuckle.

"Oh, yeah? You haven't seen the signs? Heard the fucking Guardianistas rattling on about higher alcohol taxes, curbs on advertising and the health warnings on bottles and cans? That's how it all started with this, remember," Jackson held up his already spent cigar, stubbed out the butt and reached for another, "Duck and cover, old boy. Duck and cover. And, I can tell you, they won't stop there. Anything that they deem even slightly bad for you, they'll try to stop because they can't trust us to look after ourselves. Christ, before long they'll be after soft drinks because they're too fucking fizzy. Probably bring in some sort of burping tax."

"Oh, don't be ridiculous, Jackson," Max guffawed, "Nobody's going to try and ban soft drinks!" Max laughed until tears ran down his face while Jackson cut, warmed and lit his next cigar. One of Max's, a Bolivar super corona. "Anyway," Max continued, "Speaking of Jackson's, if you're not running the place today, who is?"

"I left Sandy in charge."

Max nearly dropped his cigar into his drink. "You're letting Sandra handle front of house?"

Jackson gave an uncharacteristically nonchalant shrug. "Why not? She's more than capable." Then he narrowed his eyes and gave Max a look of doubt. "You think she's capable, don't you?"

"Oh, I have no doubt," Max chuckled, "I'm just amazed you do. Jackson Grimes, the greatest of all control freaks."

Max shook his head and gave a wry smile at Jackson who, suddenly subdued, sat back, stared into the smoke and wondered if he'd made the best decision…

***

…"You need to talk to Sandra," Max soberly stated, wrenching Jackson back from their sentimental visit to the mid-noughties.

Jackson heaved a reluctant sigh, finished his whisky, gestured to Frankie for a refill and flatly asked, "And, why would I want to do that?" with a bored stare.

"Because she came over to the house yesterday, in floods of tears, and made Deborah's afternoon a living hell. Because then Debs took it all out on me and made my evening a living hell. But mostly, Jackson, because she's your wife. And she hasn't seen or heard from you in almost a year."

"Ex-wife."

"Not until she signs divorce papers."

"You see? I knew you were a lawyer."

"Jackson, for God's sake."

"Well, then she should just sit down and sign the bloody papers, Max. Instead of just tearing them up and throwing them away. Shouldn't she?" Jackson hissed, ending by slamming a tightly clenched fist onto the table. Max raised his palms. Rarely had he seen Jackson genuinely angry, properly enraged, but he could see this was getting close. As did Jackson who, taking Max's lead, raised his hands and nodded an apology.

"Pretty good, huh?"

"What?" Jackson snapped as he turned to face Frankie, looking slightly taken aback, beside him with the next round of Hanyu. "Oh. Yes indeed, Frankie," he forced an apologetic smile and winked, "As the Major once said, 'Damn clever, those Japanese'."

Frankie nodded, feeling a little perplexed, set down the drinks and returned to the bar.

Jackson returned his attention to Max. "And, another thing. I want my fucking dog back."

"I will see what I can do. But you need to talk to her."

Jackson shrugged. Then looked to the floor like a guilty schoolboy. Max knew this was as close to an agreement as he was going to get. He sat back, smiled and returning to the past, asked, "Do you remember the rest of that night?"

"What?" Jackson, again, snapped, then caught the gear change. "Oh. Yeah. Most of it, I think."

The duo had stayed at their corner table in the Fumoir Bar until they'd consumed all of their cigars along with a bottle of malt, before moving on to Soho and The Pub That Dare Not Speak Its Name. Jackson's and Max's sin-stained, Soho bolt-hole. Jackson, Max and a disparate gathering of misfits and miscreants. They caroused and chain smoked until dawn the following morning, until the ban officially started, when they all stumbled their separate ways into the new, smoke free dawn.

"I think I still have one of the ashtrays," Max wistfully sighed.

Chapter 5

Yesterday, I found myself watching an inordinate amount of daytime television. Did you know, there is a 'reality documentary series' (yes, that's really what they're called) about, of all the cunts one could possibly choose to document, bailiffs? I use the expletive not to shock or provoke but with genuine, nauseated fury because, let's face it, it takes a special kind of cunt to even consider becoming a bailiff.

I shit you not, I've seen it for myself. A camera crew following a bunch of jackbooted thugs as they bully their way into people's homes and either forcibly remove their belongings or chuck the poor souls out onto the street. When asked to justify their actions the reply is, inevitably, the same: "I'm only doing my job." Personally, I thought that excuse lost all currency back in the late 1940s, but perhaps that's just me.

And, here's the kicker. We, the audience, are supposed to be on the side of these neckless, knuckle-dragging Neanderthals!

And people wonder why I drink.

***

"Everybody hates you."

The habitual salutation came from the grizzled, old man in the mirror. Jackson frenziedly whipped soap into a thick, frothy lather with an oversized, badger-hair brush. He covered his bristled face with the warm, comforting foam and began scraping away the coarse, greying evidence of another day's survival. He used a single-bladed, double-sided safety razor with an antique, mother-of-pearl handle. A gift for his sixteenth birthday which he had proudly used, the calendar reminded him with such cold detachment, for nearly thirty-four years.

The calendar. He'd finally hung it up that morning. Over

the antique, oak desk with the leather-bound hotel information package, headed writing paper and free pen. *Not a bad free pen, not bad at all,* Jackson had thought as he'd held it in his hand. A reasonable weight and well balanced. He'd made a note to pocket it and see if the cleaning staff would leave a replacement – a game Jackson played whenever he stayed in a hotel for a prolonged period. His record was over a fortnight at Four Seasons in New York, until they switched to pencils. He ended up checking out with sixteen of those beauties. He never used them, of course, deploring any sort of ball point and being dedicated to the nib. But he always thought they might be handy to have around in case of emergencies.

The Venetians hadn't been so generous. One Gritty Palace pen was all he'd been given for several months of custom. *What a gyp*, Jackson thought, as he wiped the remnants of the soap from his fresh, clean face and returned to the living room where, once again, he turned his attention to the calendar.

He'd picked it up in Marco Polo airport on his way back to London. On sale, since there were only four months of the year left. A bargain, as far as Jackson was concerned. One month was all he'd need. September.

He threw aside the towel, poured a cup of coffee from the room service trolley and, sitting at the desk, removed the calendar from the wall. With mild curiosity, he flipped through the preceding, spent months giving each accompanying photograph a cursory examination. Mostly random, clichéd images of the usual Venetian monuments. The Piazza San Marco, Rialto Bridge, Saint Mark's Basilica. All taken at a ridiculously early hour, judging by the lack of tourists. Still, even these third-rate photographs, cheaply printed on cheaper paper, couldn't hide the majesty and beauty of this once great city state.

For September, much to Jackson's amusement, they had chosen the Bridge of Sighs. So aptly named by Lord Byron as the condemned man's final walk from the Doge's Palace to the notorious dungeons, where the only two options on offer were life imprisonment or execution. On that short walk, the prisoner would get a last fleeting look at the, then truly magnificent, city of Venice, before entering the wretched stone and iron squalor of the Doge's Dungeon. Cold, dank, windowless and hopeless.

Jackson shifted his attention to the page below. A grid of blank dates. The days of the week, Sunday through Monday, across the top. He pushed the hotel ballpoint aside, popped a brand new, sturdy marker from it's package and, with the air of one of the Doge's Ministers for Justice signing the fate of a convict, he carefully inscribed a thick, purposeful 'X' through the twenty-sixth. Then, with equal care, he drew a diagonal line through the first two, already played-out, days, before hanging the calendar back in its place.

Satisfied, he took a sip from the coffee. Then winced. *Christ*, he thought, *how is it that the one thing the best hotels in the world can never make is a decent cup of black fucking coffee?* He made a mental note to, on his way out, mention the issue to George. First, he attended to his breakfast, pouring out a glass of chilled champagne and removing the silver dome from a generous portion of creamy scrambled eggs topped with caviar.

***

A couple of hours later Jackson brightly skipped out onto the steps of Savile Row Police Station. He felt the elation of a teenager leaving a school-hall for the last time. Secure in the knowledge that, after all that hard work, they had aced that all-important final exam. At least, that's how he assumed he felt, since Jackson had never aced an exam in his life, important or otherwise.

Of course he'd recognised the villain. Or, as Bad Cop, scowling at Jackson across a set of photographs spread out on a scratched, metal table in a stark, windowless room, insisted on calling the swine, "suspect".

41

Jackson didn't *suspect* the delinquent of anything. He'd made that clear, in no uncertain terms, when he triumphantly slammed his fist onto the blackguard's photograph with a victorious cry of, "That's the bastard!"

"Are you sure?" they'd insisted on asking him. Jackson, full of confidence and righteousness, looked back down at the twelve mug-shots. Each thug looking more villainous than the previous. But none, to Jackson's assured eye, more villainous than the rat-faced, greasy-haired, beady-eyed wrong'un he'd seen leaning out of that window. Looming over the destruction he'd just caused with, what Jackson could have sworn – indeed, would be willing to swear to, in any court of the land, if required – was a glowing sense of triumph.

The officers assured him that this would not be required, thanked him for his time and, moments later, Jackson brightly skipped out onto the steps of the Savile Row Police Station.

Looking forward to his eleven o'clock Martini, Jackson was disappointed to see that the time was only just approaching ten. A good hour earlier than he'd anticipated leaving the cop-shop. He admonished himself for mistiming the morning so badly. Then decided that, actually, it was the police officers' fault for bringing him in too early and taking about half as long as they'd said they would. They'd actually managed, he rationalised, to waste his time by saving time and letting him go half an hour earlier than promised. A remarkable feat of incompetence of which, surely, only a government institution could be capable. Still, the idea amused him, and Jackson decided it would be a fine thought to mull over while taking in a West End walk to kill the hour before respectable drinking time ensued.

This had always been Jackson's favourite time of the year in London. The last vestiges of the summer-silliness were finally slipping away as, with the return of the school year and the end of the tourist season, the city's streets were finally free from both gaggles of screaming, snotty-nosed children and hordes of screeching tour groups. The latter consisting of up to fifty in each gang, vulgarly uniformed with matching baseball caps and back-packs as they raucously maraud the streets and stations of this great city.

Of all great cities, Jackson reminded himself, reflecting on how he had, during his recent travels, spent so much time apologising to his hosts for the various British mobs moving through the Champs Elysées or San Marco Square. Profusely sweating through polyester red, white and blue outfits. Their harsh laughter and shrill cries negating any and all elegance of their surroundings as they play follow the leader. The leader usually being some poor, dispirited soul forcing a pained smile while holding aloft some sort of extendable aerial with a tatty Union Flag to steer their miscreant crew of jabbering gabblers.

He crossed Regent's Street, dodging various black cabs and red double-decker buses as he ventured from Mayfair towards Soho. The latter, he recalled hearing somewhere, named after a popular hunting cry during the time of Henry VIII. He glanced towards Piccadilly Circus and, as he always did, felt a sense of warmth while regarding the elegant curve taken by the wide, iconic avenue. A happy accident, Jackson had once been told by a random acquaintance with whom, some years back, he had spent a pleasant and educational afternoon in a local watering hole – imbibing liberally while chatting seriously. The original plan, according to his best friend of the day, had been for a straight thoroughfare down to Piccadilly Circus, until John Nash's design had to be altered to accommodate some hold-out land owners. *Property developers verses NIMBYs*, Jackson smirkingly thought, *nothing new for the good old streets of London.*

Once in the narrower, grubbier streets of the village of Soho, Jackson inhaled deeply. Even the smell, he always thought, altered dramatically as one passed from one London area to another. Mayfair's fragrant aroma of expensive leather, high-end perfumes and richly scented creams now gave way to Soho's stench of stale beer, cheap wine and the festering rot of uncollected rubbish. A pungent aroma which, as he turned onto Wardour street, Jackson drew in with a perverse pleasure.

The shift in mood was further demonstrated by a loud, angry conversation creeping up behind him, to which he matched his pace in order to listen.

"Properly vexed, man! That's what I am!" a youthful, male voice, barely broken but already full of rage and desperation, furiously ranted, "I mean, she just started slapping me, man. Like, slap! Slap! Slap! One after the other, you know? And, man, I just stood there! Taking it like a bitch! You know what I mean?"

"Yeah, man!" his comrade supportively yelped.

"Yeah. Coz, you know. I thought, you can't hit a girl. Can you? I mean, that just ain't right. Is it?"

"No, man. No way that's right."

"Yeah, but look. I mean, is it? Because, you know, I was thinking, when I got home. If she can dish it out then she can take it. Right? I mean, that's equality, yeah?"

"Yeah," the friend replied, with a rising note of wariness, "Suppose so. Equality."

"Right. So, you know what? The next time she tries that shit, I'm just gonna punch her fucking lights out!"

"Yeah... no, man. That's not equality, that's assault."

The conversation drifted out of Jackson's earshot as the duo turned a corner behind him, but he could hear the vexed youth's colleague's pitch rise with stern disapproval. Jackson hoped the boy would adhere to his friend's admonishments. They were, after all, supposed to be a kinder, more evolved generation than any previous. Generation Z, Jackson had heard them labelled. More morally centred than his Generation X or the preceding Baby-Boomers and less selfish than those humourless, sanctimonious Millennials, who had crept up behind him and his peers with such predatory stealth and guile. A breed conspicuously evident in Soho as they scurried in and out of the various shiny, high-tech veneered media companies. Palms welded and stares locked to their 'devices' as they zig-zagged around each other. Blinkered to the real world while desperately searching the virtual one for short-cuts to validation and 'safe' paths away from loneliness. Tapping exuberant, desperate messages to strangers they tag as friends in the deep, dark echo chambers of the digital ether.

He checked his watch again. Half an hour until his destination opened, which was about a twenty-minute walk away. His morning was looking up. As he turned the corner from Cambridge Circus onto Charing Cross Road, taking care to avoid passing The Pub That Dare Not Speak Its Name for fear of temptation, Jackson's thoughts returned to the police interview.

He'd signed his statement, identified the culprit and, he'd felt, done his civil duty. He felt good about himself. He wondered how long the Violinist would be locked up for. Life, if Jackson had his way, after what he'd done to poor Julia. There'd be a petition to bring back the death sentence, he fantasised, if he was on the jury. Could he be on the jury? No. Jackson was no lawyer, but he was pretty sure there'd be some sort of killjoy rule against that.

Again, his mind wandered back to Julia. And just as her face popped into his mind, he stopped dead in his tracks. He focused on the spot his eye had chosen to wander, the front window of a book shop specialising in rare publications, and stared. There, on a stand in the front window, was a mint condition, first edition of *Venice*, by Jan Morris.

Chapter 6

"You're Jackson Grimes," Julia sleepily pointed out, through an opiate filtered half-smile.

"I am he," Jackson replied in as deep and throaty a voice as he could muster, "And how good of you to remember."

"Well," Julia replied, hitting a button on a remote control causing her bed to, with a loud arthritic whirr, elevate her to a seated position. Once there, she set the remote aside and continued, "I suspect one is unlikely to forget the last face one will ever see with stereoscopic vision."

"Ah," Jackson awkwardly replied while searching for an appropriate response, failing and, as usual, opting for the untoward, "I suspect you won't miss much. Most people are fairly two-dimensional, anyway."

"Present company excepted, of course."

"Speak for yourself. I'm little more than a poorly drawn cartoon. Hanna-Barbera on a bad day, at best."

"What are you doing here, Jackson Grimes?" Julia asked with a tired sigh. Jackson couldn't gauge whether her tone was one of suspicion, accusation or genuine curiosity. He sensed a cocktail of all three. Nonetheless, it was a question he felt a sudden and panicked urge to avoid. At least until he had an answer other than, *I have no idea, but here I am.*

"We made the papers," he said, attempting to divert the conversation with an abrupt cheeriness and high-pitched tone that surprised even him. As he did so he held up a copy of the *Evening Standard*, which he'd picked up from a stand outside the bookshop. There was a photograph of Julia, taken at a recent charity function, with the headline 'Kensington Charity Worker Injured in Freak Accident'.

Julia nonchalantly picked up a copy of the same edition from her bedside. "I think you'll find it was I who made it into the papers," she pointed out, her initial lethargy giving way to sharp rationality. "No mention of any debonair boulevardiers that I read, anyway. Besides, it wasn't exactly what one would call quality reporting."

"Ah. More fake news, then."

"No, I wouldn't say fake news. Just bad journalism. For a start, I don't live in Kensington and I'm not a charity worker. That's two errors in the headline alone."

"Three."

"How so?"

"Well. Would you really describe it as an accident?"

"How would you describe it, then?"

"Oh, I don't know. Misadventure? Assault? Grievous bodily harm?"

Julia cocked her head and queried, "Are you a lawyer, Mr Grimes?"

"Christ, no," Jackson chuckled, "But I have a friend who's a lawyer. Well, I thought he was a lawyer. In fact, I thought he was my lawyer. But now he says he's not."

"Not your lawyer or not your friend?"

"Not my lawyer. But I'm sure he knows a few. Why? Would you like me to find you a lawyer?"

"No, Mr Grimes," Julia replied with a hint of mockery, "I'm sure I can find some perfectly good legal representation of my own, should it be required."

"Really? Well, perhaps you should introduce me. I appear to be down on one."

"Do *you* need a lawyer?" she asked with an amused half-smile.

"Not at the moment. But it's only just coming up to lunch time and you never really know how the day's going to go. Do you?"

"No," Julia sighed, "You most certainly do not." Her smile melted and she brought her hand up to the large, pristine bandage which covered her entire forehead, right eye and most of the cheek below.

Jackson's stomach tied itself into a tight ball and he felt his face redden as he looked down to the floor.

"Good Lord, Mr Grimes. Are you actually blushing?" He could hear the smile returning to her voice and he looked back at her as she, again, asked, "Why are you here?" This time he was sure it was suspicion, with a touch of curiosity. No accusation but he strongly detected a sudden lack of patience.

Just as he was about to answer, a stern voice of authority resonated, "Yes, that's just what I was about to ask."

Jackson turned to face a tall, cadaverous man in a black, three-piece suit. "Jesus Christ, it's the Grim Reaper himself," he exclaimed, "You're a little early, old boy."

"This is Mr Robertson, Mr Grimes," Julia explained with a slight tension in her voice, "My consultant. He has, I suspect, come to give me the verdict on whether or not I shall lose my eye entirely or merely its use."

Again, Jackson felt a rare twinge of embarrassment twisting his gut. He turned back to Julia and quietly said, "For you," as he handed her a brown paper package, "Yours seemed a little worse for wear." He gestured to the stained and battered book on her bedside table.

Julia responded with a surprised arching of her visible eyebrow and a warm smile of gratitude.

"Page thirty-nine," Jackson added, "About two thirds of the way down." He threw a sideways glance of suspicion towards the consultant and dryly tagged on, "I marked it for you."

As Jackson turned to leave Julia piped, "They're moving me into a general ward tomorrow, Mr Grimes." Jackson turned back to face her as she mischievously added, "They actually allow visitors there, if you feel so inclined."

"You mean they don't allow them in here?"

"No, sir!" the consultant impatiently answered, "This is a high dependency unit. A supposedly sterile environment."

"Supposedly," Jackson purposefully repeated, "How very reassuring." He gave Julia a parting bow and continued on his way.

***

Having finally navigated his way out of the labyrinthine hospital, Jackson decided to walk back to Mayfair. He felt he needed a good march of introspection and self-examination. What, he demanded to know of himself, did he think he was doing? He had a plan. It was a solid plan. A good plan. A plan he had thought about for decades, considered carefully for the last year and one that could, in no way, accommodate any new emotional baggage. Yet, he felt a sense of elation he had not experienced for years. Perhaps even decades.

He reached the centre of Westminster Bridge and looked down at the river traffic, particularly busy during the Thames's slack water, and paused to watch a flotilla of brightly-coloured, spear-shaped yachts approaching as they cut their way towards the estuary. He'd read about them in the same paper the article about Julia appeared. They were on their way to Limehouse Basin to begin a year-long, around-the-world race. Brave folk, he thought.

And the word struck a chord in his head. Brave. Perhaps that was the quality he saw in Julia that was so foreign to his own, pitiful nature. Jackson wondered, if the Violinist's rage been that little bit stronger, if he had launched his instrument just a few inches further out and, rather than Julia, caught Jackson full in the face, would he show such stoicism and courage? *Of course not*, Jackson though, adding aloud, "Ridiculous notion, Grimes!"

Then again, perhaps bravery had nothing to do with Julia's apparent fortitude. Perhaps she was still in shock, under medication and, sometime in the near, or even distant future, it would suddenly hit her – like a second, even more vicious blow. Perhaps, rather than a tower of strength, she was merely a ticking clock.

The yachts neared the bridge, one of them pulling ahead as the skipper raised the mainsail to its maximum height. A flapping sheet tattooed with a collage of corporate logos. Then the boat turned slightly, the canvas bellowed and she lunged forward. As she glided beneath Jackson a yachtsman standing near the bow, head to toe in brand new, bright yellow oilskins, looked up.

Jackson, waving both his arms, shouted, "Ahoy, yachtsman! Lovely day for the sea, me hearty!"

The yachtsman grinned and waved back – letting go of the rigging and tumbling overboard.

"Oh, shit," Jackson mumbled.

The yachtsman's arms flailed as he desperately tried to reach the tethered life-belt that the skipper had managed to deploy while bringing the vessel back into the wind and attempting to drop the mainsail.

Bravery suddenly becoming idiocy and panic, Jackson thought, *that's more like it*. Feeling disturbingly reassured he briskly walked on, leaving the sailors to their voyage's auspicious start.

He looked over at the Houses of Parliament, covered with plastic sheeting and scaffolding as construction crews worked to fix the eroded facade – even though most would agree that the decay within was beyond repair. He eyed the concrete barriers and armoured police officers, all carrying heavy-duty carbines. From the river below he could hear the high-rev engines and sirens of the arriving Marine Rescue boats.

Normal life had resumed. Perfectly on cue, the sky darkened and a few bloated raindrops began to fall. *Time for that postponed drink*, Jackson decided, and he made a sharp turn onto the riverside, changing course from Mayfair towards the Embankment, and setting himself onto a constant bearing for the candlelit, vaulted cellar that is Gordon's Wine Bar.

Chapter 7

By the time Jackson finally got back to the hotel his late afternoon spent lunching on heavy cheeses, cold meats and several flights of sherry was beginning to get the better of him. Exhausted, he found himself in that all too familiar state of discomfort where he was beginning to feel the effects of an approaching hangover without the benefit of ever being properly drunk. A premature darkness over the city, bringing with it an unceasing deluge, along with the unseasonably stifling heat, had also served to sap what little energy he could draw from his stiff muscles and heavy bones. Even though it wasn't yet seven in the evening, all he wanted to do was sleep. Sleep, room service, more sleep, then breakfast. These were his only thoughts as he trudged into the lobby and slogged his way towards the stairs.

"Mr Grimes," George's, now familiar, sharp greeting came from behind him.

Jackson elected to ignore whatever message George had to relay. He engaged his selective hearing and started his laborious ascent towards his room.

"Mr Grimes, sir," George called again, this time closer. Jackson relented, halted and turned.

"George," he said, flatly and with a tone he hoped implied *please leave me alone*.

"It's your wife, sir."

"I have no wife."

George's eyes widened at the abrupt retort and he was about to respond but he was pre-empted.

"Jackie?" The shrill, long-drawn greeting, with its simpering rising cadence, had the bizarre effect of causing both the temperature of and the expression on Jackson's face to freeze. He turned forty-five degrees to look to where George had glanced and saw Sandra. The Diminutive One. Looking particularly small in the vast, marble-floored and high ceilinged, Art Deco lobby – for which, he noticed, she

51

had attired herself to complement. A monochromatic vintage silk dress, patent high-heels of a make he did not recognise but could be sure was as famous as it would be expensive, and a luxuriant, antique mink coat. All set off by silver bracelets and long, looping strands of black and white pearls. He couldn't help but crack a small smile of admiration. She really did look like she'd stepped through a fissure in time, from a decade when the hotel in which they now faced each other would have been at its glorious zenith.

"Sandy," he instinctively replied, then mentally kicked himself for addressing her with, what used to be, such habitual affection. He dropped the smile and corrected the mistake with a harsh and rebuking, "What the fuck are you doing here?"

"What do you mean, what am I doing here? I heard about your accident. Are you okay?"

"Well, how did you hear...? Never mind." He made a mental note to shoot the lawyer, or accountant, or whatever Max was calling himself these days. "I'm fine," he snapped, and then abruptly added, "But, since you're here, where's my dog?" The effect of which he should have, but failed to, predict.

Sandra appeared to shrink down to even smaller than her normal size as she bowed her head and slumped her shoulders. Her enormous oval eyes, still firmly fixed on him, widened as they moistened and her lower lip began to quiver. Then came the whine. A quiet, whimpering mewl at first, rising in both pitch and volume, and which Jackson knew from years of experience would, if not swiftly interrupted, flare up into an unstoppable torrent of wailing and tears that would make the tempest outside look like a light April shower.

"All right, all right," Jackson said, as calmly and soothingly as he could, while raising his hands in surrender. "Jesus. Let's go and have a chat in my office, shall we?"

As if a switch had been flipped the crying ceased. Sandra smiled brightly and, with an enthusiastic nod, advanced towards him – placing one of her size four shoes onto the first carpeted step.

"No, not that way," Jackson exclaimed, suddenly panicked at the idea of her getting any closer to his suite than she had already reached and, his muscles miraculously waking up, he jogged down the stairs to cut her off.

Sandra stopped dead and threw him a withering glare.

"This way," he indicated, and led Sandra towards the Fumoir Bar.

***

"Thank you, Frankie," Jackson said with a boyish smile as Frankie poured two glasses of champagne, leaving the bottle in a silver ice-bucket next to the table.

"You're welcome, Mr Grimes," Frankie replied with an over-emphasised formality, throwing him a sly wink as she returned to her post behind the bar.

"Who's she?" Sandra spat in a loud whisper, just loud enough for Frankie to hear.

"That's Frankie, Sandra," Jackson tiredly replied, "She works here. I'm surprised you didn't pick up on that."

"Frankie," she huffed, "Frankie and Jackie. Well, doesn't that just sound special?"

"Well, it would, were it not for the fact that nobody calls me that. Except for you, of course. In spite of me asking you not to for years."

"You used to like it."

"I never liked it!" Jackson snapped in a hoarse, exasperated whisper. In the fraction of the second it took for the words to spontaneously erupt from his mouth he could feel the back of his scalp contract, causing a sharp pain and a microsecond of almost blinding tunnel vision. A flash of pure anger which dissipated as quickly as it appeared, lasting just long enough for Sandra to pick up on.

She looked down at the champagne flute in her hands and nervously picked at the rim with a perfectly manicured, blood-red thumbnail. Then she muttered, "I always thought you liked it," and looked back up at him with a wounded half-smile.

"Oh, Christ," Jackson sighed. He downed his drink, reached for the bottle and refilled his glass. "What do you want, Sandra?"

"What do you mean, what do I want?" Sandra emitted the second phrase in a deep, masculine-mocking voice, "And, what do you mean you don't have a wife?" she added in a thin whisper, with a tilted head and an affronted squint.

"What?" Jackson was already losing focus on the conversation.

"You said to that young boy in the lobby..."

"George. His name's George. And I don't think he's actually that young. It's just we're getting old."

"You said to George," Sandra continued, ignoring Jackson's attempted deflection, "After he said 'your wife'... You said..." She paused to take a long sip from her drink, pre-empting any potential interruption by keeping her other hand raised with the index finer pointed upward, then carried on, "You said, when he said 'your wife', and I quote," again, she deepened her voice and, by way of impersonation, rolled her shoulders, "'I have no wife'."

"Well, I rather assumed that, by now," Jackson spoke slowly, purposefully and patiently, while refilling their glasses, "you would have signed the last round of divorce papers I had Max send you. Perhaps," he added with a tone of exaggerated optimism, "you've even come here to deliver them to me, yourself, in person?"

"Oh, silly," Sandra laughed, "I tore them up."

"Of course you did. You know, if you tear up many more of them you'll be in danger of finding yourself single-handedly responsible for the destruction of an entire rainforest."

"Paper doesn't come from rainforest trees. And I recycle."

"Well, good for you." He topped up Sandra's glass to the brim and emptied the last few drops into his own. "I swear, they're putting less into these bottles than they used to," Jackson grumbled as he tossed the dead soldier, neck first, into the ice bucket.

"It's the glass," Sandra matter-of-factly replied, "Thicker glass and a deeper dent in the bottom. True fact." She punctuated her thought by raising her flute and, with a sharp click of her tongue, giving Jackson an exaggerated wink. Again, Jackson couldn't help responding with an affectionate half-smile.

"True fact, indeed," he agreed, while raising his nearly empty glass, not to Sandra, but to Frankie, "But a little off topic."

"What do you mean? What's the topic?"

"Divorce, Sandra. Our divorce. Or, rather, lack thereof."

"Oh, silly," she playfully jeered, giving him a gentle nudge with her elbow, "No. I do have something, though, that I really do want to talk to you about."

"You do."

"I do."

"Not divorce?"

"Not divorce."

"Okay, fine," Jackson defeatedly sighed, "I'm too tired, and I'm too drunk, or too hungover, or too somewhere in between to really care right now. Although, by-the-by, what about my dog? You really should have brought him with you, you know."

"No dogs in here, I'm afraid, Mr Grimes," Frankie interjected as she replaced the used glasses, topped up a fresh pair and placed the second bottle in the bucket.

"That remains to be seen, Frankie. But thank you for your input and, more importantly, the reinforcements. Please keep an eye out for further requests."

Frankie rolled her eyes as she retreated to the safety of the of the oak bar.

Sandra, after throwing Frankie another hateful look, continued, "No, not Hugo, either. And, what do you mean your dog? He's *our* dog."

"Now, I think we both know that he would have other ideas on that one."

"I think you'd be surprised, Jackie. Jack. Jackson. Sorry."

"Oh, never mind. For Christ's sake, Sandra, get to the point." He knocked back his drink and, with a frustrated splash, refilled the glass.

"Well," Sandra began. Then she took a deep breath, sat up straight, crossed her hands on her lap and, with clarity and precision, pitched, "How would you feel about us... That is, you and I... How would you feel about us, so to speak, getting the band back together?"

"The what?"

"The band," she sang, "You know, us. You and me."

"Yes, I know what 'us' means, Sandra. It's this 'band' bit that's throwing me a little sideways. What fucking band?"

"Oh, it's just a figure of speech, silly! I just mean..." She paused. The finger went up. She sipped. Jackson simmered. She continued, "You know."

"No! I don't know, Sandra!" Jackson snapped. He could feel his chest tightening. The sheer frustration, which only Sandra could ever raise, beginning to swell. "I mean, here I am asking where our Goddam divorce papers are and you're telling me that you want to get back together again?"

"Oh, no, no, sweetie. That's not what I mean at all," Sandra explained, resting a reassuring hand on his knee and smiling at him with a condescending tilt of her head, as if he'd become terribly confused through his own fault entirely, "I don't mean 'us' like that."

"Oh, forgive me. Clearly you're using some obscure, esoteric meaning of the word 'us' which I, and possibly the rest of the English-speaking world, are as yet unaware. Do continue. But please, for the love of God, try to do so at a half-decent pace. It's already taken you three bottles to get this far and I think at least one of us should be relatively sober by the time you finally get to wherever it is you're going."

"Two bottles."

"Guess again!" He drained the remnants of the second

bottle into Sandra's glass, threw the empty into the bucket with an icy crash and signalled to Frankie for emergency support.

"Okay. I have a little business project I've been working on."

"No."

"But you haven't even heard what it is yet!"

"Okay, fine. Get on with it." Jackson sat back, ready to listen.

"Well," Sandra began, "Okay. Just, take a look at this." Sandra reached into her oversized, leather handbag and produced a manila envelope.

"Well. At least I know what's *not* in this," Jackson jibed as he opened it and removed a few sheets of pristine, freshly printed paper. With a dramatic flourish, he drew from his inside pocket a pair of bright blue, half-moon reading glasses and perched them on the end of his nose.

"New specs?"

"Please. I am trying to focus," Jackson superciliously replied.

As Jackson began to read, Frankie delivered the next round. Sandra lifted her fresh glass and quietly sipped as Jackson leafed through the pages. She studied his face, the scrutinising eyes and the veins pulsing at his temples, trying to judge his response.

Finally, he finished. He carefully slipped the proposal back into the envelope, put away his reading glasses and sat back.

"Well?" Sandra asked with a wide smile, beaming with expectation.

"Well. Looks like a great idea. It's perfect for you, well done."

"The first event's next week," Sandra said, sitting forward and almost bouncing with excitement, "And it's a biggie!"

Jackson felt himself giving another, small smile. This was the Sandra he had fallen for all those years ago. Full of energy, passion and ambition. "Well, congratulations, Sandra," he said warmly, "I'm sure it will be a triumph. You deserve it."

"No, silly. Not *you* deserve it. *We* deserve it!"

"Come again, m'dear?" Jackson sat up straight, feeling his stomach tighten into a knot of anticipatory dread.

"This is for us, Jackie!" Sandra declared, her voice high with elation, "Just think! It'll be just like the good old days. Only without the hassles of an actual premises. I can do all the food and the menus. All you have to do is be there and sorta be, like, front of house. You know. Entertain people. Mix those wonderful cocktails. Pour drinks and run the staff. There'll be lots of staff. The key to this whole thing is outsourcing to freelancers and part-timers. You know, zero hours peeps. Only the house is whatever event venue we happen to be working! This is our second bite at the cherry!" She ended with a wide, proud, beautiful smile that lit up her entire face.

Jackson froze. Stared at her. Tried to determine whether or not she was in any way serious. When he realised she was he looked down at his glass and, trying to remain composed, replied, "Our second bite at the cherry, you say."

"Exactly! Now, I'm only suggesting a trial–"

"And it'll be just like the good old days."

"Yes! Just like the good old days!"

Jackson calmly nodded, then sat forward and quietly asked, "Sandra. How well do you remember the good old days?"

"What do you mean?"

"Well, for one thing, and if you think about this rationally for a moment then I suspect you'll agree me, they really weren't that good."

"They were the best!" Sandra protested.

"They were a fucking disaster, Sandra!" Jackson exploded, abandoning what little restraint he'd managed to retain, "We argued constantly! We had stand-up fights in the kitchen! In the dining room! Sometimes with a full house, for God's sake! Christ, Sandra, we ran, not one, but two restaurants into the ground just because we drove each other so far up the fucking walls!"

"But we were a power couple."

"A what? A power couple? Jesus, what does that even mean?"

"Everybody loved us!" Sandra cried, her pitch rising and tears beginning to flow.

"Are you insane? *Everybody* loved us? Maybe in the early days. And I mean the very early days. But towards the end, there? Nobody loved us! People loved you. And a few misguided fools may have been quite fond of me. But us? Together? Sandra, everybody, and I mean everybody, hated us! Christ, by the end of it all, we were positively toxic! Just ask your friends! Ask our customers! Ask the critics! Oh, God, the critics," Jackson shuddered and took a long, medicinal sip, "Even *we* hated us, Sandra. Which is why you need to get on and sign those Goddam divorce papers. Because, you know what?" Jackson leaned forward and with a cruel, venomous sneer, hissed, "One way or another, Sandra, you're either gonna be a divorcee or you're gonna be a fuckin' widow!"

"Oh, fuck you, Jackson!" Sandra screamed. She tossed the remains of her drink at him, stuffed the envelope back into her bag and stood up. Her cheeks burning red and her eyes wide and wild, she leaned into his face and with a raw, furious scream repeated, "FUCK YOU!" She snatched up her empty glass and, as she turned to march out of the bar, hurled it at Jackson's face. It bounced from his forehead and shattered on the table.

Jackson lurched backwards, momentarily stunned, and stared down at the fine, glass shards and broken stem. Scattered chaotically across the dark, reflective surface and surrounded by globules of liquid, each one beaded into an almost perfect sphere by the richly polished oak. He listened to Sandra's sharp footfalls receding through the lobby at an angry quick march.

Momentarily, Frankie appeared beside him. She removed the broken glass and began to wipe the table. She handed him a napkin and quietly said, "You're bleeding."

Jackson, still looking down, took the napkin and dabbed his forehead. As Frankie finished wiping the table, he smiled up at her and said, "Terribly sorry about that, Frankie. I really don't know what came over her."

Frankie tossed the cloth and broken glass into the ice bucket and returned Jackson's smile with a hard glare. "Really?" she frostily replied, "Because, I'm pretty sure I do." She picked up the ice bucket and walked away, leaving Jackson alone at the empty table to nurse his freshest wound.

Chapter 8

"Any idiot can handle a crisis. It's the day-to-day living that grinds you down."

I'm not sure where I heard or read that. I'd like to think it was from a motto in a Christmas cracker. Stuffed between an undersized tissue hat and a useless plastic widget by some disgruntled, zero-hours contract worker in whatever godforsaken sweatshop such novelties are produced. Someone who then went home and chuckled his way to sleep as he imagined it being read aloud at a festive family gathering.

However, I suspect this is most improbable. More likely, it came from the frustrated mind of some hack writer masquerading as a great philosopher, trickled its way down through the pseudo-intellectual collective psyche for a few decades and, finally, came to my fleeting attention when I spied it on the back of a cheaply printed T-shirt in some over-commercialised street market.

Whomever the originator, it's a sentiment that resonated with me for many years. One of numerous pithy mottos, sayings and pseudo-profundities I would lean on for support. These days, however, I've come to the conclusion that it's nothing more than tautological twaddle. After all, surely day-to-day living is nothing more than a succession of catastrophic and traumatic events, each one requiring immediate attention, urgent triage and, more often than not, professional crisis management skills?

...I shan't miss that.

***

"What the hell did you say to her!"

"I'm sorry, Max. You're going to have to be a little more specific than that. It's turning into one of those weeks. What did I say to whom? A where and when might be helpful, too."

Jackson had the telephone receiver wedged under his chin as he poured his morning coffee. He smiled at a fellow guest, a suited business type in his early thirties, who had glanced over with a quizzical frown. Wondering, Jackson supposed, what that strange device was sitting on the table, with the coiled cable winding its way to the part into which Jackson now spoke and listened, and why it needed to be plugged into the wall.

"Jackson! Are you still there?"

"What? Sorry, Max. My mind went elsewhere. Look, old boy, why don't you come over and join me? Apart from anything else, I'm hogging the house phone and I'm sure other guests are waiting to use it."

"Nobody is waiting to use the house phone, Jackson. Nobody's been waiting to use the house phone since about nineteen ninety-six. I'm amazed they even managed to find you a house phone."

Yes, that had been a problem, Jackson silently admitted. "Nevertheless. I'm breakfasting downstairs today. Hoping the coffee's going to be a little more palatable than room service," he gave the cup he'd just poured a sniff and grimaced, "Why don't you come and join me?"

"No."

"Okay, then. I'll see you in about fifteen or twenty minutes. Yes?"

"No. Jackson, look, you need to–"

"Fantastic. I'll have them set a place for you. See you shortly, old boy."

"Jackson!"

Jackson dropped the handset back onto the telephone's cradle and flagged down a passing waiter.

"No more calls until after breakfast, I think," Jackson said it in the manner, he fancied, of an early twentieth century aristocrat.

"Of course, sir," the waiter replied, in a tone and with a smile that suggested he was playing along in the same fantasy. He removed the telephone and unplugged it from the wall.

"And might I trouble you for a second place setting? My former lawyer has decided to join me. Damn cheeky, if you ask me. Encroaching on a man's breakfast. Let alone a paying client's. But, there you have it. Such is the way of the world today."

"Indeed, sir." The waiter marched on. Jackson smiled to himself, feeling strangely satisfied as he looked about the elegant, graceful surroundings of the dining area, and took a sip from his coffee.

"Oh, fuck me." he quietly winced.

***

Some forty minutes later, Max finally bustled into the dining room

"Maxwell, old boy. What took you so long? I thought you'd been run over by a bus. Or, worse still, attempted to take one. Here. Have some coffee. The first two were pretty grim and I had to send them back, but this pot isn't too bad." He poured Max a cup.

"I'm not staying," Max firmly stated.

"Well, at least have some breakfast. I've just sampled the kippers and they're excellent."

"I've had breakfast, Jackson. At home. In my kitchen. Before I left for work, which is where I should be now."

"You seem a little ratty, old boy. Are you quite all right?"

"I'm a little ratty, Jackson, because I didn't get any sleep last night and it's your fault."

"My fault? How could your insomnia in any way be my fault?"

"I don't have insomnia, Jackson. Do you know what I do have? I have a wife."

"Yes, so you keep telling me, although we have actually met–"

"A wife whose best friend kept her up for nearly three hours last night in what can only be described as a state of hysteria on account of her... what was the phrase? Ah, yes, that was it, her 'selfish, arrogant bully of an ex-husband'."

"*Ex*-husband? She really said *ex*-husband? You mean, she's finally signed the papers? Because she told me she'd thrown them away."

"No, Jackson," Max sighed, leaning forward onto his elbows and drawing a tired, frustrated breath, "No, she hasn't. And, yes, I think she did throw them away." Shaking his head he stirred three heaped teaspoons of sugar into his coffee, then continued, "But I think she could be convinced." Max sipped his coffee and instantly clacked his tongue against the roof his mouth while throwing Jackson an offended scowl. "Jesus, that's rough! I thought you said this wasn't too bad?"

"I know, I lied. It's foul. But, as you know, I hate to suffer alone. Convinced how?"

"Well, she's got this new business venture," Max gestured for the attention of the waiter, "As well you know."

"Oh, for fuck's sake, Max. Is she seriously proposing that, in return for divorce, we become business partners? Because that's heading towards the bat-shit end of the crazy spectrum, even for her."

"No, that's not what she wants, Jackson. Which you would know if you'd just listened to her instead of throwing a hissy fit."

"That's not what happened. And, hissy fit?"

"Yes, hissy fit. And I can see you're on the verge of having another one now so just shut up, for once in your life, and listen. Excuse me," he said, aside to the passing waiter, "May we have a fresh pot of coffee, please?"

"Well, what does she want, then?"

"It's one night, Jackson. Just one event. Her debut, so to speak."

"But why? Why does she want me there?"

"Christ, I don't know. Maybe to show people that there are no hard feelings between you?"

"But there are."

"Oh, come on! Okay. Maybe she just wants some moral support from the man to whom she gave twenty years plus.

Maybe, God help me for saying this, because you're actually good at what you do. Or what you used to do, anyway. And maybe, just maybe, she values your opinion?"

"Well, that goes without saying, I suppose," Jackson thoughtfully replied. As if, for the first time, he had heard something rational. "What is this thing anyway?"

"No idea. Will you do it?"

"She'll definitely agree to a divorce?"

"I shall see to it myself."

"And I want my dog back. That's important."

"Yes, I'm sure that won't be a problem. He's been acting up lately, anyway. Apparently, after you left he started knocking Sandra over and pissing on her shoes."

"Really?" Jackson beamed and, like a proud father, boasted, "It took me weeks to teach him that one."

"Oh, Jesus. You really are psychotic. Seriously, Jackson, you need help. Professional help." Max shook his head, then looked down in a poor attempt to hide a guilty chuckle as he poured two cups of the fresh coffee. "Here, try this."

They both sipped.

Jackson nodded with surprised approval and said, "Very good. Smooth, quite mellow, not too bitter," then he then gave an indignant frown and moaned, "How can they do it for you and not for me?"

"They do, Jackson. But I don't let it sit there stewing for half an hour before drinking it. Look. Can I tell Sandra that you'll be there?"

"And you'll come with me?"

"What? Why?"

"Like I said, I hate to suffer alone. Divorce papers signed, dog back and you have to come too. Those are my conditions and, quite frankly, I think they're rather generous."

"Oh, bloody hell. Fine. It's next Thursday." Max hurried his words and glanced at his watch. "God, I'm late again." He downed the rest of his coffee and stood to leave.

"That's it? You've got what you want and now you're off?"

"I have a long day ahead, Jackson."

"As do I. But I can still make time for the niceties."

"Really," Max growled, becoming increasingly exasperated. He sat back down, plonked his briefcase onto the floor and placed his elbows purposefully on the table. "Do tell," he testily queried, "What are your plans for this busy, busy day?"

"Well," Jackson began, "First, I'm going to have to the main course of my breakfast. For which you are more than welcome to join me. They do superb devilled kidneys, although this morning I'm leaning more towards the steak and eggs. Don't know why. Perhaps I need the protein.

"Then I'm going to wander down to Jermyn Street so I can swing by Franco's for an espresso before visiting Trumper's for a long overdue haircut and a proper shave. I have an appointment for ten fifteen so, allowing for a brisk walk afterwards, I should be finished in good time to make it up to Dukes for an eleven thirty martini. Very dry. Two olives. I might even have a second. That should carry me over to lunch time. Something simple and stodgy today, I think. Cod and chips at Langan's.

"From there, down to Foxes for an afternoon of cigar sampling. Catch up on the newspapers while I'm at it. I'm sure that'll build up a thirst in perfect time for cocktail o'clock. I've got a hankering for a Negroni at the American bar. Again, probably a brace.

"That said, I had a minor disagreement with them last time I was there. I mean, when you're paying a hundred and fifty quid for a drink you expect it to be properly chilled, am I right? Of course I'm right. Anyway. If they're still sore at me and it doesn't work out there then, I suppose, I'll just toddle on back here.

"Which, now that I think about it, might suit better. I can have a quick change of clothes before heading out to dinner. Where, I hear you ask? Well. That has yet to be decided. Thought I'd mull it over throughout the day. Maybe find somewhere new. Preferably local. Do you have any suggestions, old boy?"

"No," Max replied in a low, simmering timbre, "No, old boy. I have no suggestions. But I do have one question."

"Fire away."

"What the hell is the matter with you?" Max snapped to his feet and snatched up his briefcase. "And get a new mobile phone, will you?" Before Jackson had a chance to respond, Max had spun on his heels and was half way across the dining room, marching towards the exit.

"Okay. Cheerio, then," Jackson called after him, "I'll see you tomorrow. Come by for dinner, yes?" Then he beckoned the waiter, in search of a bloody steak and a pair of runny poached eggs.

***

Twelve hours later, Jackson found himself having dinner, not luxuriating in a local Mayfair eatery, but perched at the end of the grubby bar in the sticky-floored pub with the nicotine-yellow ceiling, across the road from the hospital. There he, once again, stared into the bottom of an empty whisky glass, cursing himself and his moth-like draw to whatever flame he saw glowing within Julia. From whom, he had emphatically decided, it was imperative for him to stay as far away as possible.

Chapter 9

"He may have a point about the mobile phone," Julia concluded. She then popped a shoestring French fry into her mouth and, on the first chew, gave Jackson a nod of approval. "Good chips."

"A bit soggy, if you ask me. Badly packaged. Langan's aren't used to putting together takeaways. Not that they're wonderful, anyway. To quote the original owner's alleged reply to a complaining customer, who was seated between a table with Liz Taylor and Richard Burton and another occupied by Sophia Lauren, 'you don't come here for the fucking food'."

Julia gave a single, dry laugh, took a bite of the battered cod and said, "Well, if you ask me, the fish is excellent."

"Culinary speaking, they have improved in the last half-century, I must admit."

"I would imagine so. I'm no expert on the restaurant business but I suspect, at the very least, they'd have replaced the chef by now."

"You could be right. May we get back to talking about me, please?"

"Oh, by all means," Julia pantomimed, "I mean, who am I, bedridden and half-blinded by a lunatic violinist, to compete with the woes and misfortunes of the great Jackson Grimes?"

Jackson sat back and folded his arms, regarding her with a squint of feigned indignation. "It could have been worse, you know," he playfully, if tentatively, replied.

Julia's visible eyebrow arched. "It could have been worse? Really? How, pray tell, could it have been worse?"

"Well…" Jackson leaned forward and plucked one of the remaining fries, "He could have been a lunatic cellist."

Julia's eyebrow remained raised, her mouth open, and she stared at Jackson for a good five seconds – before the sides of her lips curled upwards as she lolled back and broke into a fit of unbridled laughter.

Jackson softly chewed and, through soft eyes and with a warm smile, watched her. Mesmerized…

***

…Jackson's day had gone precisely as planned until about halfway through his shave.

The steak and eggs came about fifteen minutes after Max's unceremonious exit, for which Jackson profusely apologised to anybody who would listen. Shortly thereafter, he set forth on his walk to Jermyn Street.

"Morning, George," he enthusiastically cheered as he marched towards the revolving doors, looking over just long enough to acknowledge George's courteous reply in the form of a restrained nod as he checked in yet another wide-eyed, one-night-only guest.

Out on the street, Jackson was pleasantly surprised to find that the previous day's rain clouds had given way to clear, blue sky. Were it not for the slight golden hue of the low sun and the occasional brown leaf dancing in the warm, light breeze, it could easily have been midsummer as opposed to early autumn. He checked his watch and, seeing he had time to spare, decided to turn left and take the slightly longer route to his destination, via Berkley Square.

What a pity men don't wear bowler hats anymore, he found himself thinking. Imagining that, if they did, then this particular village of London would be teeming with them. They'd go perfectly with the innumerable couturier, pinstriped suits. All matched with wingtip brogues and tightly rolled up umbrellas. Uniforms for self-important estate agents and high minded art dealers. *Desperately trying to look respectable but fooling nobody*, Jackson judged, as one swerved around him in a manoeuvre designed to let everyone know what a hurry he was in. What a busy day lay ahead of him. How vital his next meeting was to the future of all humanity.

Jackson was in no hurry at all. A point not lost on the irate taxi driver who revved his low base, diesel engine and frustratedly tapped his steering wheel while Jackson, chest out and grinning inanely, casually sauntered across the zebra crossing.

As Jackson stepped onto the pavement on the park side of the street, the driver leaned out, rested a thick, heavily tattooed arm on the sill and angrily squawked, "What's the matter with you? Got a stick stuck up your arse? Wanker!"

"You wouldn't be so upset if you had a fare in the back, would you?" Jackson shouted back. Purely for the benefit of himself and any other pedestrian who may have heard him since, by the time he'd reached the word 'wouldn't', the taxi was a good fifty feet away. The engine wailing while the exhaust pipe exhaled a thick plume of acrid, black smoke.

Jackson ambled across the small park that was Berkeley Square. The gnarled plane trees, these the oldest in London and dating back to the 1600's, had yet to start turning and were still fully green. To the best of Jackson's knowledge, aside from being home to expensive private members clubs and shifty tax lawyers, these ancient trees were one of Berkeley Square's only two claims to fame. The other being one of the most haunted houses in London.

There were two legends as to the nature of the restless spirit residing at Number Fifty Berkeley Square. One of a man held prisoner in isolation until he finally went insane. However, the one that ran through Jackson's mind was the tale of the girl who threw herself to her death after years of abuse at the hands of her uncle. Now, it is said, if she appears before anyone, she makes such a frightening spectre that all of her victims die of fear. *Quite right*, Jackson thought, *Leave no witnesses*. He looked across the square at the house in question, to the top floor, from which she was said to have leapt, and wondered, *is that really high enough to guarantee a swift exit?* Looked a bit risky to him, he thought, and wandered on.

A feeling of slight nervousness began to weigh on his

jubilance. As he traversed another zebra crossing, back off the island square and onto Berkley Street, he found himself patting his pockets for cigarettes. Empty. He saw a Sainsbury's ahead and was about to change course when he remembered that Franco's was opposite Davidoff. *The more you pay for tobacco the better it tastes*, he reminded himself, and picked up his pace.

Fifteen minutes later he was sitting outside Franco's on Jermyn Street, waiting for his double espresso with a white Sambuca on the side, and lighting the first Lucky Strike from a packet of twenty. For which he had happily paid an exorbitant twenty-six pounds and fifty pence – along with a further six hundred and fifty pounds for the solid gold Dunhill lighter…

***

…"Hang on. Let me get this straight," Julia interrupted, leaning across the table over her bed – on which sat the as yet unopened fish and chips, "You went into the most expensive tobacconists, on the most expensive street, in the most expensive area of the most expensive city in the world. To buy a packet of cigarettes. And, while you were there, you thought, Oooh, I need a lighter, too. That one'll do. Six hundred and fifty quid? Pfft! What the hey."

"Firstly, I've never said 'what the hey' in my life. And secondly," Jackson defensively shrugged, "What can I do? That's what these things cost, Julia. I can't help that. Now. Do you want to hear the rest of this or not?"

"I honestly don't know. But you did bring, what looks like, a wonderful lunch, saving me from the horrors of yet another NHS meal. So, please. Do continue."

"Thank you. Now, where was I?"

"Franco's on Jermyn Street. A little after ten in the morning. Drinking espresso, knocking back Sambuca and smoking cigarettes. All terribly manly, I am suitably impressed."

"Good. Now…" Jackson leaned forward, proceeded to open the Langan's takeaway packages, and continued to expound upon his morning…

***

…Of all the luxuries in life in which he adored revelling a wet shave was, without a doubt, Jackson's favourite. To repose in the creaking, warm leather chair, close his eyes and feel the comforting warmth of the towels covering his face. To draw in the clean, caring scent of the foaming soap, then feel it's effervescence as the barber briskly, and generously, lathers it into his beard. To have the last twenty-four hours of the grind scraped away from his face by another. Allowing him to visit a world of his own fancy instead of being forced to stare into those reflected, raging eyes, grimacing at the horrors of his own truth.

As he lay back, smiling through the froth, the images of the last few days glided across his mind's eye. The final views of Venice as the water taxi bounced its way towards Marco Polo airport. The first glimpse of London's lights from the privileged vantage of his first class window seat.

Then, like an involuntary spasm, an image from a year ago. Sharp, pale-blue eyes. Kind but piercing. A perfectly preened, white beard. This image flashed faster than all the others. Just a brief glimpse. A still snapshot of an encounter that had lasted for thirty minutes, endured for an eternity and which, in the barber's chair, Jackson could only look at for one terrifying microsecond.

He forced his memories back to the sanctuary of recent days in Claridge's. The safety of the various elixirs, intoxicants and sauces to which he, as always, had returned to for solace. His new friend, George. His old friend, Max. His former love, Sandra. And Julia.

Julia. The violin. Her face shattered. The bloodstained pages of the book. *Venice.* One of his own favourites.

The Violinist, staring down. Cold. Still. Uninvolved and

uninterested in the carnage he had caused.

Julia again. Eye bandaged. Bandage seeping. But still with that smile. Wry. Defiant. Unconquerable. Fascinating.

As the barber wiped away the remnants of the soap, Jackson could feel that his smile had altered. He looked in the mirror and splashed on some Floris aftershave. He flashed the barber a well practiced, exaggerated wince with a playfully accusatory glare, then looked back at the mirror. What was it that had changed? He couldn't quite put his finger on it but, as he glanced at his watch, became reasonably sure that the pre-lunch martini at Dukes would hold the answer.

Jackson watched the bartender slowly stir the vodka and ice. Probably, for the first time in his life, without any sense of judgement. His mind, usually pathologically critical of any mixologist, was distracted. It kept wandering back to that hospital ward across the river.

Absentmindedly, he watched as the bartender poured in the slightly viscous liquid and, afterwards, slip in a pair of plump, green olives – married by impalement on a sharp, wooden cocktail stick. He plucked out the couple and took one into his mouth, slowly divorcing it from its partner with his incisors before crushing it with his molars.

While chewing he brought the glass to his lips for that first, cold sip and, as he did so, caught sight of his freshly shaved reflection in the mirror. He paused. He noticed the shift. The change. His well practiced dry and sardonic smirk had become tainted by a strange flicker in his eye. An odd lifting at the corner of his mouth. Corrupted by, what he could only surmise, was a form of curiosity. Warm, caring curiosity.

Jackson let out a single, surprised laugh, took a long sip from the martini, and wondered if Langan's would be able to make up a pair of takeaways…

***

..."Which, obviously, they were," Julia brightly concluded, having listened to Jackson's highly redacted and hugely embellished account of his morning. Then, pushing her tray aside, she declared, "Probably the best fish and chips I have ever had, Mister Jackson Grimes. And, I'd venture to say, definitely the most expensive. Thank you."

"You are most welcome."

"And, thank you for this," Julia reached to her bedside and took the copy of Jan Morris's *Venice*, "A signed first edition, Jackson. Where on Earth did you find it, and that quickly?"

"Truth be told, it was pure chance. I just saw it in a shop window while I was on my way somewhere. Then I ended up on my way here. If that makes sense."

"It doesn't. Interesting quote you selected, though." Her cadence took on a sing-song quality, as if she was preparing to tease him as she opened the book, leaned forward and pointed at the sentence.

Jackson moved towards her and, for a moment, their bare forearms lightly brushed. At the same time, Jackson caught the scent of her perfume, floral and light, interrupting the sterile, institutional odour of the ward. It caught him off guard and he felt compulsively drawn to her. A base instinct, a reckless impulse, commanding him to move closer.

He managed to quash the urge as quickly as it appeared, only to have it replaced by an acute sensation of embarrassment. He could feel an uncomfortable, un-controllable warmth redden his face. A sudden prickling at the back of his neck. Instinctively, he pulled away.

"Here," Julia laughed, misreading his sudden lurch for a moment of clumsiness.

Jackson gave a weak smile, looked back to the text and silently read, *'May God protect me from the man I trust, I shall protect myself from the man I do not'*. "Ah, yes," he said, regaining his composure and sitting upright, "One of my favourite mottos."

"Oh, I'm sure you have many."

Definitely teasing, Jackson decided. He grinned and

nodded – of course.

"But, surely, a lesson learned too late?" Julia suggested.

Jackson frowned, not understanding.

Julia looked down to the book and read him the accompanying line, "'Etched into the wall of the *dungeon* of the Doge's Palace'."

Jackson grinned. "I see what you mean," he agreed, "A lesson learned far too late. But, then again, the important ones usually are."

"Important what?" came a sharp, boyish interruption.

Every sinew in Jackson's body stiffened and his jaw clenched with fury. Instinctively, he spun around, glared at the intruder and demanded, "Who the fuck are you?"

"Jackson!" Julia shrieked, completely taken aback.

The interloper, a scruffy character with a patchy beard and a multi-coloured beanie cap, stood rooted to the floor. Staring at Jackson with equal measures of surprise and horror.

Jackson looked back to Julia, whose initial expression of dismay rapidly turned into one of shocked amusement.

"Jackson!" she repeated, and began to chortle, "This is my brother!" She'd barely finished the sentence when she peeled away with laughter.

"Oh," Jackson awkwardly replied, "Shit. I mean… Hello," he stood up, extended his hand and, attempting a late return to form, assertively added, "Pleased to meet you."

"Who *are* you?" The youthful face under the beanie cap whined.

"You mean you don't know?" Julia managed to reply through her increasing howls, "Everyone should know him. He's Jackson Grimes!"

Jackson flashed her a sly glance, suppressed his own laughter and then turned back to the boy.

"Julia! It's not funny!" the brother whined.

Julia attempted a reply but, unable to speak, merely nodded that it was, while drying the tears from her good eye with a tissue.

"Jules! You're gonna split your stitches!" he droned with

a lazy inflection – the antithesis of his sister's perfectly clipped speech pattern.

Again, Julia failed to produce an audible reply. Then she shook her head, raised her palms as if asking for silence and, with a few deep breaths, finally regained her composure. "Okay," she sighed, "Jackson, this is my brother, Julian. Julian, this is Jackson."

"Pleased to meet you," Jackson repeated.

"Yeah. Hi," Julian moped.

"Well. I think it's probably time I was... Wait," Jackson looked back and forth from sister to brother, "Julian?"

Julian rolled his eyes, knowing what was coming. Jackson looked to Julia, who wore the same, tired expression.

"Julia. And Julian," Jackson couldn't resist a slight smirk as he glanced from one to the other, "Julian and Julia, Julia and Julian. Really?"

"Really." Julia testily replied.

"Wow."

"Yes. Wow. And, as you can see, we're not exactly twins. Merely cursed from birth. Well, from his birth, to be precise."

"Oh, thanks, sis."

"And thank you for coming," she continued to Jackson, ignoring her brother, "And for the book. And for the food."

Jackson smiled, giving her a small bow.

"Perhaps," Julia added, "If you get that mobile phone then, before you next visit, you could call ahead?"

"I'll shall do just that."

"And, perhaps, you could try not to swear, quite so much. Particularly at total strangers? Just a thought," Julia lightly suggested and offered him a final, amiable smile.

Jackson returned her gesture, attempted one of apology to her brother and then left the siblings to their business, while reconsidering his own.

***

Jackson began this reconsideration in earnest, minutes later, slumped forward at the long bar of the grubby pub across the street from the hospital. Staring into another whisky glass and contemplating the day. Both the one he'd lived and the edited version with which he had regaled Julia.

He had, naturally, neglected to mention the magnetic and, as far as he could tell, unexplainable draw he felt towards her. And he made sure to leave out the purchase he'd made in the barber shop: a stunningly crafted, mother-of-pearl handled straight razor. He'd told himself he'd bought it because its handle matched, almost perfectly, that of his antique safety razor. But now, as he looked down at the blade in his hand while waiting for the next whisky, he could hear a small, cold whisper, from the darkest recess of the back of his mind, taunting him. Reminding him, *stick to the plan. The path is set*. And for it to carry on then, for both of their sakes, it was imperative for him to stay as far away from Julia as possible.

He stared back into his drink and saw, staring up from the bottom of the shallow glass, the man with the white beard. The memories of whom he'd also redacted from his account to Julia and, with another long sip, he tried to erase from is own mind.

Chapter 10

"I'd like to buy a mobile phone. Please."

"Great!" Came a chirpy, toothy-smiled reply, "What sort of contract are you looking for?"

"Contract? What do you mean, contract? I want to buy a mobile phone, not a mobile phone company."

"No. I mean, how long are you planning on being with us?"

"Interesting turn of phrase," Jackson growled with a wicked grin.

"No, no," the Teenage Salesperson floundered, "I mean, *us*. The company. What are you looking for? Twelve months? Twenty-four months? Thirty-six? Longer the contract, better the deal. And, with the thirty-six month contract we can offer you another free SIM card and a great half-price bargain on a twelve inch device."

"Well, thirty-six months would definitely be pushing it. And what the fu…" Jackson managed to stop himself, then took a deep, calming breath before rephrasing, "What on Earth is a SIM card, or a twelve-inch device?"

The Teenage Salesperson gave Jackson a sideways glance. "Maybe it would be easier if you took a seat over here where I can run you through a few options?"

Jackson looked around the spectacularly illuminated shop, which managed to appear both minimalistic and cluttered at the same time. Walls and display cabinets were crammed with row upon row of glowing screens, all of varying sizes and dimensions.

Jackson looked back to the teenage salesperson and warily replied, "Yes. I suppose it would."

A few minutes later, Jackson found himself sitting in a chair that was far too low at a table that was far too high. The Teenage Salesperson, clipboard and clicky-pen in hand, sat opposite, looking down at him from a high stool.

"Okay. What do you think you'll mostly be using your phone for?"

"I want to be able to talk to people who aren't in the same room as me," Jackson replied, as if it were the most obvious thing in the world. He sensed discomfort from the Teenage Salesperson and decided to play his faux pas off as a joke. "You know. As the man once said, 'it's good to talk'."

"Who said that?"

"Bob Hoskins."

"Bob who?"

"Hoskins."

"Oh." The Teenage Salesperson looked momentarily bewildered before, as if inspired, flashed the toothy-smile and cheerily asked, "Was he on last year's X Factor?

"No! X what? Last year's X what? What are you talking about!"

"Nothing. Doesn't matter," the Teenage Salesperson flushed red and returned to the questionnaire, "Apart from voice calls, what will be the most useful function for you?"

"The off switch."

"Okay. But really I was meaning in terms of apps."

"Apps?"

"Apps. Applications. You know like, I dunno. Maps. Could you see yourself using maps?"

"Why would I need to do that?"

"Well, in case you're going somewhere and you get lost."

"I already know how to get to anywhere I'll ever need, or want, to go."

"But what if you don't?"

"But I do."

"But, what if you don–?"

"Well, then I'll take a… blinking taxi!" Jackson could feel his restraint on the verge giving way. His internal promise, to try and follow at least one piece of Julia's advice by not swearing, particularly at total strangers, was in danger of taking a catastrophic nosedive. He took a breath, forced a smile and politely asked, "Could we move this along, please?"

"Of course, sir," The Teenage Salesperson looked back down at the clipboard, clicked the clicky-pen and continued, "What about data?"

"What about it?"

"How much do you think you'll need per month?"

"Well, that depends. What's it for? When you say 'how much', what does data come in? Pints? Or, is it metric?"

"Well," the Teenage Salesperson's voice began to waiver, "It comes in... I mean... Well, you use it for emailing. And the internet."

"On my phone? Why in God's green Earth would I want to do that? I'm sure the hotel has a perfectly good computer for that sort of thing, should I ever actually require it."

"The hotel?"

"Yes. The hotel in which I live."

"You live in a hotel?"

"I do. Claridge's, if you must know. Now–"

"You live in Claridge's?" The question came with wide-eyed awe.

"Yes. Now, please. For the love of God. In the name of all that is good and holy. I beg of you. May I buy a mobile phone?"

The wide-eyed stare held for a few seconds. Then the pen clicked and there came the next, thin-voiced question, "What about messaging?"

"Yes!" Jackson exclaimed, profoundly relieved to hear something that sounded vaguely familiar, "Yes! Messaging! That is something I can use. That is something I *do* use."

"Ah, but how do you message?"

"Oh, fffff-fiddlesticks!" Jackson sat back, fought the urge to tear out his own eyeballs, then gritted his teeth and grumbled, "Go on."

"Well, will you be using a third party service? Like WhatsApp? Or Snapchat? Or iMessenger? Or, will you be texting?"

"Texting!" Jackson snapped his fingers and pointed at the

Teenage Salesperson, as if awarding points in a quiz, "Definitely texting. I texted my friend Max only a few days ago, just before I lost my last phone."

"Okay, now where getting somewhere – wait…"

A long pause lingered between them. Jackson's proud grin began to fade as the Teenage Salesperson stared at him, the toothy-smile melting away before, with a new, slow confidence saying, "Let me get this straight. The last time you sent a text was a few days ago."

"That's right."

"Then you lost your phone."

"Indeed. Well, sort of lost it."

"Then you, sort of, lost your phone. Again, few days ago. Is that right?"

"It is."

"And you're only replacing it now. You haven't missed it until now."

"Again, that is correct."

"Hmm." The pen gave a final click. The clipboard went down. "Two questions. Firstly, why do you now want to replace it?"

"Because I've only, now, met somebody worth calling."

"Okay. Good reason. I mean, weird. But good. Second question. When did you buy the phone you, sort of, lost?"

"Oh, I don't know. I suppose it was back around nineteen–"

"Okay!" the Teenage Salesperson interrupted, almost snapping at Jackson, who was on the verge of exploding when the Teenage Salesperson smiled. Not the toothy, adolescent grin of before but a warm, canny beam. As if suddenly understanding Jackson better than anyone who had ever known him while asking, "Do you know what you need, sir?"

"What's that?" Jackson asked with growing interest.

"A dumb phone. A pay-as-you-go, no-contract, dumb phone." Jackson had no idea what any of that meant, but it sounded perfect. Particularly when the Teenage Salesperson added, with a shrewd squint, "A burner."

Jackson finally relaxed. With a warm smile, and regarding the Teenage Salesperson with a newfound respect, he sat back and asked, "What is your name?"

***

Jackson frantically struggled with the heavy-duty plastic in which his new mobile phone had been hermetically sealed.

"For fffffaaaaargh's sake!" he groaned, tossing the package aside and rising from his seated position on the bed. As he passed the muted television he paused, noticing the graphic appear on the screen: *The X-Factor*.

"Ah-ha," he chirped, his curiosity piqued, and turned up the volume.

Jackson went into the bathroom, removed his Swiss Army knife from its place in his leather wash bag and returned to the bedroom. All to the soundtrack of Hear No Evil, See No Evil, Speak No Evil and Pure Evil berating and belittling a thoroughly demoralised singer – now shattered, humiliated and stripped of all confidence for the amusement of a baying, bloodthirsty mob.

"Ah, ha," Jackson spat as he returned to the bedroom and, with a wince of anger, muted the cacophony. *Christians and lions*, he thought, *the amphitheatre lives on*.

He sat back on the bed and returned to his own gladiatorial battle – Jackson Grimes verses The Plastic Menace. The campaign was short but the casualties were high. Mainly due to an early, tactical error within the Grimes camp when he elected to attack with the long blade instead of the scissors. He made his first offensive with a stabbing thrust, followed by a sideways slice, across the top of the package. However, due to the slippage effect of two pieces of slick, heavy-duty plastic between a piece of thick, glossy cardboard, he lost control of the strike. The blade swerved inwards and Jackson managed to lacerate his own palm.

"Oh, Christ!" he screamed, throwing both weaponry and

enemy aside, "Not another fucking trip to the fucking emergency room! I can't fucking take it any more!" And, clutching his gushing hand, he ran for the bathroom – abandoning both the battle for the phone and his newly moderated lexicon.

***

"What happened to your hand?" Frankie curtly asked.

"I bought a new mobile phone."

Frankie gave a single nod, accepting Jackson's reply as a complete and sensible answer, then placed two whiskies on the table and returned to her post behind the bar.

"It's a burner," Jackson proudly continued. He removed the small, plastic flip-phone from his pocket and handed to Max, who sat across the table.

"What's a burner?" Max asked, quizzically examining the phone, "And, good Lord, look at that. Actual buttons and no touchscreen. Where did you get this, nineteen ninety-eight?"

"Just up the road. And, that's what the spooks call them," he gave another childish, wide-eyed grin, "Burners".

"Spooks?"

"Yeah, spooks. You know. Spies. Secret agents"

"Really. That was the sales pitch you fell for. Buy this and you will be Bond. Only you, Jackson." Max gave a warm, amused grin. He handed back the phone and raised his glass for a toast. "But I am honoured to have been the recipient of your first call from your steam-powered device. Tell me, can you text? Or does it send up smoke signals instead?"

"Funny," Jackson took back the phone, "And you were the second call. The first was to the hospital."

"I'm assuming it wasn't about that." Max gestured towards Jackson's hand, around which a blood-spotted Claridge's emblazoned flannel was taped, "Because, if that was a professional job, then the NHS is even further up the creek than everyone thinks."

"As if the NHS would use a wash-cloth of this calibre. No,

I was just… looking for a patient. Fruitless exercise. Turns out they don't have bedside phones anymore. Bastards."

"Oh, Christ, Jackson. Please tell me you're not harassing that poor woman while she's trapped in a hospital bed convalescing."

"Never mind that. And, not that it isn't a pleasure to see you, old boy, but to what, exactly, do I owe the pleasure?"

"Dinner, Jackson. You invited me for dinner."

"Of course I did. Where shall we dine?"

"Anywhere. But first let's talk for a moment."

"Oooh. You've got your serious face on. Talk about what?"

"Take a wild guess, Jackson."

Jackson frowned and gave a flummoxed shrug.

"Or, should I say," Max added, with a mischievous smirk and an exaggerated whine, "Jackiiiee."

"Oh, God-dammit, Max. Why you gotta go and fuck up a perfectly good evening by bringing up this shit? And what's so funny?"

Max shook his head and chortled, "You, Jackson. I've told you before and I'll tell you again. When you get flustered like that, you betray your roots."

"Do not."

"Do too. You even said 'wash-cloth' a few minutes ago. Nothing to be ashamed of, you should be proud."

"Yeah, says you."

"Yeah, says me," Max replied in a deep and unconvincing New York accent.

Jackson cracked a smile and retorted, in a perfectly natural, Brooklyn accent, "Fuck you, you fuckin' fuck."

Both of them roared with laughter, remembering the infamous Circle Line party back in the late 1980's. When Max, the dirt poor, full-scholarship law student destined to become Max, the fabulously rich wealth manager, met CJ Grimes, the Brooklyn-Boy Bartender fated to become Jackson Grimes, the more British than British restaurateur. The train car had been commandeered by mutual friends as a cheap venue for Max's birthday party. Which, after Jackson finally disclosed to Max that it was also his birthday, became a joint celebration. The first of what would become an annual tradition.

Jackson looked around the opulent Fumoir Bar, then back to Max.

"I wouldn't be sitting here without you, old boy," he said, quietly. Shifting back from his natural to his naturalised accent.

"Nor I you," Max replied, "My number one client. My first client. Don't think I'll ever forget it."

"Don't think I'll ever let you," Jackson playfully retorted.

Max rolled his eyes and raised his glass. They air-toasted and sipped. Then Max put down his glass, leaned forward and quietly added, "But you wouldn't be sitting here without her either, Jackson. You must know that."

Jackson took a deep, frustrated sigh. Flexed his jaw. Then he let out a loud, defeated laugh, looked at Max and said, "I will do my bit at this event. Then I get my freedom and my dog." He sipped his drink and, suddenly suspicious, asked, "What is this thing, anyway? Birthday party? Anniversary do? God, it's not a bloody wedding, is it?"

Max took a long, health sip, put down his glass and, with a wicked grin, replied, "Oh, Jackie. It's much worse than an of those."

Chapter 11

Mitchell Mitchelson's latest series, *Life, Death and Glass*, was to be debuted in the main exhibition space of the Tate Modern Gallery, formerly the turbine hall of Bankside Power Station. The massive ground floor and mezzanine expanse, made up of of sharp edged concrete and glass rectangles, had been dotted with a multitude of glass globes, spheroids, elongations, bubbles and bubbles within bubbles. All of various colours and sizes. All containing a sinister, grey powder. Some just a few, infinitesimal grains. Others filled to the brim.

Mitchell had spent nearly two years on the island of Murano tirelessly studying the art of glass-blowing until, as he would less than modestly claim, he felt he had mastered the art as well as any expert the tiny Venetian isle had to offer. When reminded that many of those great experts under whom he studied could work just as tirelessly for up to two decades on their craft and still only be considered apprentices, and that they came from artisan families with a heritage dating back centuries, he would flamboyantly reply, "Yes. *Artisan* families studying their *craft*," he, on the other hand, was "an *artist*".

This, apparently, was a reply that would sufficiently impress most experts, dealers and collectors in the fine art world. It was certainly enough to bamboozle Sandra, who now stood before the exhibition's centrepiece. A grand affair titled *Three Sixty-Five*.

"Is it all that you expected?" Mitchell asked in a soft, feminine timbre with a slight German accent.

"Oh, it's magnificent," Sandra gushed, "Just... Just magnificent."

The young artist, the blackness of his attire matched only by that of his glossy, dyed hair, stood close behind her. He rested his hands, both adorned with heavy, silver rings and bracelets, loosely on her hips. As he lent down to kiss her neck, Sandra tilted her head to one side, closed her eyes and gave a warm, comfortable smile.

"Time and place, Mitchie-Mitch," she coyly whispered.

"Any time, any place," he replied with a quiet, mischievous chuckle. Sandra let out a weary sigh, placed her hand over his and gave a gentle pat.

"Mmm," Mitchell murmured. He nuzzled her neck and impishly whispered, "Why don't we make a quick visit to the side office?" Sandra rolled her eyes and was about to push him away, when she felt a tickle on the back of her hand. She looked down and saw that Mitchell had produced a tiny baggie of white powder.

"Oooh," she beamed, "Well. Don't mind if I do." Sandra turned, stood on the tips of her toes to kiss him, and then plucked the baggie from his hand. "Merci, mon cheri," she chirped and, taking his hand in hers, led him towards the nearest door.

Just as they reached the side office they were interrupted by a tinny-sounding Kylie Minogue singing, "You Should Be So Lucky, Oh-So-Lucky, Lucky," emanating from Sandra's handbag.

"Oops," Sandra blurted, stopping dead in her tracks and rummaging through the bag, "Gotta get that. It could be my peeps."

"Peeps?" Mitchell repeated, with a tone of charmed amusement.

"Yeah, peeps. My party-peeps. You know. Staff. For Thursday. Hello?" The last word was spoken into her phone as she raised her silencing index finger towards Mitchell, "Max!" she chimed followed by an eager, "Well?"

Mitchell retrieved the baggie from Sandra's finger tips and, with a petulant whine, whispered into her free ear, "I'll leave you some crumbs."

Sandra frowned, waving him away like a pesky fly while saying, "What was that, Max?"

***

"I said we'll be there," Max replied with the hoarse voice of a man whose morning after was about to be spent wondering what happened the night before. He sat at the writing desk in Jackson's suite, his throat parched and his head throbbing. Slumped forward and staring at a tall glass of fizzing Berocca, praying for it to settle. "It may well cost me my marriage, it's already cost me most of my dignity, and you know what it's going to cost you. Yes?"

"Okie-dokie. My place in a couple of hours?" Sandra cheerily replied, then hung up.

"Okay, a couple of... Sandra?" Max listened to a moment of silence before heaving a heavy, exhausted sigh and throwing aside his phone. "Strange girl," he muttered.

"Thank you! That's exactly what I've been telling you for years!" Jackson bellowed from the bathroom.

Max gave a wince of pain. He looked around the chaotic shambles that was Jackson's suite. A pile of blankets on the sofa on which he had, eventually, passed out. A heavy, glass ashtray with several thick, dark cigar butts mashed into the bottom. A near empty bottle of forty-two year old, cask-strength Glenfiddich and two glasses.

"Did we drink all that Scotch last night?"

"Whisky, old boy. Only amateurs call it Scotch," Jackson corrected, "And, you mean you don't remember? What a waste." Jackson poked his head from the bathroom and gave Max a knowing grin. "It was staggeringly good." He returned to the bathroom, continuing at a roar, "Not only that, but you paid for it."

"Oh, Christ," Max shuddered and looked back at his effervescent drink, which had finally dissolved. He drank it in three gulps, put the glass down, groaned, refilled from a water jug and plopped in two more tablets. As he did so he noticed the calendar, hanging just above the desk. The days crossed out. The thick 'X' through the twenty-sixth of the month.

"What's this about, then?" Max called, curiously.

"What's what about?"

"The calendar. All the days of the month crossed out and this big, dramatic 'X' on the twenty-sixth. Our birthday. What's on the agenda?" He managed a mischievous grin. "Big one for you this year."

"Always a bigger one for you, old boy. Or should I say, old man."

"Yes, but yours is milestone big." Then he shook his head and muttered, "Then again, every year's a milestone for an outright narcissist."

"What was that?"

"I said absolutely, old boy," Max called back, wearing a sly smile.

"Oh, who cares?" Jackson emerged from the bathroom. Shaved, showered, and donning a particularly well-pressed Armani suit and pristine white shirt. Looking, through Max's desiccated eyes, disturbingly refreshed.

"How can you look that together after the night we just had?"

"Practice. Besides, I've got to look sharp for my boy. Hey? But first..." he checked his watch then gleefully declared, "Breakfast! I don't know about you but I don't really fancy the idea of going into battle with the Diminutive One on an empty stomach. Shall I call down, or should we crawl down?"

Max stared at him with a cocktail of expressions comprised of exhaustion, accusation and utter amazement.

***

"Oooh. That wakes ya up!" Sandra exclaimed, standing up straight after hungrily sniffing in a stout, white line. She licked the tip of her finger, wiped the remnants from the glass table top and rubbed it on her top gums. Then she gave Mitchell a sweet smile, a kiss, and began to gather her belongings.

"Where are you going?" Mitchell whined, "Aren't you going to stay and help me finish everything?"

"I've got my own prep to finish, Mitchie. And, believe me, this is just as important for me as it is for you. Besides, I literally have to go and see a man about a dog." She shook her head and chortled at her own joke, leaving young Mitchell looking bewildered and, as he watched her totter away, beguiled.

**

Having feasted on smoked salmon and duck eggs – followed by, after growing tired of watching the green-faced Max reluctantly picking at it, an omelette stuffed with cheese, ham, onions, mushrooms and red peppers – Jackson felt ready to face anything the world could throw at him. Except Sandra. She, he decided, he would leave to his increasingly long-suffering friend, confidant and, as he was incessantly reminded throughout the previous night's drinking session, non-lawyer.

Although not a lawyer, Jackson had maintained that Max was, surely, more than capable of witnessing the decree nisi. Which, after much cursing and raging at all things modern, he had managed to download from a DIY divorce website and print. This had been achieved sometime in the wee hours of the morning, after they had returned from Tramps nightclub but before Jackson had broken the seal of the stupendously expensive bottle of whisky procured by Max.

As the three sheets printed off Max, slurring and barely able to keep his eyelids from falling, suggested that this particular document, with its American syntax and that had been found on a Nairobi based website, then received as an email attachment with the suspiciously boyish subject heading, 'Free At Last!', might not be entirely legal in this United Kingdom of Great Britain and Northern Ireland. Jackson reasoned that since, as he kept reminding all and sundry, Max was not actually a lawyer, his opinion mattered not a jot.

"Besides," Jackson reckoned, "It's the thought that counts."

Max attempted to argue that this sentiment generally applied to disappointing birthday presents and lame Christmas cards. But, by then, the whisky had been opened, Max had made the mistake of putting ice in his and Jackson was irately lecturing him on how and why he had just committed an act verging on sacrilege. One which, up in Scotland, would at best see his, "tiny English balls tarred and feathered".

Now, sitting alone in the back of Max's Maybach and satisfied from a double breakfast, Jackson felt a comfortable warmth as he ran through the fuzzy memories of the night.

"Okay, you can wait here," Max had said, moments earlier before leaving him to go and meet Sandra, "But when I'm back, you're off. I'm damned if I'm going to have that beast of yours slobbering all over the inside of this brand new s600. And, yes, feel free to help yourself to anything in the drinks cabinet."

"Well, that's mighty generous of you, old boy."

"No, just realistic," Max sighed before alighting.

Jackson stayed in his place and watched his friend trudge past the Georgian fronted houses towards the flat that had been his and Sandra's home for the better part of two decades. "Too true," he happily muttered, opening the drinks cabinet and finding, to his delight, a chilled half-bottle of vintage Veuve Clicquot. "Oh, Max. Bravo," Jackson purred. He twisted out the cork with a civilized hiss, as opposed to a plebeian pop, and poured the champagne into a crystal coupe. Then he held the saucer-shaped glass up to the light and examined the soft, rising bubbles. "And a proper glass, too," he murmured with approval, "I have taught you well." Jackson downed the drink, refilled and relaxed into the plump, warm seat.

Momentarily, he looked around and examined the richly luxuriant interior. Young, soft hide and old, dark oak, exuding the deep, heady scents of lacquer and leather. A thought stuck him and he suddenly blurted, "Why don't I have one of these?"

"I beg your pardon, sir?" the chauffeur, somewhat confusedly, replied.

"I said, why don't I–" Jackson was interrupted by his door opening and Max reappearing, breathlessly struggling with a taunt leash. "Max! Why don't I have one of these?" Jackson again demanded to know.

"What? One of what? Here, for Christ's sake, put down my champagne, get out here and take control of your dog. NO!"

"Hugo!" Jackson roared. He threw his arms open, allowing the Chauffeur to take the half-full coupe from his hand, and Hugo, an excited mass of legs, paws and slobber propelled by a gigantic, whipping tail, leapt into the car and onto his chest. "There's my boy!"

Jackson wrapped his arms around the Hugo, whose elation was matched only by his energy. The dog spent the next ninety seconds wailing with delight while covering Jackson, along with most of the Maybach's interior, with as much saliva as any Great Dane is capable of producing. Max, meanwhile, watched helplessly from the street.

Finally, both master and dog settled down, and Jackson said to Max, "Well, he's in here, now. Surely you could give us both a lift?"

Max just stared at him. Stupefied and defeated.

***

Fifteen minutes later the Maybach crawled through thick traffic with Jackson, champagne back in hand, reclining in the rear. Next to him sat Hugo, staring out of the open window with a combination of pride and curiosity that only big dogs can muster. Max, no longer seeing the funny side of anything, sat in the front passenger seat, desperately texting and emailing from a range of devices.

"You didn't answer my question, old boy," Jackson suddenly said, interrupting Hugo's heavy panting.

"What question was that?"

"Why don't I have one of these magnificent vehicles?"

"Because you can't afford one, Jackson."

"Oh, I'm sure I can."

"No, you can't," Max argued with a touch of irritation, "Nobody can. I certainly can't. This isn't my personal property, you know. This is a company asset. Normally, reserved only for VIP clients. Several of whom I am now attempting to send apologies to on account of my most difficult client hijacking me last night and, as a consequence, utterly messing up my morning. It is not my own personal plaything. And it is certainly not a taxi service for my reprobate friends and their livestock. So, no. You cannot afford one. In fact, at the rate you're going, you'd be lucky to afford a third hand Skoda. And you certainly can't afford to live in five star hotels for the rest of your life. Or, for that matter, the rest of the month. When are you going to back to work, Jackson?"

"So, you mean you don't take this to the office every day?" Jackson asked, purposefully ignoring most of Max's sentiment.

"No, Jackson," Max tiredly confirmed.

"Taxi still cheaper then?"

"The tube, Jackson. I take the tube," Max glared at Jackson via the rear view mirror, "Sometimes, if I have time, the bus. Like every other normal Londoner. Christ. What planet are you living on these days?" Max put aside his iPad and, his frustration building, turned and leaned into the back to face Jackson. "Really. When are you going to find a permanent living solution? This is getting serious, Jackson."

Serious. Jackson began to feel a tension within him. Unseen, dark forces closing in. A face flashed across his mind. The white beard and those pale, blue eyes. Serious. He feigned a smile, shrugged and cheerily replied, "A month, you say? Well. Not to worry."

"What? Jackson, this combination of gibberish and riddles is getting very old. I mean, you should have heard yourself last night you were..." Max frowned, looked out the window, and then back at Jackson. "Is that the Houses of Parliament?"

"It is," Jackson confirmed.

"Jackson, where are we dropping you?"

"Just up here," Jackson brightly replied, "Nearly lunchtime. Thought I'd grab a bite around here before taking my boy for a good, long walk back up to the hotel. You know. Through the parks." He lent forward and, addressing the chauffeur as if he were a cabbie, said, "Just up here will be fine, mate."

The Chauffeur pulled over.

Max looked out at the road and despondently shook his head. "Of course," he sighed, then reached into his breast pocket and took out the three sheets of paper, "Here. Don't forget this. God knows, we've all been through enough for it."

"She signed them?"

"Yes, for whatever it's worth, and I suspect it's worth nothing, she signed them. But you have to be as good as your word, okay? Thursday night?"

"Thursday night, old boy. And you'll pick me up. As agreed, yes?"

Max gave him a suspicious glance followed by a reluctant nod. Then a warm, wicked smile as he said, "Fun night, hey?"

"Fucking epic, old boy!" Jackson laughed, "Hope Debs forgives you sometime before the turn of the next millennium." Jackson gave his old friend's shoulder a warm squeeze and opened the door. "Come on, Hugo!"

With a sense of concern and foreboding rising from his gut, Max watched Jackson and Hugo alight the car, cross the road and make their way across Westminster Bridge towards St Thomas' Hospital.

***

"Well, I got my dog back! Although the fascists who run this place wouldn't let me bring him up – who the fuck are you?"

Jackson switched gear mid-sentence after pulling the curtain of Julia's bed open and discovering that she had been replaced by an elderly woman with a phenomenally angry countenance.

"I beg your pardon?" the infiltrator screeched.

"What's going on here?" a third voice, as angry as the patient's glare, came from behind. Jackson turned to face the owner – a stone-faced, steely-eyed nurse who snapped, "Who are you?"

"That's just what I was wondering," Jackson said, looking back down at the bedridden woman, whose demeanour had shifted from fury to fear.

"No, sir! You! Who are you?" the nurse demanded.

"Me? Well, I'm Jackson Gri– never mind who I am! Where's the patient who belongs in this bed? The young and attractive one." He threw the last line at the increasingly worried looking woman, who shrank down and began to slowly draw her sheet up to her face.

"Please, sir. You're frightening the patient."

"Well, so she should be frightened. I'm a consultant physician in this hospital and if I can't find my patient then I'm going to have to find someone else to operate on. And I shall take great relish in removing various, vital organs," again, he looked down at the increasingly terrified looking invalid and, with a malicious sneer, added, "Just for fun."

"Right! That's it!" the nurse exploded, "Out!" Then she leaned down to the now terrified woman, all but her wide eyes hidden by the raised sheet, and said, "He's not a doctor."

"Don't you believe it!" Jackson thundered.

"GET OUT!" The nurse screamed, snapping the curtain closed.

Chapter 12

"You are stalking this woman," Max said, with a tone that was both advisory and admonishing.

"I'm not stalking her," Jackson protested, "I'm looking for her. How can I be stalking her when I don't even know where she is?"

The two sat together in the back of the Maybach, as Jackson and Hugo had done two days earlier. After which time Jackson had, as far as Max could gather, spent almost every waking hour trying to locate Julia…

***

…Following his altercation with the nurse and ejection from the hospital, Jackson retrieved Hugo from a nearby outdoor cafe – the maître d' of which he had bribed to feed and water his canine friend. The duo then set off through the heat and haze the late, London heatwave, back to Claridge's. While Hugo thought of nothing but squirrels, several of which he attempted to catch in the parks, Jackson mulled over two issues: how he was going to find Julia, and how he was going to check in his new roommate.

"Mr. Grimes! You can't bring that in here!" George protested.

"For the rate I'm paying you, George, I can bring in a team of horses if I want," Jackson boldly replied.

George assured him he couldn't.

"Fine. No horses, then. A fine place to begin our negotiations."

And negotiate they did, long with the grey-faced General Manager who, up until that point, had succeeded in avoiding any direct contact with Jackson – although she did know him, "all too well," by reputation. Jackson assumed that by "reputation" she had meant his professional heyday. The General Manager allowed him to hang onto this delusion and hence, suitably flattered, Jackson instinctively turn his charm up to its highest level. This secured Hugo access to the room, the main lobby and, discreetly, the Fumoir Bar.

"A good place to start," Jackson agreed.

"And to end, Mr Grimes. Enjoy the rest of your stay," the General Manager replied in an authoritative tone, before returning to the back office.

"Right," Jackson sighed, content that his first mission had been a success, and he prepared to move onto the second – for which he returned to the computer room he vaguely recalled from his and Maxes search for divorce documents the previous night.

Jackson then spent the rest of the day clumsily navigating the internet, searching for Julia. He started with the newspaper articles about the accident, before remembering that she had told him they were wholly inaccurate. Then he resorted to *The Google*, hurling at it a plethora of *key search words*, some relevant and others random, in the vain hope of finding, if not an address, then at least an area to which she might be local.

Julia. Julia Someone. Horrific Chelsea Accident. Beautiful Woman Loses Eye. King's Road Bistro Mayhem. Deranged Violinist. Lunatic Musician Nearly kills Julia. WHERE THE FUCK IS JULIA? ...

***

..."I thought you couldn't use the internet?" Max interrupted, "Which was why you shanghaied me for a night to get you those stupid bloody papers?" then he shook his head in frustration at the stand-still traffic ahead, "Christ, this is going to take forever. We should have just taken the tube. Why do I let you talk me into these things?"

"I can't imagine," Jackson replied, relaxing back into the magnificently comfortable seat. Having depleted the champagne, he handed Max a pink gin and took a long sip from his own. "And, although I've often said I don't use the internet, old boy, I've never that I can't. I'm a Neanderthal, not a Luddite. Anyway, this is case and point as to why I avoid the bastard. It's fucking useless."…

***

…"Fucking useless!" Jackson bellowed at the screen, much to the consternation of a bleary-eyed Canadian beside him, wearing a crumpled grey suit and long-haul flight stubble.

"You having trouble with the browser? Want some help?" the Canadian asked in an enthusiastically helpful, if tired, tone.

"My what?" Jackson grumbled. The Canadian repeated the offer, which Jackson declined on the grounds of irate frustration with all things technological. Instead, he suggested that they repair to the Fumoir Bar saying, "I could do with an impartial opinion on my next course of action and you look like you could use a drink."

The Canadian agreed, more from politeness than thirst, and minutes later they settled into the corner table, under which Jackson attempted to hide Hugo. The Canadian transpired to be an advertising consultant called Jacque, visiting London to deliver a keynote lecture at a conference. Teaching people how to sell overpriced thingamajigs and pointless doodahs to gullible suckers who can't afford them, Jackson supposed. Jacque respectfully informed Jackson that his supposition was both erroneous and possibly slanderous – then listened patiently while Jackson, plying them both with copious quantities of whisky and bourbon, described his conundrum. How he met Julia at that crucial moment. How he visited her in hospital, twice, but neglected to acquire either her contact details or last name. The brief meeting with her brother who, frankly, he just didn't take to. His fruitless online search. Finally, he came to his question – what to do next.

"Well," Jacque slowly replied, carefully sipping his third bourbon, "I don't know what the laws or cultural customs are in this part of the world, Jackson. But, to my mind? It sounds to me like you might be stalking this woman."...

***

..."Well, I have to concur with your new friend, Jackson. You are stalking this woman," Max said, with a tone that was both advisory and admonishing.

"I'm not stalking her," Jackson protested, "I'm looking for her. How can I be stalking her when I don't even know where she is?"

"Regardless, we're nearly there. So let's not mention this again until we've left, okay?"

"Fine. One hour."

"You'll stay for as long as required, Jackson. To the bitter end if needs be. That's the deal."

"Jesus," Jackson sulked, "Well, okay. But if she starts doing the French thing, I'm off. I fucking hate it when she does the French thing."

Max gave a sympathetic smile, nodding in agreement. Then, in unison, they both sighed, drained their pink gins, quit the Maybach and, with equal unwillingness, trudged their way towards the Tate Modern.

***

"God, I despise conceptual art," Jackson grumbled as he swiped two champagne flutes from a passing waiter. He handed one to Max, took a sip from the other and spied another tray, this one laden with canapés. "Ah. The main event." He spun around to try and catch the passing food, only to find himself face to face with Sandra smiling up at him.

"Oooh!" she chimed, "Don't mind if I do." Sandra plucked Jackson's drink from his hand, took a long sip and winked.

"Sandra," Jackson dryly said, "Care to explain what, exactly, I'm doing here?"

"Oh. Silly," she replied with a half-suppressed laugh while giving Jackson a dig in his ribs, then linked her arm through his and walked him into the room. "Since when have you ever complained about playing co-host at a great party?"

"Co-host?" Jackson queried with a cocked eyebrow. Again, Sandra winked. As she led him through the space they passed one of the sculptures – a colourful sphere half-filled with the fine, grey substance.

Jackson gave a curious squint and asked, "Are these Venetian glass?"

"Of course. Haven't you done your homework?" Sandra handed him a brochure, the title of which read 'Mitchell Mitchelson's *Life, Death and Glass*'.

Jackson let out a cross between a single laugh and a snort. "Really? Is this actually his name?"

"Yes, it really is. And, please, you're not here to make fun, Jackie."

"Jackson. And, about that. Once again, I ask you. Why the fuck am I here?"

"Shh. Less of the gutter talk, please. You're here to make me look good. To work the room. Like we used to, Jackie."

Jackson clenched his teeth and snapped, "It's Jackson!"

"Sandie and Jackie. Together again, I see?" a middle-aged, lugubrious man greeted them, extending a hand towards Jackson.

"You could say that," Sandra replied with a teasing, rising tempo.

"Or maybe you couldn't?" Jackson added, matching Sandra's cadence while adding a sardonic smile. Just as Sandra flashed him a rebuking glare, Jackson took the man's hand in a firm but friendly handshake, drew him in and, as if letting him in on the greatest secret the world had to offer, said, "Have you tried any of the food yet? All made my Sandra's own fair hand, you know. She's truly excelled herself this time. Truly excelled. Especially the lamb." He whispered the last sentence, nodding towards a nearby platter.

The man looked over with suddenly ravenous eyes and

replied, "Yes. That does look good."

As another tray of champagne passed, Jackson took three glasses, two in one hand and one in the other. He handed one to the man and added, "Vintage, of course."

The man smiled, took the drink and moved towards the lamb. Jackson looked down at Sandra – whose rebuking glare had melted into a wide smile.

"You know full well why you're here," she said. Jackson replied with an eye roll and handed her one of the glasses as she asked, "Have you even tasted the lamb yet?"

"No, but it smells exquisite."

Sandra beamed and gave a slight bow. Again, she linked her arm through his and sluggishly guided him towards the stairs. Jackson could feel the back of his neck bristle as he tried to restrain his naturally long, purposeful strides.

"Come on. I want to show you the main piece. The one all the aficionados are going to be writing about tomorrow."

"Good evening, Sandra. Wonderful spread," greeted a passing guest.

"Ah, enchanté," Sandra replied with a simpering titter.

Jackson flexed his jaw. He flashed a rebuking glare to Max, who stood laughing with a group of fellow suits. Max squinted back and Jackson silently mouthed, "*She's doing the French thing! The fucking French thing!*" to which Max responded with a helpless shrug. Jackson, leaning behind Sandra, replied in some sort of frenzied, improvised sign language that he hoped told Max, firstly that he and Sandra were going up to the mezzanine level. Secondly, that it was imperative Max should follow them – swiftly and armed with several drinks. And, finally, that Jackson was not at all happy about anything.

"Jackson? You with us?"

"What?" Jackson barked, snapping his attention back to Sandra. A moment, he could tell from her piercing glare, too late.

"The literature. Did you read any of it?"

"Yes, of course. I've read plenty of literature. You know

this. What are you talking about?"

"No, *the* literature. About the exhibition," Sandra spoke with a nervous giggle and, gesturing towards the brochure in Jackson's hand, took a step back. Jackson realised that a third party had joined their conversation. A tall, thin man, probably in his late twenties. Pale, gaunt and clad from head to toe in jet black. "Jackie, this is Mitchell Mitchelson. The man of the hour."

"Jackson," Jackson corrected, "It's Jackson."

"Oh, and she calls me Mitchie, too," Mitchell giggled, "But it's funny, no? And a pleasure to meet you, Jackson."

Jackson reached forward and shook the artist's unsettlingly flaccid hand, heavy with a multitude of silver rings and bracelets.

"Oh! Not so tight, please," Mitchell exclaimed in a sharp, feminine voice, high pitched and overly excited. The excitement, along with his constant sniffle, Jackson put down to pharmaceutical causes. "These hands are my life, yes?"

"Oh, yes, of course," Sandra replied on Jackson's behalf.

"Yes, of course, old boy. Drink?" Jackson added, swiping a couple of glasses from yet another passing tray.

"Don't mind if I do!" Sandra chirped, much to Mitchell's easily tickled amusement.

"She never says no, and neither do I!" Mitchell said, copying Sandra's metre and inflection while mirroring her body language.

Jackson smiled, looking from one to the other, then cocked an eyebrow as he noticed the casual manner in which Mitchell rested one of his bejewelled hands on her hip.

"Oh, but I must go," Mitchell continued in a more serious register, "and, you know, press the flesh, as the saying goes."

"Oh, I'm sure you've been doing plenty of that lately," Jackson replied in a low and gravelly voice. His narrowed eyes suggestively flicking between Mitchell and Sandra.

"Jackson!" Sandra hissed, flushing red and pushing Mitchell's hand away. Mitchell's eyes popped and he gave another sharp sniff. Then Jackson flashed him a boyish wink and, with a dry whisper, added, "Touch of a Soho sniffle there, Mitchie?"

"What? Oh, you know!" Mitchell chortled, "You know I have, Jackie! I see you upstairs later, yes?" Mitchell mimicked Jackson's wink but directed it at Sandra. With another quick sniff he walked away to join a nearby group of guests.

Jackson glowered down at Sandra. She looked back up at him with the puppy eyed, guilt-ridden expression of a child caught raiding a biscuit tin.

"What?" she asked in a small, defensive voice as she involuntarily brought her finger up to touch the tip of her nose. Jackson shook his head.

"Nothing," Jackson said, "None of my business. Come on. You can tell me all about this fantastic work of art the entire world's going to be talking about tomorrow.

"Well…" Sandra began – again, linking her arm through his and, ploddingly, walking him up the stairs.

"But can we, please, pick up the pace?" Jackson groaned, "Other people are waiting." Jackson drew her attention to the growing crowd behind them waiting to ascend the stairs. All of them far more eager to reach the top than him. With the possible exception of Max who, Jackson was relieved to see, was only a few yards behind them – laden with a bottle of champagne in one hand and a clutch of glasses in the other.

***

The oversized hourglass was six feet and eight inches in length. The entire piece, including the wrought iron stand on which the glass was centrally hinged, stood at well over eight feet. The glass was simple, elegant and delicate. Finely crafted and perfectly symmetrical from every angle, it was slightly opaque with a few lines of smoke running vertically from tip to tip.

By contrast, the iron stand was remarkably ornate. Elaborate strips and bands protruded from the centre at various, irregular angles. All of them looping to twist around and eventually rejoin each other back at the centre, and each of them tattooed with finely detailed, intricate etchings.

Like the pieces on the ground floor, the hourglass contained a grey, sand-like substance. As Jackson, Sandra and Max stood gazing at it, all of this was resting in the bottom of the lower bulb. The plan was that, when Mitchell gave his speech, he would ceremoniously turn the glass over, allowing the sand to begin its journey downward. This descent would take exactly three hundred and sixty-five days. It was, so to speak, a year glass.

The fine grey substance had been ground, treated and measured, as had the central aperture, to ensure that this would be accurate to within one minute. It has been a painstakingly challenging task since this substance was ash. The fine, light crematorium ash of three hundred and sixty-five souls. The tiny etchings inscribed in the ironwork were the names, birth dates and death dates of these deceased time travellers.

"The man is a genius," Sandra gushed, staring at the year glass.

"The man is a sociopath," Jackson corrected, with a tone that was more impressed than judgemental. "I mean, where did he get three hundred and sixty-five urns of crematorium ash? One or two, I can understand. You know. An uncle here, a cousin there. But three hundred and sixty-five?"

"eBay?" Max suggested.

"Oh, Max!" Sandra laughed, "No, they're bequeathals. People who've left their remains to the arts."

"You can do that?" Jackson asked, with a touch suspicion.

"You can," Sandra assured him, edging a little closer to Jackson and quietly adding, "You know, a lot of the guests here tonight are relatives."

"No shit," Jackson and Max replied in wide-eyed unison.

"Yes shit," Sandra confirmed, continuing with a hushed tone verging on reverence, "So, you know, this is almost like a funeral for them. Or a memorial service, maybe. Woah!"

she exclaimed the last word, stumbling slightly and catching Jackson's arm.

"Easy there, old girl," Jackson chuckled, "You might spill a bit."

"I might if I had any to spill," Sandra giggled, holding out her empty glass.

Jackson, who now held Max's champagne bottle, leaned over to oblige.

"Don't mind if I do," Sandra again sang. Jackson clenched his teeth as he felt the catchphrase grating on his ever-thinning nerves.

"Don't you think she's had enough?" Max whispered, standing on Jackson's other side.

"Oh, almost certainly," Jackson caustically replied, filling her glass to the brim.

Max let out a disapproving tut before returning his attention to the year glass and saying, "You know, I must admit. I'm a lot more impressed than I thought I'd be."

Jackson returned his attention to the sculpture and was about to offer his opinion when Mitchell joined them from behind and cheerfully interjected, "Why thank you, Max. Or, is it Maxwell? Or, perhaps we could call you Maxie?" he finished with a high-pitched giggle.

"Yes, I think Maxie. That would be just grand," Jackson grinned.

"Max is just fine," Max firmly stated.

"Ah, you boys and your fussiness over your names. Maxie, Max. Jackie, Jackson. But, no. Jackson," he became serious, looking up at the sculpture and cocking his head, "What do you think?"

"Well," Jackson again looked up at the piece, mirrored Mitchell's tilt and quipped, "My first thought is that you're going to overcook your eggs."

Mitchell frowned, taking a silent moment to register, then smiled and let out a loud, high-pitched giggle. "Oh, that is funny," he cried, while extended an empty champagne glass, which Jackson began to fill. "A good crack, yes? I see you make many of these. Perhaps we should call you Jackson Crackson, hey?"

"Now *that* would be grand," Max goaded.

"Indeed," Jackson snarled, then he once more topped up Sandra's flute. As he did so the glass shook in her fingers and a drop spilt onto her hand.

"Oopsie!" she tittered. Max gave Jackson a surreptitious dig in the ribs. Jackson responded with a nonchalant shrug.

"But really," Jackson continued to Mitchell, throwing back his shoulders, locking eye contact and effortlessly switching into his charming, professional guise, "I think it's a triumph, Mitchell. And I'm both honoured to be here and thrilled that these two convinced me to come. Although, if they'd said in the first place that you'd been working in Venice, especially with Murano glass, then they wouldn't have had to work nearly as hard. I particularly like the light, almost imperceptible smoke trails you've managed to get running through the glass from tip to tip. Nice touch. Really draws the eye. And the signature of a true master." He raised his flute and gave a slight bow. "Congratulazioni, Signore. E veramente magnifico."

Mitchell smiled and returned the gesture, replying, "Jackson, you make me blush. Now, I must go and prepare my words so I can do my bit. Yes, Sandra? Perhaps you could gather the attention of our guests below?" He took another bow and moved towards the year glass.

"A little OTT, old boy. Don't you think?" Max jibed in a low whisper.

"OTT is the only language us narcissists understand, old boy," Jackson retorted with a gravelly whisper and a wily grin.

"Nicely done, Jackie," Sandra interrupted, "Now, a little help?" She looped her arm through Jackson's and, somewhat unsteadily, manoeuvred them towards the edge of the mezzanine.

Behind them, Jackson noticed, a crowd of eager art lovers had already gathered. They were watching Mitchell, who stood on the other side of the year glass, flipping through a small stack of index cards.

Jackson and Sandra stepped toward the year glass, nearing the wall overlooking the massive space below, and Sandra moved to pass Jackson her champagne flute saying, "Here. Hold."

As she spoke and turned to give him the glass, one of her stiletto heels slipped and she stumbled towards Jackson, who caught her.

"Easy there, old girl," Jackson laughed as he pulled her up when his champagne, still half full, spilt onto the front of her dress.

Sandra flushed red with anger and snapped, "Jesus, Jackson! Watch it!" while pushing him away and, in doing so, stumbled again. This time, she turned her ankle and fell away from Jackson. Backwards, just knocking the year glass which, in turn, toppled slightly.

Jackson pulled Sandra back towards him. He almost had her back on her feet when he saw the sculpture was, rather than righting itself, leaning backwards. Resting against the edge of the low wall and teetering over the floor below.

"Oh, mein Gott!" Mitchell shrieked, his index cards falling from his hands as he brought his hands up to face.

"Oh, shit," Jackson muttered, then shouted, "Watch it!" He shoved Sandra aside and lunged for the falling sculpture.

Max caught Sandra and both looked on as Jackson managed to catch one of the metal struts and pull the sculpture back, just as it was on the brink of falling down into the main space.

"I've got it!" Jackson shouted. He gave a proud, almost heroic grin and repeated, "I've got it!"

"Oh, Gott sei Dank," Mitchell sighed, allowing his hands to fall back to his sides. He looked to Max, Sandra and the rest of the mezzanine level crowd and puffed his cheeks, exhaling with relief.

Then, a quietly concerned, "Oh, shit," came from Jackson, his voice laboured with physical strain. Once again, all eyes turned to him. His heroic grin had become a concerned frown. His face was red and beading with sweat as, gripping the metal struts tightly with both hands, he struggled with the weight.

In a slow, pendulous move, the glass pivoted on its central hinge. The bottom bulb, weighted with ash, now hung on the other side of the wall, swinging over the main hall below. Pulling Jackson along with it.

"Oh, mein Gott!" Mitchell shrieked again, bringing his hands back over his face.

"Oh, Christ," Max sighed. He let go of Sandra, who slumped to the floor, and ran to help Jackson. Together, the two of them pulled with all their might. Sandra and Mitchell, along with the guests gathered around them, apprehensively looked on – as enthralled as they were astonished.

The guests below – of whom Jackson and Max, from their precarious positions, now had a clear view – appeared utterly oblivious. Huddled in small groups, they laughed and sipped champagne while enjoying Sandra's canapés.

Jackson and Max managed to raise the sculpture another few inches.

"Yes! We have it now, Max!" Jackson shouted, "We have it now!" As he declared victory the year glass, once more, pivoted. Swung further out. Pulled them further forward.

"No, we don't, Jackson," Max strained to shout.

"Yes, we do!" Jackson insisted through clenched teeth as, again, the sculpture slipped a fraction away from them.

"No, we don't."

"Yes, we do!"

"No, we don't! MOVE!" Max screamed the last word to the people below – just as the sculpture slipped out of their hands and tumbled towards the floor.

Then crashed into the floor – and detonated.

The glass shattered into thousands of splinters, explosively releasing the remains within. In one fraction of a second a plume of grey, fine ash rushed outwards and upwards, filling the entire space.

Lingering moments stretched into drawn out seconds of dark, grey silence. As the ash settled, a tableau reminiscent of Pompeii emerged through the haze. A still, silent crowd of smoke-grey statues. Appearing lifeless, apart from their wide, luminous eyes, vacantly staring into the ash cloud that had engulfed them with such sudden ferocity. Unblinking as they tried to make sense of the moment.

Jackson and Max found themselves sitting on the floor, their backs against the wall, facing the fossilised mezzanine level group. Sandra, sitting on the floor before them, stared at Jackson. She opened her mouth to speak, struggled to find words, and failed. So, instead, she laughed. And her laughter rose into a fit of chuckling. Jackson joined her and, while everyone else remained quiet, their laughter built into hysteria. Feverish cackling which harshly echoed through the massive, concrete space. They rocked back and forth – tears running down both of their faces creating clean, flesh-toned streams through their grey makeup.

Then Sandra wiped her face, looked down at her begrimed hand and her laughter stopped. The convulsions, however, continued. Morphing from hysterical laughter to uncontrollable, inconsolable weeping.

Jackson became silent and, his eyes softening and his lips settling into a doleful half-smile, he stared at her. Helpless. Hopeless. Feeling as empty as she appeared crushed.

Sandra's sobs eventually quietened and a moment of silence lapsed between her and Jackson, until it was broken by a distant cough. A splutter, echoing through the grey, noxious haze. Then another, and another, as the smoke-grey statues wakened. And their screams began.

***

Jackson and Max sat together on the curb. Both leaned forward and stared silently at the ground – dejected, despondent and utterly drained. A little over an hour had passed since, as it would forever be known, the Tate Incident had occurred. Thanks to the efforts of a small coalition army comprised of all three emergency services, the chaotic pandemonium that had immediately ensued was beginning to settle into a semblance of organised mayhem.

Red and blue lights flashed, reflected in the black, glossy tarmac between Jackson's feet. He looked up. The massive, brick slab, with a monolithic tower at its centre, had once been a power station. Then an art gallery. On this night, however, it looked more like a post-apocalyptic disaster site. Ash-covered victims, their wide eyes still haunted, leaned on each other for support as they shuffled forward. Some wept. Others confusedly jabbered. A few, helped by police officers and fire fighters, lumbered towards waiting ambulances for oxygen or treatment for shock. Others disappeared into the night, desperate to get home to clean off the cinders. Wash away the dead. Cleanse from their pores the remains of their loved ones.

Jackson produced his Lucky Strikes and, with dry lips, slowly drew out a cigarette. He was about to put the packet away when he paused and offered one to Max. Max replied with a hard glare and shook his head. Jackson lit his cigarette and took a deep drag, which he exhaled with a sigh of profound relief.

"Twelve years," Max quietly stated.

"What?" Jackson asked.

"Twelve years, Jackson. That's how long it's been since I last had a cigarette."

"Really? Impressive. I can't remember the last time I went twelve hours without one."

Again, Max responded with a stony glare. Then he looked across the road. Jackson followed his gaze. On the steps of the gallery's main entrance sat Sandra and Mitchell. A paramedic held an oxygen mask over Mitchell's face while Sandra, staring vacantly into her own thoughts, limply held his hand.

"Well," Jackson said, flicking the glowing butt of his spent cigarette into the night, "I've always said she throws a

110

great party. And, as the saying goes," Max turned back to face Jackson, who grinned as he finished, "It ain't a party until something gets broken."

Max's face remained frozen. A hard stare of incredulity. Meanwhile, Jackson chortled and reached for another cigarette. Again, he offered one to Max.

"Bloody hell! No!" Max batted the packet away, "Jesus, what is wrong with you, Jackson? I mean, Jesus Christ. Look. Just look around you," Max fumed. He leapt to his feet and moved to walk away.

Jackson frowned, momentarily confused, and then a thought stuck him. "Wait a minute," he protested in a tone that was as injured as it was astonished, "You're not blaming me for this, are you?"

"Of course I'm blaming you for this!" Max screamed, rounding on Jackson, "Who else could there possibly be to blame?"

"Well, nobody. It was an accident. And we nearly had it, you know." Jackson looked down at his right hand. He flexed the fingers and pressed hard into the palm with his left thumb. Testing the grip. "Hands just aren't as strong as they were," he muttered, as if his mind had momentarily gone elsewhere. Then he looked back up at Max and snapped, "And anyway who's to say you shouldn't shoulder at least part of the blame? We definitely would have had it if you'd come over a moment or so earlier."

"Seriously?" Max's eyes popped, "Christ, Jackson, wake up. This is vintage Jackson Grimes. This is exactly the sort of mayhem that follows you around like a determined groupie. Face it. When this shit happens around you it's always your fault. Every bloody time. Do you want to know why? Because you wind people up, Jackson. You poke at them. And you prod at them. And you needle them. And you stretch their patience. Their tempers. Their entire psyches until they finally snap. The way you did with Sandra tonight while you filled her with booze. And deep down, you know it. You pretend that you think it's all for a laugh but you know

111

the damage you're causing. And you enjoy it."

"That's a bit harsh, old boy. We are friends, after all."

"Friends, Jackson? Are we? Do you even have friends?"

"I have many friends," Jackson remonstrated, hoisting himself to his feet.

"No, you don't, Jackson. You have acquaintances. Temporary playmates who find you amusing while they're taking a break from their real lives," he gestured towards Sandra, "You have disgruntled former lovers and angry ex-wives."

"Ex-*wife*. Only one of those."

"And you have babysitters."

"What do you mean, babysitters?"

"I mean me, Jackson! Me and all the mugs like me who get sucked into the vortex of your chaos, who spend their lives running after you and cleaning up the flotsam and shitsam left in your wake. My God, if the Four Horsemen of the Apocalypse saw you coming, they'd turn around and go back home. They'd take the day off. They'd just look at each other, shrug their shoulders and say, 'wasted trip, chaps. Jackson's here. Job done'."

"Oh, now you're just being silly," Jackson laughed.

"Am I? Tell me, *old boy*," Max taunted with a suddenly venomous edge, "Guested on any breakfast television shows lately?"

"How dare you!" Jackson exploded, "How dare you! You promised you'd never mention that again!"

"Oh, please. I'm going home," Max huffed and, shaking his head, walked towards the car.

"Yeah, good idea. Helluva night," Jackson concurred, joining him. Max stopped in his tracks. Jackson mirrored him.

"Where do you think you're going?" Max asked.

"You said we were going home."

"I said *I* was going home. I don't know where you're going. I don't care where you're going."

"Really? You're abandoning me? Here?" Jackson's face fell and his voice became shallow with disbelief as, in an almost fearful whisper, he added, "On the south side of the river?"

Max looked down at the ground and took a moment to think. Then he returned his hard stare to Jackson and, with a slow, quiet and deliberate metre, he said, "Jackson, before we part ways, I'm going to say one more thing to you. And I want you to listen carefully. Very carefully. Because it comes straight from the heart. In fact, I would say, in the three decades we've known each other, that it is the most heartfelt sentiment I have ever expressed to you."

"What's that then, old boy?" Jackson softly asked.

And Max, with a resonance of barbed wire and steel, calmly and firmly said, "Fuck off."

Chapter 13

There are, as far as I can ascertain, three main methods of making a grand exit. And any self-determined departure must be grand. At least as grand as the life led beforehand.

The first appears to be overdosing. The second, asphyxiation of some sort. Be it by hanging, exhaust fumes or whatever. And the third is leaping from a great height. All pretty grizzly, if you ask me. Risky, too. How much is enough? How tight is tight enough? How high is high enough?

What a pity we don't, in this country, have the right to bear arms. It would save an awful lot of bother.

Perhaps, as a Goodfella once pointed out, the Romans had the best approach. A hot bath, a glass of wine and a sharp blade.

***

Jackson pushed aside a half empty whisky bottle and placed the calendar flat on the desk. He drew another thick, black line through another empty, wasted square. Another day spent. Three days since the Tate Incident. Ten more to go.

Jackson moved to stand when he caught sight of himself in a mirror. He paused to inspect his appearance: unkempt, unwashed and unruly. He rubbed his heavy facial growth, left to go wild since the Tate Incident. Since he'd last spoken to Max. Since he'd last spoken to anyone, apart from Marco.

"Everybody hates you," he recited with a toxic, hateful growl.

The reply came as a meek whimper from Hugo, lying on the bed and staring at Jackson with big, soft eyes. Full of concern.

Jackson cracked a half-smile and quietly said, "Except for you, old boy. You love me. Don't you?"

Hugo replied with a small bark. He jumped off the bed and plonked his massive head onto Jackson lap. Jackson gave him a loving hug when there came a knock at the door.

"Ah-ha!" Jackson announced, attempting an upbeat tempo, "Time for my breakfast and your constitutional."

Hugo replied with another small whimper, this one of protest, while Jackson stood and pulled his bathrobe around his flabby girth. A moment later, he clipped a leash onto Hugo's collar as he opened the door. A fresh faced uniformed man, accompanied by a heavily laden room service trolley, stood on the other side.

"Morning, Marco," Jackson greeted with a low, listless tone.

"Good morning, Mr Grimes," Marco replied with a nervous edge. In the manner of a well-practiced routine, he pushed the trolley just inside the door and then took the end of Hugo's lead from Jackson, while asking, "Still under the weather, then, sir?"

"'Fraid so," Jackson replied, feigning a hoarse, dry throat. "Maybe tomorrow, hey?"

"I hope so, sir," Marco replied, looking past Jackson at the various whisky, vodka and gin bottles strewn around the suite, most of which had been delivered by him or his enabling compatriots. Then, as Jackson ushered him and Hugo, who kept his worried eyes on his master, into the hallway, Marco asked, "Around the square and then back?"

"Please. Very kind of you, Marco." Jackson fretfully replied.

"Oh!" Marco suddenly added, "There's a letter–"

Jackson, his selective deafness engaged, closed the door. He moved around the trolley and inspected the various items. Coffee, steak, eggs (fried and scrambled), hash potatoes, a separate bowl of black pudding for Hugo, and several types of fruit – which Jackson was reasonably sure he had not ordered. However, Jackson first turned his attention to the most important items on the trolley – a large jug of tomato juice accompanied by Worcestershire sauce, Tabasco, horseradish, celery salt, a variety of spices and a bucket of ice. He splashed a couple of fingers of vodka into a tumbler and got to work on his new life mission: to perfect his once famous Bloody Mary recipe.

As he picked up the jug of tomato juice he found, leaning against it, an envelope addressed to 'Jackson Grimes, Claridge's Hotel – By Hand'. The stationary was made of a stiff, ivory linen mix. The handwriting, in teal ink, was elegantly looped and aligned to perfection.

Jackson slit the envelope open with a fruit knife and removed a card. The writing style was the same as on the envelope. The message was short and brief, but still too long for him to finish reading before, as if he'd just had a shot adrenalin straight to the heart, he burst out of the door, ran along the corridor and barrelled down the stairs.

"George!" Jackson bellowed across the lobby.

"Mr Grimes!" George protested, "We've discussed the inappropriateness of bathrobes in public areas, have we not?"

"Never mind that!" Jackson snapped, pulling the robe tight and refastening the loose knot, "When did this arrive?"

"Sometime this morning, I suspect."

"Who delivered it?" Jackson demanded, suddenly breathless and leaning against George's marble counter.

"Well, I'm not sure. It was here when I–"

"Never mind that! Where's my dog?"

"Yes, about your dog."

"Never mind." Jackson rushed over to the revolving doors to intercept Marco, with Hugo obediently at his heel, who he'd spied trotting past. He tapped vigorously on the glass and beckoned them in, then turned back to George and continued, "George, I need a tuxedo. No! A smoking jacket. Yes, definitely a smoking jacket. Do you think you could make me an appointment with the house tailor for later on this morning?" He turned to Marco as he entered and, barely pausing to drawing breath, said, "Thank you, Marco, but I'm suddenly much improved. I'll take him out today."

"Very good, Mr Grimes," Marco smiled.

"Mr Grimes, we don't have a house tailor," George finally managed to insert.

"Well, bloody find one," Jackson called back as he ran up the stairs with Hugo, equally excited, bouncing at his side. Then added with a roar as he rounded the corner towards his suite, "And make sure he's Italian!"

***

Jackson stood on the doorstep of the Georgian townhouse, shuffling his feet like an anxious teenager waiting for his first date to appear. Hoping it would be her who opened the door and not a narrow-eyed, suspicious parent. He nervously ground a spent cigarette butt into the flagstone with his foot. Then, as an afterthought, kicked it down onto the street.

Satisfied, he stood tall while taking deep, even breaths, smoothing the velvet of his new, burgundy smoking jacket and preening a bouquet of long-stemmed red roses. Finally, he reached towards the door when, just as he was about to make a well-rehearsed, confident, three-sharp-taps knock, it opened.

Jackson gave his most winning smile – which instantly collapsed. "Oh. It's you," he flatly commented.

Julian responded with a stiff nod. Then frowned, looking Jackson up and down with a touch of curiosity, a pinch of amusement and a healthy dollop of disdain. "A little overdressed, aren't you?" he queried with nasal condescension, followed by a derisory snort.

"There's no such thing," Jackson haughtily rebuffed. He looked the younger man up and down, taking in his threadbare, paint-stained jeans, hemp shirt and open-toed sandals and continued, "The same, however, can certainly not be said of the opposite," then he focused on the sandals, with a cocked head and a raised eyebrow, and added, "Are those imitation leather?"

"They're vegan friendly."

"Really," Jackson wearily replied, "Well, aren't you just full of goodness and virtue?"

Julian gave Jackson a cold stare, stepped aside and halfheartedly said, "Suppose you'd better come in, then."

"You're too kind." Jackson gave a small bow and stepped into the house.

"I can take those for you, if you like," Julian offered, reaching for the roses which Jackson held crooked in his arm, leaving his hand free to carry a bottle of vintage Dom Pérignon.

"I don't," Jackson defensively snapped, then instantly regretted the effusion and added, "But thank you for offering."

"Suit yourself," Julian shrugged and walked away, leaving Jackson by the door to survey the room.

Elegant, expensive and inherited, were the first three words that came to Jackson's mind. The occupants of this house had, he guessed, lived here their entire lives. As had their parents before them. Old money. London aristocracy.

The parquet floors were covered with antique Persian rugs. Chintz printed sofas and deep, wingback armchairs were placed haphazardly, adjacent to highly polished oak and mahogany tables. The whole place gave a warm aroma of beeswax furniture polish and fresh flowers – the latter of which, as he looked around, Jackson saw he had not been the only one to think of bringing. He gave a quick shiver at his lack of originality, then continued with his cursory examination. Heavy velvet curtains hung on either side of French doors that, he could just make out through the darkness beyond, led out into a large garden.

As he took a step forward, Jackson could feel a floorboard gently give, letting out a small, tired squeak of complaint. He looked down and could see that the Persian rug, discreetly angled to cover the damaged board, was indeed antique, but probably valueless as it verged on the threadbare. A further inspection of the room revealed that much of the furniture was in a similar state.

The desks and chairs, although well-maintained on their surfaces, were adorned only occasionally with the odd, semi-expensive heirloom. A grandfather clock stood tall and proud at one end of the rectangular space. Beautifully, lovingly polished – but silent and still. Stopped rather cryptically, Jackson thought, at precisely one minute to twelve. The cushions on the sofas and chairs appeared flat and limp having, over the years, lost most of their down stuffing. Although the yellow, tungsten lights were all dimmed, he could see that the ageing silk shades veiling them were also showing signs of fatigue. The walls and ceilings on which they cast their shadows were dull and water-stained. Oil paintings by unknown artists, beautiful but worthless, hung side by side and top to bottom, crookedly and close together, covering the more severe patches of dampness and distress.

Old money now gone, Jackson thought, revising his original assessment, *impoverished aristocracy*.

As he took another step forward, Jackson noticed a pillow on one of the sofas that appeared incongruously modern. Bright yellow polyester emblazoned with brash, red text. He squinted and could just make out the slogan, which read 'Nouveau Pauvre, F**k Lloyd's'. Jackson couldn't help give a wistful half-smile, as he briefly recalled how his old friend had saved him from that same fate.

"You can't get something for nothing!" Max had vehemently argued when Jackson was ready to sign along the dotted line, committing everything 'down to his last set of cufflinks' as collateral for the promise of a luxuriant lifestyle at the age of twenty-four. Jackson had pointed out that, so far, he had succeeded in making a career out of doing precisely that. But Max was not to be budged and, as his new financial adviser and manager, flatly refused. The one and only time he had truly denied Jackson.

There but for the grace of God, Jackson now thought, *or rather, there but for the sense of Max*.

"Are those for me?" Julia's sing-song greeting snapped Jackson back from his memory and he spun to face her. She gave him a crooked half-smile, which he knew matched his own, as she reached forward with both hands and took the flowers.

119

"They are," Jackson replied, "Although, I see I've joined a herd rather than lead a pack." He nodded around the room towards a collection vases and baskets displaying a variety of competing floral displays.

"Well, you know what they say. A girl can never have too many flowers," Julia chimed, with a hint of sarcasm.

"This is true."

"No, it really isn't," she then sighed, almost mournfully, glaring at a particularity ugly basket that exploded with an assortment of wild, twisted branches. Each one brandishing a fierce, jagged blossom that looked like it was about to attack its neighbouring counterpart. "But these are lovely," she reassuringly added, glancing down at his roses.

"Perhaps this will achieve a more convincing review," Jackson said, holding aloft the bottle of champagne.

"Ah. Much more convincing," Julia concurred.

"J-One? You want me to take that?" interjected Julian, who Jackson had sensed hovering nearby during his brief exchange with Julia, as he made a move towards the bottle.

"No, thank you," Julia replied, sweetly but firmly, "But, could you be a dear and get these into some water?"

"Yeah, alright," the brother huffed, throwing Jackson another suspicious glare, "But I think we're running out of vases."

"I'm sure you'll think of something," Julia assured him with a touch of condescension as she thrust the bouquet into his arms, the foliage covering his entire head.

As Julian clumsily struggled with the flowers while turning to leave, Jackson gaily suggested, "And don't forget to cut about an inch off each stem once submerged."

Julian halted, turned his head slightly and, Jackson could just about make out through the stems and flowers, stared at him with smouldering fury.

Jackson smiled back and, in as helpful a tone as he could affect, added, "At an oblique angle with a sharp pair of secateurs is best. Makes them last twice as long, you know."

Julian's cold stare, of which Jackson could only see one

eye through the greenery, lingered for a moment before he turned on his heels and marched away.

Jackson returned his attention to Julia, who regarded him with an amused smirk, while also shaking her head with minor disapproval. "How do you know so much about cut flowers?" she asked, her head slightly cocked.

"Quarter of a century running, managing and owning some of the finest bars and restaurants in town," Jackson replied with boastful authority, "Believe it or not, cut flowers are one of the biggest expenses. You want to make them last as long as possible."

"You just heard about it in a pub once, didn't you?" she stated rather than asked.

"Yes, I did," Jackson admitted, "But then I tried it and, I can assure you, it does actually work."

"Oh, I know," Julia replied in a low voice which, Jackson felt, implied she knew something he didn't and that, once he did know, he'd feel a bit of a fool. "Come on," she continued, her pitch raised and the bottle held high, "We'll pour out a few glasses and then I'll introduce you to the others."

Jackson took another look around and, to his surprise, noticed that there were, indeed, other people in the room. Some stood, some sat, but all stared, rather unsettlingly, at him as he followed Julia to the kitchen.

***

Wooden chairs with thick comfortable cushions surrounded a large, roughly hewn pine table. On one end of the cornflower yellow room a large, solid fuel stove radiated far too much heat for the current weather. Pots steamed, pans simmered and Jackson could smell the welcome, warm aroma of roasting duck wafting from the oven.

A duo of nervous twenty-somethings, dressed professionally in black and white uniforms, tended to the food preparation in a clumsy yet well-rehearsed manner which betrayed them, at least to Jackson, as novice caterers. First timers on a trial run.

Doing a favour for a friend as the friend was doing a favour for them. One of them made brief eye contact with Jackson and nervously flinched, nearly dropping one of the pans. Jackson winked back, then attended to his own task.

He and Julia stood at the other end of the kitchen where a deep, enamel sink had been filled with ice, in which several more champagne bottles, buried to their chests, stood to attention. Jackson stood next to the sink with one of the bottles in his hand, pressing the base onto the adjacent slate counter. Holding the cork tight, he slowly and methodically twisted the bottle.

"Why were all your friends staring at me like that?" he asked, leaning down as he felt the cork begin to ease upwards.

"Well, obviously they were staring at you because you're Jackson Grimes," Julia teased, carefully lining a row of flutes onto the table, "Doesn't everyone stare at Jackson Grimes?"

Jackson shook his head as the cork gave way with a relieved hiss.

"Aw. No pop," Julia pouted.

"Never. A champagne cork removed should sigh like a well satisfied..." Jackson stopped mid-sentence, as if regretting having started it, then looked down to the table and began to pour.

"Like a well satisfied what?" Julia asked with a provocative lilt.

"Never mind, I forget. Anyway, I asked first. Your friends. Why were they staring?"

"Jackson." Julia's voice hardened. She moved around to the opposite side of the table, placed her hands flat on its surface, straightened her arms and leaned forward. "Look at me."

"What?" Jackson laughed, with a touch unease, while continuing to top up the glasses.

"You heard. Stop what you're doing and look at me."

Jackson carelessly shrugged, put down the bottle, matched Julia's stance with his palms on the table and locked his stare onto hers.

Her expression was serious without being stern. One corner of her mouth curved slightly upwards. Waiting to turn into a half-smile but not quite ready. She stared unflinchingly, unblinkingly into Jackson's eyes with laser-like intensity, which Jackson tried to match but couldn't. His own gaze kept flicking to the other side. To the patch that covered her other eye. Her damaged eye.

After a few moments, he gave in and focused on the injury. The patch was immodestly, almost proudly on display as Julia had worn her hair swept back and raised high. It was not black plastic, as he had expected, but a smaller version of the one she had worn in the hospital. Perforated aluminium covering white, soft gauze. From beneath the gauze, three scars branched out, still fresh under a light dusting of makeup. One extended up her high forehead, ending just before her hairline. The second crossed the hollow of her temple and vanished behind her ear. The third, a more prominent wound, ran down the side of her face. Traversing her high cheekbone, crossing the shallow indentation below and then fading away as it reached her strong, proud jawline.

Jackson looked back to her good eye, still locked on his own with a demanding, dissecting stare. Then he glanced down at her mouth as, finally, the slight curve of at the corner rose into that wicked, knowing half-smile he had been waiting for.

"That is why they are all staring at you," she quietly answered, "Because you were there. Because you saw everything that happened and can tell them all the sordid, grizzly details. I mean, they say it's a 'welcome-home-get-well-soon-we're-all-here-for-you' party. But, let's be honest. It's really a 'gosh-I-wonder-what-she-looks-like-underneath-the-patch-and-what-exactly-happened' ghoul-fest." As she spoke, she carefully placed the drinks onto a small round tray.

"And why, exactly, am I here?"

"The same reason. Because you were there. Also, so that you can carry these drinks. I'm still getting used to this blind spot and lack of depth perception, I'm afraid, so I keep running into walls and dropping things next to tables instead of placing them onto them. Bit of a bore, really. And you are, after all, a pro at these things, are you not?" She flashed a smile, turned and strutted towards the door through which they had entered.

Jackson delayed, looked down at the tray of champagne and took a beat. After a quick glance to make sure that Julia's back was turned, he looked down at his hands, splayed his fingers and examined them. Still. Steady. He smiled, nodding with self-approval.

"What on Earth are you doing?" Julia called from the door as she held it open.

"Nothing," Jackson replied, a touch defensively, "It's just been a long time since I've been a front line soldier instead of a barstool general. I want to get it right."

Julia gave a frown of suspicion to which Jackson reacted with a smile she thought unusually weak and unconvincing. But before she could comment he lifted the loaded tray, casually balanced it onto his fingertips and raised it to chest level. He then plucked another bottle from the ice and, making a show of holding it behind his straight back and hoisting the tray up high, swept across the kitchen to join Julia.

As he neared, Julia stepped in front of him and looked at him with a wicked grin. "Of course," she slowly, mischievously whispered, "the *other* reason that they might be staring at you is because they have all, undoubtedly, read about that catastrophic debacle you caused at the Tate Modern earlier in the week."

Jackson's face fell in unison with Julia's lighting up. "Ah, that," he sighed, "Okay. Now, that was not my fault."

"Yeah, says you."

"No, really. There were extenuating circumstances and many, many factors that were beyond my control. And, what's more, I nearly saved the day!"

Julia responded with a derisory chortle as she led him back into the drawing room.

"…I mean, I'm not saying that he doesn't deserve to be punished. Or that he shouldn't have to make amends. I'm just saying that maybe he has a story to tell, too. That maybe he deserves a little compassion and sympathy, too. Or, whatever. I mean, look. I know about these things, perhaps better than most. I work with people suffering from stress and emotional struggles every day. I see what the world does to some of them. And it can be so cruel. Some people are so fragile. They just can't take it. They just snap and, yeah, sometimes end up doing horrible, terrible things. But they don't mean to. They don't plan to. So, is it entirely their fault? Entirely? Surely, society has to accept a share of the blame? Or, at least, accept a share of the burden to take on? Maybe, just maybe, he too is a victim, of sorts? Don't you think, Sis?"

Jackson looked around the table. For once remaining quiet and, rather than barrelling in, gauging the temperature – which, depending on the seat, varied from searing to below freezing with nothing remotely comfortable in between. Except for Julia who, patiently and stoically, looked across the table at her brother with astounding kindness. The other guests, who Jackson felt he had come to know extremely well during the hour of drinks followed by the four-course dinner, all stared into their desserts. Silently, awkwardly and uncomfortably.

For his own part, Jackson could feel the back of his neck warming. Prickling. His hairs bristling. He thanked God that he had decided to limit control of his alcohol intake throughout the evening and, hence, was able to restrain his simmering temper. He looked from one sibling to the other, as infuriated by the brother's wide-eyed, cloying gawp as he was intrigued by the sister's levelled, even-tempered return.

Finally, Julia smiled and softly replied, "I think it would be nice if you made us all some of your lovely coffee, Julian. The one with the hazelnuts." She smiled to the rest of the table and, moving to stand, suggested, "Perhaps we should take it back in the drawing room, yes?"

A collective murmur of relieved agreement rose, along with the murmurers, all of whom turned towards the drawing room door while Julian, looking strangely irked, shuffled towards the kitchen.

As they all stood, Jackson leaned in to Delia, a silver-haired lady in her mid-eighties wearing a dress that almost matched the chintz sofa, who he'd been sitting beside at the far end of the table from their hostess. "I think you and I could do with something a little more medicinal than coffee," he mischievously whispered, "Don't you, Dee?"

Delia grinned, nodding in agreement and quietly replied, "And perhaps another one of your Lucky Strikes?"

Jackson winked, patted his pocket and extended his arm.

"This time, instead of the stoop, let's go out to the garden," Delia suggested, looping her frail arm through his, "You'll see what I mean, then. I'm sure you'll find it impressive."…

***

…The two had met at the beginning of the evening when Jackson, upon Julia's instruction, had ensured that none of her guests were without refreshment. As they had upon his arrival, they had all eyed him with curiosity, intrigue and, in at least one case, judgement.

Dee, a friend of the family since before Julia's birth, was the last to be served and the first to command Jackson's attention. Brazenly and unashamedly asking him if he had seen the "Villainous violinist".

"Oh, indeed," Jackson had replied, "And, what an abominable, wretched wrong'un he is!"

Jackson went on to regale Dee with a ludicrously exaggerated account of that fateful afternoon's events. Dee hadn't believed a word of it, which they both knew and accepted, but he amused her and the two joined forces for the duration of the evening.

The alliance was entertaining and, for both parties, useful.

Dee, by her own admission, found these social gatherings incessantly and increasingly dull. At her age, being the eldest veteran of this little tribe, she knew everybody present and, more to the point, everything about everyone present. Any new arrival was a welcome arrival, in her books. By way of reciprocation, anyone who knew anything, let alone everything, about Julia and her world was a welcome asset in Jackson's ledger.

Over pre-dinner drinks, in return for a cigarette and the overly embellished account of Julia's accident, Jackson learned that his initial deductions were, in essence, correct. The home had been in the family for several generations. Although well off, the family could never have been considered rich. Especially by today's disproportionate London standards set by gold-plated Saudi princes and diamond-encrusted Russian oligarchs. Julia's parents, descended from minor peerage long forgotten and historically inconsequential, had both been academics. The mother a lecturer on classics. The father, now deceased, a well-respected, if cautiously received, expert on an obscure, utterly useless field of mathematics that only he seemed to understand – and even he never seemed entirely sure. One thing that was certain, to Dee's mind, was that it didn't involve economics. Julia's father, it transpired in later years, had been an appalling investor. His final act of naivety had been to become a name at Lloyds of London just a few short months before the entire house of cards collapsed.

As they filed into the dining room to commence dinner, Jackson made sure to stay at Dee's side – offering his arm for support, which she obviously did not need but accepted with a sly glint of flattery in her eye. Once securely seated by her side, Jackson took control of the nearest bottle of wine, several of which had been generously dotted around the long, extravagantly laid table – which was also adorned with monogrammed silverware, antique china and a stunningly colourful, if utterly pointless, floral centrepiece.

While plying Dee with wine, he amused her with various anecdotes from his past. All carefully selected to lionise him for when, as he knew was inevitable, the tall tales would make their way to Julia's ear. As quo for his quid, Dee completed the fateful story of Julia's parents. How, within months of what he thought had been ensuring a safe future for his family, the insurers did, indeed, come after Julia's father for his cufflinks – along with all his other goods and chattels. After months of wrangling, an agreement was made whereby everything of value but the house was taken. The house, however, would only remain with the family until the end of his and his wife's lives.

Jackson looked around the table and, seeing no sign of Julia's mother, gave Dee a look of curiosity that begged her to continue. She appeared on the verge of doing just that when, to Jackson's frustration, the soup arrived. Although, his frustration rapidly vanished when he saw that the soup was a perfectly seasoned lobster bisque. As he slurped up the first spoonful, another curious thought struck him. He looked across the table to Julian and saw that, sure enough, the younger sibling had elected to forgo the crustacean decadence in favour of a guiltless, dressing-free green salad.

"That was spectacular," Jackson reassuringly whispered to the male caterer as he removed the gleaming, empty soup bowl, "You're doing a terrific job."

The young man, more of a boy, flushed red, attempted a thank-you, failed and swiftly moved on.

Jackson looked back to Dee, who smiled with approval and, as if rewarding Jackson for giving kind words to a child, continued with the sad account of Julia's parents.

Shortly after the humiliating agreement with the robber barons from the City, Julia's father retreated into himself until, just a few months after the sordid incident, he died in his sleep. This, in turn, sent her mother into a downward spiral until about a year ago when, as Dee indelicately yet loving phrased it, "her last, remaining marble finally rolled away."

Since then she had been living in a care home, where Julia visited her most days. Although, recently, the old dear had succumbed to a coma from which she would, in all likelihood, never return.

As Dee finished the story, the female caterer from the kitchen appeared and, nervously, placed the duck before Jackson. He sensed her linger for a moment and, realising he was expected to play some sort of role, made a show of deeply inhaling the aroma, smiled up at her and purred, "Sensational."

Like her partner before, she flushed red, then moved on with, Jackson was both amused and pleased to see, an extra spring of confidence.

"Oh, you are kind," Dee teased.

"Believe me, I'm not," Jackson firmly replied, "And I never lie about food or drink." He sliced through the soft, pink flesh, held it up and, looking at Dee, repeated, "Sensational." He popped it in his mouth and began to chew. As he did so he glanced around and, this time by accident, caught Julian glaring back at him. Jackson looked down at Julian's plate to see what he guessed was nut loaf of some sort. He gave Julian a sorrowful shrug, sliced off another forkful of duck and gleefully raised his eyebrows as he continued to chew. Then, turning back to Dee, he asked, "What's the deal with the brother? I get the distinct impression that he really doesn't like me."

"Ah, ha," Dee teased, flashing Jackson an all-knowing grin while wagging her finger. She then returned to her food, letting Jackson know he'd have to wait until dessert for any further revelations.

Although the dessert arrived as planned, Dee's accompanying disclosures did not. Not long into the main course conversations across the table, encouraged by exquisite food and lubricated by fine wine, began to overlap and merge.

"How are you finding your duck?" The question came with quiet confidence from a well-spoken, ginger-haired man wearing a seersucker suit and a club tie.

"By looking towards my wine, then slightly down and to the left," Jackson replied, offering a good humoured smile. The man laughed, as did his American wife, which had the effect of declaring the conversation open for any and all to join.

General, cross table chit-chat broke out, mostly concerning mundane topics such as the unseasonably hot weather. Then a heated debate ensued regarding a petition against a local construction project – a venture concerning a multimillionaire pop star and his desire to build a subterranean garage for his collection of classic Ferraris. The plans to extend the basement downwards by five floors and under a public street required closing off traffic, inevitably causing inordinate noise and air pollution, for at least eighteen months.

The subject had been introduced by a portly, jolly man wearing a tweet suit and sporting a luxuriant, handlebar moustache. He seemed to have a rather relaxed attitude towards the matter. His wife, however, wearing a pair of blue-tinted, prescription glasses which matched her brightly dyed hair, took a more hard line approach.

"Any local sod who doesn't sign the petition deserves to be entombed in the hole this mediocre pop fart wants to dig, along with him and his stupid, fucking cars!" she vehemently proclaimed.

To which Julia looked over at Jackson with a knowing grin that said, "*You see? You're not the only one who can swear.*"

Just as Jackson was responding with a mild smile of agreement a gaunt, sly-eyed man, pencil thin and wearing a tight, pinstriped suit to prove it, managed to steer the discussion in another direction by latching onto the petition theme and citing one in that day's paper that demanded fewer cuts to NHS funding. Jackson and Julia froze and their shared look shifted to one of seriousness, both knowing where this conversational road would inevitably lead.

Sure enough, as the empty plates from the main course were gathered, the pencil-thin man managed to shoehorn in his undoubtedly rehearsed segue, loftily saying, "Of course, Julia. You've had recent experience with our most glorious of institutions. If it isn't too delicate a subject?"

It fucking is, Jackson thought but restrained himself from bellowing. Instead, as the cheesecake and homemade ice cream arrived, he looked on in uncharacteristic silence while questions, shyly at first, came Julia's way.

Then the pencil-thin man, who Jackson noted also had a pencil-thin moustache, asked Jackson for his thoughts.

Unlike his private replies to Dee, Jackson kept his response to the group, as had Julia, quick, sharp and evasive, saying that, in his humble opinion, "The son-of-a-bitch deserves to spend the rest of his miserable life sealed up the same hole as that pop fart and his stupid, fucking cars!"

A diffusing chortle rippled around the table, Jackson and the blue haired activist clinked classes, and the subject seemed closed.

However, Julian, with an earnest passion, felt the need to add, "But, what if there's more to it than that? What if there are aspects that we don't know about it, or circumstances leading up to it that we're not aware of? I mean, I'm not saying that he doesn't deserve to be punished. Or that he shouldn't have to make amends. I'm just saying that, maybe, he has a story to tell, too..."...

***

..."Impressive indeed, Dee," Jackson agreed, looking out across the garden as he lit two cigarettes and handed one to his new friend and ally. By way of return, she passed back his glass of cognac, which Jackson had purloined from a drinks cabinet he'd spotted near the grandfather clock within moments of arriving, nearly three hours previously. They both took deep drags and released the grey, swirling smoke with relieved sighs.

"That is lovely. Really, I don't know why I ever gave up."

"You didn't, Dee. You just haven't had one for a while. And, after tonight, you probably won't have one for another while. A day, a month, a year, a decade. Doesn't matter. You're still a smoker and always will be."

"Jackson, you do talk a lot of twaddle!"

"Oh, I'm an expert twaddler," Jackson purred, "I excel in twaddle. Twaddle is my currency."

"Well, you've not wrong there," Julia interrupted from behind. Jackson and Dee both turned as, clutching her own glass of cognac, she stepped out to join them and gestured towards Jackson's side-pocket. "Got one of those for me?"

"Here, darling. Have this one," Delia offered, "Silly habit, anyway."

"Thank you, Dee," Julia smiled. She took the cigarette and, as Dee retreated back into the house, sat down on the steps. Tentatively, Jackson moved towards her. She shifted to one side and, accepting the invitation, Jackson sat next to her. Julia took another drag, held it in for a thoughtful moment and, while exhaling, said "He's a good person, you know. That little brother of mine."

"Yes," Jackson tentatively replied, "A proper virtuous one, by all accounts."

Julia nodded, but did not respond.

Jackson felt momentarily awkward. He looked down at the moonlit garden, which was large by any standards, let alone those of central London. Past the rows of flowers, all arranged in uniform, rectangular beds more reminiscent of a farm than a formal garden, he saw a long, plastic structure.

"What's that?" he asked.

"A polytunnel," Julia replied, exhaling another plume, "Poor man's greenhouse, really. Some of the more exotic plants can only flower under cover. Most of them are on the lot but I keep a few here, where I started. After it all went pear shaped and I had to do something."

"Started what?"

"My business," she replied. Jackson surveyed the garden

for another moment, then looked back at her and, joining the dots, glanced past her into the drawing room. At the various bouquets that he and the other guests had brought.

"You're a fucking florist?" he exclaimed.

Julia grinned and nodded, also looking back to the bouquet strewn room. "Most of those probably came from my shop," she sighed, "I wouldn't mind so much but they all get friends and family discount. I must have lost a fortune."

"Oh, Christ." Jackson shook his head and they both laughed.

As their chuckles subsided, Julia in a low, anxious voice said, "I have tickets to see him play, you know."

Jackson frowned, urging her to elucidate.

"The son-of-a-bitch," she explained, gestured towards the eye patch with her hand as she brought the cigarette up for another drag, "He's the first violinist for the London Philharmonic Orchestra. Well, he was. I'd imagine, now that he's in the clink, they'll have to replace him. Anyway. I've got tickets for the end of the week. I'd just bought them online, right there in the bistro, about half an hour before... Well," she took another deep drag, smiled at Jackson and asked, "So, will you come?"

Jackson gave a broad, wide smile, which he wished he was able to disguise but knew he couldn't.

"I'll take that as a yes." Julia put out her cigarette and stood.

Jackson followed suit, frowning with another thought. "Who were you originally going to go with?" he asked.

Julia twisted her lips into a sardonic smile and replied, "Somebody who's suddenly become rather busy and no longer responds to my WhatsApps."

Jackson nodded blankly, trying to pretend he knew what she meant but vaguely recalling that he'd heard about this WhatsApp business quite recently, and they returned to the party.

As they entered the drawing room, Jackson noticed the roses

he'd brought had been rather shabbily arranged and tucked away in a dark corner near the downstairs lavatory. He rolled his eyes, unimpressed, when a further detail caught his eye. Julian had, indeed, found a suitable replacement to subsidise the household's vase shortage. A pre-war, metal bedpan, enamelled white with ugly, institutional-blue piping and covered with rust spots.

"Oh, very good," Jackson muttered to himself, "Bravo, little brother." He looked around and located Julian across the room, glaring back at him. Jackson returned the hard glower for as long as he could, which was about a second and a half until his facade cracked into a wide grin. He raised his glass, flicked a glance at the bedpan and gave the younger sibling a long, congratulatory bow. Julian, momentarily taken aback, raised his own glass and, almost involuntarily, returned a nod of appreciation.

***

Although Jackson was one of the first to leave the party it was well into the wee hours by the time he arrived back at Claridge's. Rather than take a taxi straight from Julia's house, high up on Primrose Hill, he decided upon a walk through the Royal Parks. Partly because it was such a warm night. Partly because there was a clear sky and a bright, full moon. Mostly because he knew of an after hours bar on Portland Place – just the other side of Regent's Park and a few blocks from where he would re-emerge into the West End.

At the bottom of Primrose Hill Jackson crossed over Regent's Canal. To his left, towards Camden, a small flotilla of permanently moored narrowboats, one painted with a high gloss chessboard motif, floated silently and still in the water – opposite the ostentatiously red, two story, floating Chinese restaurant.

From the other direction, towards Embassy Row and, beyond, Little Venice, a pair of night cruising narrowboats motored towards him. Front-mounted spotlights illuminated, music blaring, the boaters squeezing every warm moment out of the Indian summer – which everyone felt would, but knew couldn't, last forever. As they passed London Zoo aviary, standing tall under the moonlight, a cacophony of multi-species birdsong cried out in chaotic unison. Petitioning the boaters, along with their engines and their general revelry, to shut up.

Jackson stood in the middle of the bridge, smoking a cigarette and watching boaters navigate their way beneath. The skipper of the second barge waved up at him and Jackson waved back – this time with no casualties. As the boats reached the floating Chinese and made the sharp left turn into Camden, where he knew their volume would be moderate by comparison, Jackson flicked away the cigarette and continued across to Regent's Park. Then through the straight and majestic, tree-lined path that cut so efficiently from North London to the West End.

When he reached the top of Portland Place Jackson picked up his speed, checking his watch and realising that even he might have difficulty getting served at this time of the night. He turned down the wide, neoclassical avenue and saw, outside the doorway that was his destination, a tight knot of men, most of whom he recognised. All middle-aged and well heeled. All raucously laughing and furiously smoking.

Jackson took a few more steps and was about to shout out a hullo but stopped, suddenly uneasy. The feeling that welled up inside him was not one of excitement, or eagerness, but rather a sense of tired apathy. He stood watching the loud, sweaty carousers and tried to put a finger on the exact emotion he was unexpectedly feeling. Then he smiled. It was boredom. The idea of venturing into the depths of yet another late night drinking den, only to re-emerge sometime in the near, or more likely not-so-near, future, with only the haziest of memories, suddenly seemed dull.

Jackson watched for a few minutes, until the smokers returned inside, and he chuckled. *Well,* he thought, *that really will put a dampener on the general proceedings, won't it?* He shook his head, turning away as a taxi with its top light illuminated came around the corner. He hailed it, boarded and made his way home.

***

A few minutes later, Jackson bounded through the revolving doors of Claridge's and, with the exuberance of a teenager returning from a first date that had surpassed even his wildest expectations, bounced up the stairs towards his suite. When he was about half way up George, stationed at his desk, called after him,

"Mr Grimes?"

"Not now, George. Whatever it is can wait until the morning."

"Well no, Mr Grimes, it's your wife."

"I have no wife, George," Jackson called back without breaking stride, "And I can show you the paperwork to prove it!"

Jackson rounded the corner and, removing the key from his pocket, approached his door.

"Hugo?" he called out as he strode into the suite, "Hugo, old boy, where are you?"

Closing the door, Jackson threw his keycard onto the coffee table. As he moved towards the bedroom he removed his jacket, tossed it onto the sofa and again bellowed, "Hugo!" as he marched into the bedroom, where he saw a large bulge under the duvet cover. "Christ, dog, how did you manage to get yourself under there?"

Hugo replied with a confused, "Huff," which came from behind Jackson.

Jackson turned to see the dog standing in the bathroom door, staring confusedly up at him and then back at the bed.

Equally perplexed, Jackson turned back to face the bed.

The duvet erupted and Sandra appeared. Wide-eyed, trembling and naked. Her reddened cheeks were streaked with makeup stained tears as she cried, "Jackie!" in a torn, broken whine, "Where have you been?"

"Jesus Christ!" Jackson screamed, "What the fuck are you doing here?"

Chapter 14

"It was terrifying," Jackson repeated, for at least the fourth time, with a low shake in his voice.

Max had only been half listening. He had been trying to continue with the organisation of his paperwork while Jackson, clutching a glass of his whisky, lay back on his leather sofa, stared up at his office ceiling and rattled on with yet another one of his own exaggerated, self-indulgent stories.

"Was it, now?" Max condescendingly muttered while shuffling spreadsheet B from pile X onto stack Y.

"It really was," Jackson earnestly replied, then impatiently added, "Why are you doing that, anyway? Don't you have a secretary to take care of all that on some sort of wretched machine these days?"

"An executive assistant. And, yes, I do. But this gives me a clearer picture of where things stand and, more importantly, it relaxes me. You're not the only dinosaur in the village, you know. And, by the way, I'm pretty sure that I'm still not speaking to you."

"Oh, come now, old boy. I think, given the circumstances, we can put all that behind us, don't you?"

"No," Max sternly replied, then cursed himself as he returned spreadsheet B to pile X and shifted memorandum C onto pile Z. The latter move seemed to make him happy and he smiled, giving himself a contented nod of approval.

"Really, Max. It was horrible. I mean," Jackson sat up, leaned forward with his forearms resting on his knees, took a slug of Maxes whisky and looked up with exhausted, dark-circled eyes, "Apart from anything else, I had no idea how strong she is."

This seemed to get Max's attention. "What do you mean by that?" he asked, his mental alarm bells ringing as he held contract twenty-seven in the air, allowing it to hover between inbox tray Delta and outbox tray Bravo...

…"What the fuck are you doing here?"

"I've been waiting for you, Jackie!"

"Well, I can see that! Christ! How long? How did you get in here? Who let you in here?" Jackson babbled, "I mean. Jesus, Sandra," he found himself back at the beginning of his confused, increasingly panicked thought process, "What the fuck are you doing here?"

"Jackie, I want you to come home!"

"I am home, ya mad freak!"

"I mean *our* home!" Sandra screamed. Then she launched herself forward, threw her arms around Jackson's neck and, as they both fell to the floor, wrapped her legs around his waist.

"Sandra! Jesus! Sandra! Get off!" Jackson shouted, desperately trying to escape Sandra's grip but finding himself trapped underneath her. "Sandra, please!" he barely managed to croak as her arms, coiled around his neck, tightened with his each and every move.

Jackson looked over at Hugo who ran up and down the room, barking excitedly while looking from master to mistress. As if he were a neutral fan unsure of which wrestler to support, so cheering for both.

"Jackie, I love you!" Sandra yelled.

"Christ, Sandra, for the love of God!" Jackson could hardly get the words out as her writhing continued and her hold strengthened. He could feel her ankles interlock behind him and her thighs clamping at his sides.

He looked over at Hugo whose cheering, for either competitor, had ceased. Now replaced with concerned, worried attentiveness.

"Do something, you useless mutt!" Jackson managed to wheeze through his crushed windpipe. Then he looked to the door as a loud, alarmed knock emanated from the other side.

"Mr Grimes!" George called out with what Jackson thought was entirely too calm an attitude, "Mr Grimes, is everything okay in there?"

"No, of course it fucking isn't!" Jackson, red-faced and blue-lipped, strained to scream but barely managed to gasp. Then he gave up, knowing that any sort of volume or projection had been crushed out of him. Instead, he looked to Hugo who, again, started to bark. This time, Jackson was relieved to hear, with an appropriate sense of urgency.

"Mr Grimes!" George again shouted from the other side and, just as Jackson felt he was about to lose consciousness, the door burst open...

***

..."I mean, my God," Jackson continued to Max, who had now abandoned his paperwork and sat opposite Jackson, "Diminutive she may be but, I shit you not, it's all muscle and sinew. Never used to be like that, you know. Has she been doing Pilates?"

"Pilates? Bloody hell, Jackson, what happened next? Is she okay?"

"Yes, of course. She's fine," Jackson blustered, then winced, "Well... Sort of."

Max regarded Jackson with a narrow, suspicious squint. Jackson shrugged, splayed his hands defensively and continued...

***

..."NO! I wanna go back to the ROOM!" Sandra's bellow reverberated around the lobby. Her eyes, black-ringed from the running makeup, were almost as wide as her mouth, in which her bared teeth glistened.

Her hands gripped the bannisters and locked on like a pair of vice grips. Jackson, standing on the stairs above her, attempted to prise open the fingers of one. George stood on the step below her and tried to do the same with her other. Between them, and behind Sandra, a uniformed police officer held a thick blanket over her, attempting to protect her modesty and rescue her dignity.

"Sandra. You've gotta come with us," Jackson pleaded.

"NO!" Sandra shrieked, "Take me back to the ROOM! I wanna go back to the ROOM!" She screamed "room" with startling volume and terrifying rabidity.

Hugo sat watching from the bottom of the stairs with perplexed curiosity. Marco stood at his side, holding a relaxed leash, and also stared up at the mayhem – equally perplexed but, rather than curious, horrified.

After a few minutes, blue and red flashing lights appeared against the darkened, plate glass windows. Marco opened a set of double-doors next to the revolving doors. Another uniformed police officer marched in, followed by two paramedics who manned a wheelchair. The wheelchair had been equipped with restraints for the wrists, ankles and waist...

***

..."Bloody hell, Jackson! You might have opened with that! They didn't section her, did they?"

"Well, I fucking hope so!" Jackson snapped back, somewhat irked at Max's lack of sympathy towards him.

Max hurriedly pulled on his jacket while gathering his mobile phone and wallet from his desk.

"Besides," Jackson wistfully continued, shaking his head and sipping his drink, "Maybe it's for the best."

"For the best?"

"You know what they say, old boy. If the straitjacket fits." Jackson winced as he uttered the line. Then gave an almost apologetic shrug.

"God, you really are a complete arsehole," Max fumed, "But, never mind. Once again, Max is here to clean up Jackson's mess."

"My mess?" Jackson exclaimed. He shot to his feet, his eyes popping, and he looked at Max with pure indignation as he remonstrated, "What do you mean, *my* mess? You're blaming me for this?"

Max ignored Jackson's affronted wail, threw open the door and marched down the hall, shouting at his executive assistant that he'd be gone for the rest of the day.

Jackson stepped over to the, still open, door and called after him, "Again?"

Max turned to face Jackson and was about to deliver a vehement response when, behind him, the elevator door pinged open. He boarded and, as the door closed, merely scowled at Jackson with disapproval verging on despair.

"Well," Jackson huffed, closing Max's office door but remaining inside.

Jackson cradled his half-remaining whisky, sauntered over to the plate glass window and looked down at the view. He took some deep, relaxing breaths and, feeling calmer, looked out at the city.

Not his favourite view of London but, nonetheless, spectacular, if in a severe and slightly sinister way. Max's office was high up in one of the glass and steel towers of the City, overlooking the modern, global, finance-centric London as opposed to the old, Empire-proud, industrial one. The jagged, sky-splitting shard, the top of which Jackson always wanted to tell someone to finish, owned by Qatar. The fat, bloated Gherkin owned by a medley of internationals. And that monstrous, shapeless slab, owned by the Chinese. The latter leaning down and looming over the older city with a menacing stoop. Ready, should the sun happen to be in the wrong place, to set fire to any one of its unsuspecting neighbours. Jackson looked up at the azure, blistering sky and wondered if this could be such a day. Then he remembered that the frontage of this monolithic nightmare had been covered with slats to prevent any more such events – while also adding a sinister, Kafkaesque quality to the concrete behemoth.

He knocked back the rest of his whisky, strolled over to

Max's drinks cabinet and picked out another first-rate malt. Just as he was about to pour, he turned back to the window and looked up at the cloudless sky. His eyes wandered across the horizon towards the tiny, distant London Eye – which he'd recently been told, in some bar or other, was British owned but American sponsored. An Anglo-American mutt, just like him. For the sake of solidarity, Jackson had no choice but to approve.

From there, Jackson's attention wandered to his own area of town and, beyond that, the other side of the city. Out of sight but still on his mind. He smiled, thinking about Primrose Hill and what a beautiful day it must have been over there.

Jackson put down the bottle and the glass, took out his mobile phone and dialled the only number saved that wasn't Max or Claridge's.

"Cracking day, don't you think?" he said, by way of hello. Julia agreed with a light, whimsical note in her voice. Then, attempting a similar tone in his own inflection, Jackson suggested, "Fancy an afternoon stroll?"

***

"Well, tell me a bit about her, then? What's she like?"

"Oh, you know. Usual stuff. Heart of gold. Soul of an angel. Only got the one eye."

"The one eye, you say?" the vendor asked with a knowing smile. He reached under the polished glass counter and removed an antique, silk-embroidered box of about six inches in length.

Jackson opened it and inspected within. Then he looked back up the vendor with an astonished gawp followed by a crooked smile and replied, "Bloody perfect."

Minutes later, Jackson skipped up the steps from the basement of Gray's Antique Market – a warren of stall-sized antique, jewellery and general curiosity shops in the heart of

Mayfair. He nodded quick goodbyes to the various other wheelers and dealers whose wares he had inspected, judged and found wanting over the last forty minutes or so. Several stiffly returned the gesture, while glancing down at the obvious bulge in Jackson's suit pocket. Knowing that it was a sale they had dropped only to have snatched up by one of their ruthlessly competitive friends.

Once out in the searing daylight, Jackson marched over to a bollard to which Hugo, sprawled out and dozing in the sun, was leashed. As Jackson untied the lead the dog gave a brief, lazy grunt of complaint.

"Oh, come on, Hugo!" Jackson blustered, "We don't have time to bugger about!"

Hugo looked up and gave a resigned whimper. With a long stretch and a wide, slobbery yawn he pulled himself to his feet.

"I hope you didn't leave that poor animal out in this sun for too long!" The censorious remark came from a stern-faced man-boy, with sun-bleached dreadlocks and a platted beard, who carried a tatty, hemp tote-bag.

Jackson shot him a hard squint and coldly replied, "This poor animal shall, tonight, dine on the finest beef carpaccio and steak tartare that this great city has to offer. What's on your evening menu?" he leaned forward and peered down his nose into the tote bag, then sneeringly added, "Lentil boy."

The man-boy flushed red, looked around for support and, finding none, scurried into the crowd.

Once the meddler was out of sight, Jackson picked up a half-empty water dish and, with Hugo at his side, approached a nearby drinks stand, cheerfully saying, "Thanks for keeping an eye, Dave," while handing the dish to the stall's grinning owner. "You're a star, as always."

"A bit harsh on the poor hippy kid, there. Weren't you, Jackson?" Dave replied.

"People should mind their own bloody business," Jackson haughtily snapped. Then he looked up at the sun, which was lower than he would have liked. "Damn," he muttered, checking his watch. He'd arranged to meet Julia near Hyde Park Corner in less than ten minutes. "Seen any taxis around?"

"Loads. None of them going anywhere, mind," Dave goaded.

Jackson gave him a sardonic smile, bought another bottle of water and made his way up to Oxford Street. There he quickly spotted a stationary taxi, opened the door and, pushing Hugo in first, slammed it behind them.

"Hyde Park Corner, my good man. Quick as you like," Jackson exclaimed with as much self-important urgency as he could muster.

The heavily tattooed, shirtless cabbie, sweat-drenched and exhausted, swivelled around and peered up from a limp, red-topped newspaper. He flashed a glance of suspicion at Hugo, then said to Jackson, "You two in a hurry, then?"

"We are."

"Well, I've been sitting here, going nowhere slowly, for half the afternoon. And then some. Had a fare in the back trying to get to Sloan Square. She got out to take the tube."

"Take the what?" Jackson icily responded.

"Tube. Hyde Park's only a couple've stops and one change from here."

"A couple of what? What are you talking about?"

"Tube, mate. Underground." He gestured towards the nearby sign for Bond Street Underground Station.

Jackson stared back at the driver, flabbergasted.

The cabbie shrugged, "I mean, I can take you if you want. But you'll be looking at the best part of an hour and not much change out of a bullseye."

Jackson continued to stare back, his bewilderment unchanged.

The taxi driver leaned forward and politely explained, "A bullseye means fifty quid, mate."

"I know what a bullseye means!" Jackson snapped.

The driver displayed his palms with an exaggerated apology.

Jackson sighed, equally apologetic, glared towards the London Underground sign and muttered, "Truth be told, if I had the time, I'd happily fork up a ton or even a monkey to avoid going down into that cesspool."

"Well, you'll get no complaints from me, mate."

"Sadly, it's not your complaints that concern me," Jackson sighed. Then he thanked the driver and, leaving him back to his newspaper, quit the taxi and footslogged towards the underground station.

As he neared the tube station's escalator Jackson stared, dumbfounded, at the throngs of half-naked, sun-soaked masses crushing their way onto the conveyance. Red, fat lumps of roasted flesh, glistening with sunscreen, sweat and stink. All pressed together as they descended into the steaming, fetid bowels of the city. Then he stopped dead in his tracks.

"You've gotta be kidding," he whined, staring at a sign which read, 'All dogs must me carried on the escalator and train'.

Jackson looked down at Hugo, who returned his master's dejected frown with a worried, sideways tilt of his massive head.

***

"Well, Julia. I have just learned one of life's great lessons."

"And what would that be?" Julia asked, slurping the end of her iced coffee.

"There is nothing great about the unwashed. Have you been on the London Underground lately? It is shocking."

Julia pursed her lips, restraining a smile, and replied, "I use the London Underground all the time, Jackson. I live in London."

"Jesus, you sound just like the Non-Lawyer."

Julia responded with a quizzical frown.

"Max," Jackson clarified as he took the seat opposite her. He then gave a flinch of embarrassment when he noticed that her coffee was empty. "I hope I haven't kept you waiting for too long."

"I've been in good company," Julia softly replied, patting the copy of *Venice* he had given her in the hospital. Jackson gave an appreciative, almost humble, nod. As he did so he looked around to inspect the surroundings.

The meeting point had been of Julia's choosing and Jackson had been in such a rush to get there that, when he arrived, he saw only her and failed to notice the setting. They were sitting at a small wicker table outside an Italian cafe on a cobbled side-street. *Outside*, thought Jackson. Cautiously, he found himself glancing upwards. Julia cracked a smile.

"Don't worry. I've already checked," she assured him, "No open windows."

Jackson matched her smile, beckoned over a waiter and ordered more iced coffee for them and water for Hugo – to whom, as Jackson tethered him, Julia gave a curious, warm smile. Hugo looked back at her with equal interest.

"And, who's this?" Julia asked as she bent down.

"This is Hugo. And he needs to lose some weight."

Julia introduced herself by offering her hand for inspection and, upon Hugo's enthusiastic approval, stroking his head while saying, "Well, I think he looks smashing. Don't you, Hugo?"

Hugo gave a happy groan of assent and rested his head on Julia's lap, which she welcomed, settling into absent-mindedly scratching behind his ears while she returned her attention to Jackson. "I must say, I was surprised to get your call."

"Why would that be?" Jackson asked, sounding slightly put out.

"I thought you didn't do mobile phones. Or any sort of phones, for that matter. I was expecting a letter. Or a telegram. Or even a message hand delivered by one of your hotel porters."

"Ah," Jackson reached into his inside pocket and, with sadly inappropriate pride, produced his late twentieth century design mobile phone. "You know, you'd have received my first call if you hadn't managed to escape the hospital so early. Mind you, I do wish I'd thought of the message delivered by the hotel porter thing. And can you still send telegrams?"

"I doubt it," Julia shrugged, "But wouldn't it be wonderful?"

"That it would," Jackson agreed, "Although, this isn't too far off. It's pay as you go." He handed her the device for inspection.

"Oooh. A burner!" Julia teased with genuine enthusiasm as she opened the flip-phone. Examining it as one would a long-lost toy from one's childhood.

"That's right!" Jackson exclaimed, with boyish excitement, "Like a spook!"

"Actually, I was thinking more like a drug dealer. Or an outlaw on the run."

"That's even better. Well, the outlaw on the run bit. I despise drug dealers. But, anyway, you get it. Max just thought I was being childish."

"Oh, you are being childish. But that's alright. Probably a good thing, all things considered. And who's this Max? That's the second time you've mentioned him in as many minutes."

"Just someone who says he isn't talking to me at the moment."

"Why do I get the feeling that doesn't really narrow things down?"

Jackson replied with a shrug of guilty agreement, just as the phone began to vibrate in Julia's hand.

"Well, he's talking to you now," Julia chimed, handing it back. Jackson took the phone and, sure enough, the display read 'Non-Lawyer'. Jackson considered for a moment, clenching his teeth, then switched off the device and slipped it back into his inside pocket.

"How's my dear friend, Dee?" he cheerily asked, leaning back into the seat and reaching for his coffee.

***

"For God's sake, Jackson. What's was the point in getting a new phone if you're never going to bloody answer it?" Max spat the message and, as he hung up, muttered, "And what's the point in me leaving messages I know you'll never bloody listen to?" As he finished talking to himself he smiled at an approaching nurse.

"You can go in now," the nurse said, then cautioned, "but not for too long, please."

Max nodded his acceptance.

The ward comprised of two long rows of beds, uniformly spaced on either side. Each one occupied by someone groaning, moaning or coughing. The ill, the infirm and the dying.

Only Sandra appeared silent. She sat still, propped up with overstuffed pillows and swathed in dull, grey linen. The sheets, tucked in protectively tight, were pulled up to her neck. Aside from her face, only her left arm was exposed, allowing access for an intravenous drip.

Her eyes appeared even larger than normal. Opened wide. Fixed and vacant, until her gaze shifted onto Max as he quietly entered. Then they silently followed him as he approached and took the seat beside her. As she looked up at him two large tears rolled down each of her reddened cheeks. Max clasped her hand and, with a warm smile, leaned forward.

"I don't even remember what happened," Sandra whispered. Her voice shaking, hoarse and exhausted. With a muted and frightened quaver, she added, "What happened?"

Max smiled, squeezed her hand and shook his head, telling her it didn't matter. Then he turned, distracted by a loud, phlegmy cough from the neighbouring patient.

"First things first," he said, with soft reassurance, "Let's get you out of here."

***

"No, thank you," Julia replied to the waiter, declining his offer of another coffee, "I was promised a walk."

Hugo, whose head still rested on Julia's lap, looked up at her and gave a low, hopeful moan.

The waiter replied with a courteous incline, placed the bill on the table and returned to the restaurant.

Jackson, to whom Julia's latter statement had been directed, responded with an enthusiastic, "Here, here," and removed from his breast pocket a well-worn, passport size wallet.

Julia tried, and failed, not to notice that it was stuffed with bank notes. All of them crisp, unfolded and filed, Queen's face front and upright, in order of denomination. She gave an embarrassed flinch when she saw that Jackson had noticed her intrusion. Then she smiled, deciding to play the moment through, and said, "Haven't you heard of debit cards, Jackson?"

Jackson arched an eyebrow and, with a deep and raspy voice, replied, "Real men carry cash."

As they stood, Julia retorted, "Real idiots get mugged."

The trio strolled towards Green Park. Hugo bounced along between Jackson and Julia, his leash hanging loosely as he happily thrashed his tail against their legs.

They sauntered past Apsley House, with its majestic, neoclassical facade. Former home of, and now museum dedicated to, the Duke of Wellington.

"And the coolest address in town," Jackson pointed out. To which they both, in unison, added, "Number One London."

They then both confessed that neither had ever been inside, like so many of the free museums in London. Each would walk past at least one every day, mentally adding it to the must-do-that-some-day list. Then time moves on and the must-do-that-some-day list gets distilled down to a wish list. Until, as time begins dwindle, the wish list is whittled down to the inevitable bucket list.

"Cheery," Julia said, taking Jackson by surprise as he had

almost forgotten that he was speaking aloud. Without the usual filters of humour and derision, these were the thoughts he would usually dwell upon in the privacy his mind.

Julia registered the slight discomfort in his demeanour and, gently changing the conversation's course, said, "I've also never been to New York."

"Oh, you should." Jackson replied, then boasted, "It's the greatest city in the world."

"And yet you moved here. Why was that?"

"Okay, then – second greatest."

Julia tilted her head and sighed, telling Jackson that this answer would not be sufficient. She then pointed out that Jackson already knew almost everything about her, thanks to the indiscretions of his new best friend, Dee, and that it was time to even the score.

Reluctantly, Jackson succumbed. As they made their through Green Park, winding through the sun-dappled paths under the canopies of the, still leafy, plane and lime trees, Jackson told Julia about his first days in London.

He had come over on a whim, mostly to spite his parents. Jackson came from a background of moderate wealth and privilege. The money had come from his great-great-grandfather: an oil baron, a steel mogul, an automotive tycoon and an aviation pioneer. Great-great-granddaddy had been a good, old-fashioned, American Captain of industry, which meant that Great-grandaddy needed to do nothing. Which is exactly what he, and subsequent heirs, had done. The result being that Jackson represented the final generation of legacy money, the rules of entropy having applied to the Grimes family purse just as stringently they do to the laws of physics. Jackson's grandparents had been born into staggering opulence. His parents had been born wealthy. Jackson, almost rich.

Nevertheless, on his twenty-first birthday Jackson came into his, not immodest, inheritance. The day after his twenty-first birthday he called his parents from JFK International Airport, airside, to announce that he'd decided that a law degree from Columbia University really wasn't for him and that he'd really much rather bum around the world for a while instead. He thought he'd start in London.

After his first week in London, he'd already started to feel bored. A new friend asked if he'd mind filling in for some bar work. Jackson hated work – but he loved bars. On the first night Jackson discovered that he had a talent for two things: mixing cocktails and selling happiness.

A month later, he met Max at the infamous Central Line Party. The friendship came first, the partnership a year later when Jackson became Max's first client. A new kind of business called Personal Wealth Management. Naturally, the first thing Jackson did was go against every piece of advice Max gave him and sink his entire worth, along some funds he'd actually convinced Max to lend him, into buying a dilapidated West End bar. Within half a year it was the hottest spot in town.

"To tell you the truth," Jackson confided to Julia, as they neared St James's Palace, "in the end we made a hell of a lot more from the real estate than we ever did the bar. Same with the restaurants. But, hey, that's the Big Smoke for you, right?"

Even then, Jackson had never intended for the move to be permanent. Until Max and his wife, Deborah, did Jackson the greatest favour, and the worst disservice, of their lives. They introduced Jackson to Sandra. The Diminutive One.

"That's not a terribly flattering moniker for someone you must have once loved enough to immigrate for," Julia lightly chided.

"True. True," Jackson quietly replied, his eyes down, just as they just reached the edge of Green Park. "Mind you, I might have stayed anyway. I mean, New York is great, but it doesn't have this." He gestured to their right. The wide, straight Mall, with Buckingham Palace at the end, lined on both sides with fluttering Union Flags. From the Palace a troop of Horse Guards, sitting tall and proud with their armour glinting in the low sunlight, trotted towards them in

152

perfect formation.

Julia accepted the digression. Again, she handled the conversation's tiller asking, "Where are you taking me, anyway?" with a peppering of light intrigue.

Jackson replied with a wide, boyish smile. He took her hand, led her across the road into St James's Park and, moments later, they stood, as the sun readied to set, in the centre of the Blue Bridge.

"The best views in London," Jackson cooed.

Julia looked out across the lake. Again, Buckingham Palace, with the Royal Standard flying overhead.

"Whichever way you look." Jackson added, gently placed his hands on Julia's shoulders and turned her around to face the other side of the lake – Whitehall. The turreted clocktower and romanesque arches of Horseguard Parade, in the distance the Tower of Westminster and, beyond, the London Eye. The lowering, bright sunlight flickered on the water beneath them on which banks of swans, teams of ducks and herds of Canadian geese gracefully glided.

Julia silently agreed.

In the quiet moment, Jackson removed from his pocket the paper wrapped gift he had purchased from Gray's Antique Market and handed it to Julia. Julia gave a single laugh.

"You do like to give presents, don't you, Jackson Grimes?"

"Not to everybody," he assured her.

Julia sighed, took the package and removed the brown paper and string, revealing an antique, silk embroidered box.

"Jackson, it's lovely," she said, admiring the intricate design of the needlework. Red and white roses against a silver background. Their green, thorny stems platted together. Then she opened the box and paled. Suddenly nervous, she stared down at the item within, then looked back up at Jackson.

Tentatively, Jackson reached behind her head. He slowly, delicately, took in his fingers the string that fastened her eye-patch. Julia flinched, unsure, and Jackson stopped. Stayed still. Julia took a nervous breath – then looked back at him, smiled, and nodded.

Jackson untied the string and, tenderly, removed the eyepatch. Behind, the scars appeared more obvious without the makeup. Raw. Fragile. The eyelid hung limp. A tiny, flesh veil loosely draped over the plundered home of a stolen artefact.

Jackson reached into the silk box and removed the gift – an antique eyepatch. Embroidered white silk with a single red rose crafted in the centre, highlighted by a strong silver thread surround.

Jackson took the gauze dressing from the hospital's patch, placed it into the silk one and gently placed it over Julia's wounded eye. He tied the white ribbon, attached to the patch by a loop on either side, behind her head and stood back.

He smiled, and quietly said, "Just adds a bit of, I don't know... Panache."

Julia gave a small, tearful laugh and nodded. Her soft, warm smile matched his and, as cautiously as he did, she slowly moved forward. And they kissed.

Chapter 15

After the sun set, Jackson and Julia continued their walk through the park and up to Piccadilly Circus. Julia commented on the magnificence of the dazzling, dynamic billboard screens that have, for decades, illuminated the Circus. Growing only bigger and brighter with each technological leap. A fantastic, bizarre cross between grandiose architecture, loud entertainment and crass commercialism.

"Where else would a Coca-Cola advert come close to becoming a listed landmark?" she wondered aloud.

To which Jackson only just managed to restrain the proud New Yorker within from replying, *Time Square, sweetheart, which makes Piccadilly Circus look like a string of second-hand freakin' Christmas tree lights!*

There, they parted ways. Julia, much to Jackson's consternation, ventured below the streets to begin her homeward journey. She would have taken Jackson up on his offer of dinner but her brother was waiting and she had promised to eat with him.

"Ah, the Virtuous One," Jackson said, "You know, I don't think he likes me very much. Although that gag with the roses in the bedpan was above and beyond. Bravo to him on that one."

"He is a good person, you know," Julia sternly replied, defending her sibling with just a hint of reproach towards Jackson. Julia told Jackson how proud she was of him for standing up for the various causes in which he believed. For volunteering at the several community centres, outreach programmes and homeless shelters. For taking the lead in organising some of the more important demonstrations in recent years.

Jackson agreed. This was indeed good work, and he should be commended. But on the walk back to the hotel Jackson couldn't help wondering why this goodness wasn't spent closer to home. What a pity it was that the Virtuous One had only visited his sister once, for five minutes, during her traumatic stay in hospital, because of his previous, important commitments. What a shame that he spent his time looking after strangers while Julia was left to attend their aged, senile mother – visiting on an almost daily basis while he came by once a month to tell the old dear, for what that was worth, about all the unfortunates in the world he had spent his time saving. How sad that it was left to Julia to run the business and the home, ensuring that The Virtuous One was housed and well fed so he could march on with his good deeds. And how wretched that he, and so many like him, spent their lives trying to save the planet by screaming at the world, deafening themselves to the cries of those closest to them. Those who they might actually have a chance of helping. Of saving.

Then Jackson's thoughts turned to his own parents. Both gone for years now. His father from a long, painful and humiliating illness. A curse that Jackson wouldn't wish on his worst enemy, let alone a father. Or a child. His mother followed soon afterwards, from a heart attack. A broken heart, some had said, and Jackson shuddered with shame at how he had been too busy to make the short, seven-hour flight across the Atlantic before either passed. Not because he was volunteering in a centre, or working for a charity, or trying to save the planet. Rather, because he had drinks to pour, customers to please and an ego to feed.

At least, these were the reasons he told the world – with such conviction that, eventually, he began to believe them himself. The deeply buried reality being too shameful, to terrifying, to admit – even to himself. Especially to himself.

As he rounded the final corner, seeing Claridge's up ahead, Jackson spat into his own hypocrisy. That night he would drink alone, pondering the three cast iron promises he had made to himself, all those years ago, which he now found himself perilously close to breaking. Then he would sleep fitfully, his dreams invaded by the man with the white beard.

***

156

"Not that I don't enjoy our increasingly regular breakfasts, old boy, but I thought you still weren't talking to me?" Jackson called out by way of greeting to Max, who stood down in the lobby as he jogged down the stairs with Hugo at his side.

"I'm not," Max stiffly replied, "Not by choice, anyway. And I'm certainly not here for breakfast."

"Just as well. Hugo isn't welcome in the main restaurant. We're going around the corner."

"Jackson, I don't have time for this and we really do need to talk."

"And I really do need to eat. So, come. Let's do both. Wasn't it you who once taught me about the value of compromise?"

"Not with any sort of success," Max tetchily replied, then he shook his head and flung out his hands. "Alright, alright. Lead the way."

"Good man," Jackson cheerily exclaimed, slapping Max on both of his biceps. With Hugo on one side and Max on the other he marched out of the door, turned right and, just before Bond Street, ducked into the small, quaintly cobbled Lancashire Court.

"They actually serve decent coffee here," Jackson enthused as they took a table under an oversized, square awning. While Jackson ordered a pot of coffee and a bottle of sparkling water, Max removed from his pocket a spiral-bound notebook and, with a well-worn Mont Blanc fountain pen, proceeded to furiously jot.

Jackson watched for a moment, feeling a wistful smile creep across his face as he remembered gifting Max the pen, which matched his own, on their thirtieth birthday. Then he asked, "What are you doing, old boy?"

"I am making a list, old boy," Max sunnily replied, "In fact, I am making two lists. I am then going to give both of these lists to you. You are then going to take both of these

157

lists and," Max reached into his pocket and removed a set of keys with a Hello Kitty fob, "these keys to yours and your wife's flat."

"Oh, for fuck's sake!"

"No, for Sandra's sake. And for your sake. And for my sake. And for all our bloody sakes! After you leave the flat, you are then going to take the various items you have collected to the King Edward VII Hospital."

"Where? Is that where she is?"

"The King Edward VII Hospital. And, yes, it is."

"That's the one the Royal Family use, isn't it? It must be the most expensive hospital in London. How's she affording that?"

"Yes, they do. Yes, it is. And, you're paying for it."

"I can assure you, I'm not."

"I can assure you, you are."

"Oh, for Chrissakes, Max! Why?"

"Why? Because I am your manager, Jackson. I am your accountant. I am your trustee. I am, may God have mercy upon me, your friend. And I am telling you to. It comes under the You Broke It, You Fix It rule of life."

"Are you ready to order your food, yet?" an enthusiastic waiter interrupted.

"No!" Jackson snapped, keeping a wide-eyed stare of astonishment on Max, "Seriously. You really are blaming me for her melt down?"

"Not in the way that you think I am, Jackson. I'm not saying it's your fault directly. Or that it was the result of any malicious act on your part. Or that you intended to spend two decades gaslighting your wife to the point where she has now had a full-on clinical breakdown. But I am saying that it is your responsibility. I am saying that, like it or not, your behaviour, your attitude and your constant, outrageous insanity has, to put it mildly, rubbed off on her. And not in a good way, Jackson. Not in a fun way."

"Do you hear violins?"

"What? No. Jackson, focus! Do not bring Hugo. They

158

won't let him into the hospital."

"I'm sure I can hear violins."

"Bloody hell, who cares?"

"Oh, that's coming from the Handel museum," the hovering waiter helpfully interjected, "They're having a morning recital. Just over there, see? Is your coffee okay? Would you like to order anything else?"

"In a moment. Please," Max replied through gritted teeth. "Is it free entry?"

"I'm not sure but I can find out."

"No! Christ, Jackson, who cares!" Max blurted, then looked up at the waiter and pleaded, "Will you leave us alone for just… five… more… minutes."

The waiter shrugged and shuffled away.

Max leaned forward and continued, "Now, listen–"

"My God, what is the story with this keyring?"

"I don't know, Jackson, and I don't care. The lists, Jackson. Pay attention to the lists. One is for her medications, along with any unfilled prescriptions, to be collected into a plastic bag. Mostly from the bathroom and kitchen. When you arrive at the hospital, give that bag to the duty nurse. The other is for some personal items and clothes for Sandra. Just use one of her smaller suitcases."

"She doesn't have any smaller suitcases. They're all bigger than her. What does she need, anyway? Oh, Christ. It's going to be shoes, isn't it? She misses her fucking shoes."

"It isn't shoes. Well, maybe some shoes. But that's neither here nor there. Can you do this, Jackson? Can I rely on you?"

"Yes, of course you can, old boy. Happy to be of service. Although, does it have to be today?"

"Yes, it has to be today, you idiot! What is wrong with you?"

"Nothing, nothing. You just took me off guard, that's all. And you know I'm useless before I've had my breakfast. Where is that hopeless, fucking waiter?"

***

159

For the first time in a little under a year, Jackson entered the flat that had been his and Sandra's home for well over a decade. He drew in a deep breath, inhaling through his nose. The air was familiar, but not the same. Sandra's sweet, citrus perfume still dominated, but was no longer offset by the forest scents of his own aftershave. Hugo's musk still lingered, but had now become somewhat displaced by a pungent invasion of lavender and roses. *Potpourri*, Jackson guessed, *Sandra always loved pot-fucking-pourri*.

He closed the front door and looked down the corridor. Three doors on the right and one down at the end. On the other side was the border wall between them and their neighbours – who Jackson had never met but, he wryly remembered, had on more than one occasion communicated with in the form of angry banging from their side in response to, and answered by, loud music and raucous carousing from his. Usually in the wee hours of the morning when he and Sandra were hosting one of their after-after-parties following the opening or closing of some club or bar.

He moved further down the corridor and, again, inhaled. And smiled. Beneath the initial layers he could detect the feint aromas of herbed meat. Basil, rosemary and sage. He felt a warm, familiar feeling of contentment. Sandra had been cooking lamb. Then the feeling morphed into one of discomfort as he remembered for which event she had prepared the meat.

Jackson shook the moment off before the discomfort had a chance to become guilt. Again, he looked down the hallway. He singled out one door. The only door that was closed. The room for which, for a few years, Sandra had wanted to produce an occupant. An issue, the issue, Jackson had always managed to evade. Their commitment to the thriving business. The unsuitability of their unorthodox lifestyle. Any reason. All of them true but none of them honest. Then, eventually, he took up residence in the room during that final, silent eighteen months. Until, finally, Jackson's avoidance escalated to absence.

Jackson ambled into the living room. It struck him how little she had altered. Then it amazed him that, in fact, she had changed nothing. Even the photographs of them both together, snapshots of happier times, were still in place. He caught sight of one of the earliest. One of his favourites. The two of them together, young and dynamic, standing outside their first co-venture, where he manned the bar and ran the front of house while she commanded the kitchen.

As he smiled at the image his eye wandered from the photograph to the mantlepiece below, on which he spied a small, plastic container. He picked it up and, stretching his arm out to focus on the small, typed label read, 'Hydrocodone. Do not mix with alcohol'. He snorted at the instruction. *Fat chance*, he thought, and he threw the canister into a plastic bag he held in the other hand.

As he turned to leave he stopped and sighed, having spotted its twin next to the fireplace. He knew, from what Max had said over breakfast, he'd have to search harder. There'd be, at the least, another brother or two. And probably a few cousins from another branches of the ever growing pharmaceutical family…

***

…"She can't remember a thing," Max had explained to him at the restaurant, after he was sure that Jackson understood both his task and the importance of carrying it out to the letter of Max's annoyingly specific instructions.

Over the past year Sandra had upped her already high dosage on various medications. Some for pain, others for anxiety. Then there were the non-prescription, illicit drugs, just to bring her back up. Just to keep going through the night. In case she missed out.

This came as no surprise to Jackson. Sandra had always had a penchant for the nose candy. Or, as she preferred to call it, marching powder. In the early days, Jackson set his precedent and turned a blind eye. Knowing it allowed her to work those sixteen, eighteen, sometimes twenty-two hour days.

But long before that, the long hours of standing while heaving pots and pans around had taken their toll on Sandra. The pain started after just a few short years, just when they were becoming successful. Famous. Important. They had to go on. They needed to push forward. The pain had to be driven away. Or at least buried.

The occasional Nurofen became the four-hourly Nurofen. When the Nurofen failed to cut through the pain, Sandra discovered Solpadeine.

"But why use Solpadeine when you can get Solpadeine Max, with that extra codeine kick?" a friend once joked at one of their parties, "And it's over the counter!"

They all laughed.

"Not in the USA, it isn't," Jackson pointed out a few weeks later when he suggested that, perhaps, a 'codeine kick' was not what Sandra needed. Especially when she was going through the better part of two bottles of wine a day.

"You're one to talk!" Sandra irately retorted, before storming out of the room and leaving Jackson to finish what remained of the whisky.

They never mentioned the subject again.

Jackson remained silent when, in the bathroom cabinet, he saw the over-the-counter Solpadeine Max replaced with prescription packets, the typed labels giving Sandra permission for twice the manufacture's recommended dosage. He stayed equally dumb when, as the months and years went by, these were replaced by more understated, dispassionate boxes and canisters labelled with increasingly complicated, clinical names.

It wasn't until about a year and a half before he left that he noticed the other pills appearing in the cabinet. The sleeping pills. The antidepressants. But he couldn't say anything, then. They'd stopped talking and, shortly thereafter, they stopped sharing a bedroom and the adjoining bathroom.

So Jackson could claim ignorance to any further escalation while focusing on his own decline...

***

...Now, looking into the cabinet, Jackson could see that the pharma-family had, indeed, expanded. He gave the line-up a cursory examination, all of them standing to attention on the top shelf.

Ultram – one a day. With food. Do not mix with alcohol. Diazepam – two a day. With food. Do not mix with alcohol. Flurazepam – one every evening. Do not mix with alcohol.

Paroxetine, Fluvoxamine, Vicodin, Demerol, this-as-well, that-n'all. Each to be taken with food and none, under any circumstances, to be mixed with alcohol. Dozens of containers, either canisters or cardboard boxes, procured from a sundry of chemists and prescribed by a dose of doctors.

Jackson took each of them, one by one, and consigned them to the plastic shopping bag. The five wraps of cocaine, which he found in Sandra's 'secret' hiding place within her dressing table, he flushed down the lavatory.

***

The pillows that now surrounded Sandra were plump and overstuffed. The linen that swathed her was clean, crisp and pure white. Nestled amongst it all, alone in the spacious, quiet room, she slept. Jackson had never seen her, or anyone, immersed in such a deep slumber. Almost comatose and still managing to look utterly exhausted. Jackson stood at the end of the bed, the nurse standing guard in the open doorway behind him, and felt ashamedly relieved at her unavailability.

He parked the suitcase just inside the door, turned to the nurse and whispered, "Perhaps I'll leave a note."

The nurse was about to respond when Sandra quietly rasped, "Jackie?"

163

"Shit," Jackson muttered. He forced a smile, turned and said, "Sandra," then grandly gestured towards her suitcase and declared, "I've brought you your shoes."

"Thank you," Sandra drowsily replied as she attempted to pull herself up to a seated position.

"There's a button, Sandra."

"A what?"

"A button. There. On the pad. See? A button. Oh, for God's sake." Jackson moved towards her and picked up a control pad from her bedside table. "A button. Here. See?" Jackson held down the green button on the pad and, much to Sandra's joy, the back of her bed slowly began to rise.

"Oooh," she giggled, "Big fun."

Jackson threw an accusatory glare at the nurse and growled, "I thought the idea was to get her off the drugs, not keep her on a perpetual high."

"It's a process," the nurse replied.

"That it is," Sandra agreed, "Damn fine one, too."

"Can I get you anything?" The nurse asked.

"He'll have a large whisky and I'll have a G 'n' T with ice 'n slice. What the hell, make mine a double, too."

"We're fine, thank you," Jackson firmly insisted, "I won't be long, anyway."

The nurse nodded and left, closing the door behind him. Jackson stared at the door for an uncomfortable moment, then awkwardly smiled down at Sandra.

"Quick. Before he comes back," Sandra urgently whispered, "Did you bring them?"

"What? Did I bring what?"

"My drugs. The ones I asked Max to get for me."

"No. I mean, yes, I did, but… What?"

"Relax, Jackie. I'm joking," Sandra sighed. Her face melted from wide-eyed joviality to weary solemnity. "Come. Sit."

Jackson, with only a hint of frustration, sat in the chair next to her.

Sandra glanced down and, with a sly smirk, commented,

"Mind you. Maybe you really do need a drink. Got a bit of the boozy shakes there, Jackie?"

Jackson looked down and saw that the fingers on his left hand were trembling. "God-dammit," he muttered, with a tone of embarrassment rather than anger. He pressed the thumb of his right hand into his left palm. As the dancing fingertips settled, he looked back at Sandra with a weak, thin smile.

Sandra studied his smile, his face, and saw something she had never seen in Jackson before. She thought it might be fear. "Jackson?" she asked, "Are *you* okay?"

Jackson sighed. He stared at Sandra for a long, thoughtful moment, then leaned back in his seat and, in a first step towards breaking his first promise, with a quiet and subdued voice said, "Sandy. Do you remember when my father died?"

***

Julia sat at her dressing table with three mirrors angled to give her all the necessary perspectives. She strategically applied makeup around her wounded eye, while occasionally glancing at her agitated brother's reflection.

Julian sat just outside the bedroom, hunched forward and wringing his hands. "I just don't see why you have to take *him*," he groaned, "I mean, you didn't even ask me."

"Would you have come? You never have before when I've asked," Julia replied with an even, assertive tone.

"I might have," Julian defensively retorted. His pitch rising towards the end in such an unconvincing way as to make Julia smirk.

Julia mischievously offered, "Well, in that case, why don't you? I can easily put him off for another time." She watched her younger brother squirm in his seat.

They would often have conversations like this. Julia readying herself for the world while Julian sat in the seat just outside her bedroom door. Him looking out across the garden while she glanced at him via the mirror. Gauging his mood, reading his reactions and occasionally winding him up. These exchanges had started when she was a teenager and he was just a child. They'd now gone on for three decades and, much to Julia's amusement, Julian still had no idea that she could see him in the mirror.

At this particular moment, she only just managed to stifle her laugher as she watched him writhe in his seat. Shaking his head, leaning forward and frustratedly biting his lower lip.

"Well I can't, now, can I? I've made other plans."

"Have you?" Julia asked, her voice dripping with innocence and ignorance, "What would they be?"

"Oh, you know damn well what they are, J-One!"

Julia pursed her lips with a restrained smile. She watched Julian nervously tug on his little blues beard. A recent addition and, in her opinion, a grubby little affair which, as she now watched, she secretly wished he would pull out entirely.

"Do I?" she drawled, continuing to feign unawareness. If nothing else, Julia's earnest little brother was a man of routine, to an almost obsessive degree. This was the last Tuesday of the month, when Julian and his enlightened cabal would meet to discuss the various woes and misfortunes of the world.

As Julia thought he was on the verge of becoming truly distressed, she let him off the hook. "Oh, that's right. Last Tuesday Club."

"It's a serious obligation, Jules."

"I know, Jules."

"And it's my turn to chair!"

"It's always your turn to chair, Julian," she sighed, becoming despondently serious. Then quietly added, more for her own benefit, "God bless you." She watched him for further a moment until, seeing him relax back into his seat, she continued with her own routine.

"The man's a menace, you know," Julian huffed.

"Who is?"

"You know who."

"Oh, him," Julia murmured, now becoming weary of the

topic.

"Utter menace. Did you see that clip on YouTube?"

Again, Julia paused, holding her makeup brush an inch or so form her chin as she looked back at Julian's small, fretting reflection. "Which one?" she prodded. Back to the sport.

"Exactly! Which one?" Julian repeated with a note of victory. Then sulkily added, "The American breakfast thing. *Good Morning America*, *America This Morning*. I dunno, it had *Morning* in the title and it was American."

"I know the one you mean. I've seen it."

"Well, it's shocking," Julian, again, huffed, "I mean, appalling."

"I agree. Appalling," she smiled.

"Disgraceful," Julian further condemned.

"Utterly disgraceful," Julia mirrored.

"Completely shameful behaviour."

To which Julia, finally, let out a short burst of howling laughter.

"It's not funny, J-One!"

"Oh, come on, J-Two. It's a bit funny." Julia gave one last look in the mirror, tossed her makeup brush aside and swivelled her seat around to face the door. "Julian, come in for a sec."

Julian padded into the bedroom, keeping his eyes low.

"Sit down over there." Julia gestured towards a wing-backed chair by the window. Next to a small side table on which rested the first edition of *Venice,* along with a half-finished romantic thriller hidden under the latest National Geographic.

Julian sat in the chair and stared at her with his wide, youthful eyes. Beyond youthful. Child-like. Years younger than the surrounding face, as if unsullied by any of life's experiences that a man of his age should have endured by now. Her fault, she supposed.

She wanted to tell him to stop wasting his time with his various causes and these idealistic comrades who all, she knew, took advantage of his passion and dedication. She

167

wanted to warn him that most of them, like his contemporaries who started the group with him, would inevitably become politicians, solicitors or property developers. In some cases, all three – now donning three-piece suits and filing writs instead of wearing hoodies and brandishing placards. More concerned with their bank accounts, holiday villas and legacies than fracking, poverty or pollution. Whereas he, if he didn't start looking out for himself, could end up lost. Still marching but fallen through the cracks of life.

She wanted to tell him to get out there, meet a girl, or a boy, and, just for once, have some fun in his own life instead of worrying about and trying to fix other people's. But as she looked into those teenage eyes, set into the face of an early middle-aged man, she found she could only smile and let it all go, as she always had, so instead she quietly asked, "Will you come and see Mum with me tomorrow? It has been a while."

Julian twitched, looking momentarily evasive, then meekly replied, "Yeah, of course."

Julia responded with a half-satisfied half-smile, then turned back to the mirror and, with a lighter tone, said, "Help me tie this, will you?" She turned back to the mirror and raised the silk, rose-motif eyepatch to her face.

Chapter 16

Julia had replaced the eyepatch's white ribbon with one of deep, blood red, to match her evening gown. Backless and drawn in tight at the waist, the dress flared downwards until it almost touched the floor. The hem weighted so it moved with a theatrical swish with each of her long, confident strides.

Jackson, seated at the far end of the long bar, watched her sweep through the double doors and glide down the centre of the room, an impressed crowd parting before her. He was more curious than taken aback. Every time he had seen Julia she had looked sophisticated and stylish, but always understated. Muted. This was neither understated nor muted. This was forceful. This was dynamic. Jackson wondered if the sartorial departure was something new. An anomaly, maybe, as a reaction to her recent trauma. Or, perhaps, simply another side to Julia that had always been there.

Either way, Jackson thought as he watched her, she looked magnificent. In an attempt to look casually nonchalant he waited for her to see him as she approached, until he realised that he was sitting on her blind side. Quickly, he hopped from his bar stool and moved to greet her.

"Might I say, you're looking remarkably elegant this evening," Jackson said, with an almost comically molasses timbre.

"As do you, sir," Julia mimicked.

Jackson, himself breaking form, had purchased another velvet jacket for the evening, which he wore with a matching waistcoat and silver watch-chain. A particularly ostentatious Favourbrook frock coat. Black with, Julia noticed, blood red, rose-motif stitching.

"Coincidence?" Julia commented, tapping one of the tapestried flowers on his chest.

"I think not," Jackson played along. Then he quietly added, "You do realise that almost everybody else here is wearing blue jeans and bloody T-shirts."

"Are they, now?" Julia smiled, looking him up and down. "Well, as a new friend of mine would probably say – fuck 'em."

Jackson beamed with approval, offered Julia his arm and they returned to the bar, where there waited an ice bucket cradling a bottle of Veuve Clicquot.

***

Jackson had certainly heard of Johann Sebastian Bach and even quite liked some of his music, once somebody told him to whom he was listening. Julia claimed to be no expert on classical music either, which gave Jackson great comfort. Until, during the intermission, when they sat back at the bar sipping their half-time champagne, she expounded on the importance of the piece they were about to hear. How the *Partita for Violin Number Two*, the highlight of the evening, was considered one of the most challenging pieces for any solo violinist.

"Do you know it?" she deliberately asked, struggling to keep a straight face. Jackson grinned back, knowing that, on some level, he had been duped.

"Sweetheart, I've never even heard *Part-of-a Violin Number One*, let alone the sequel," he responded, topping up their coupes. "Successful franchise, was it?"

Julia gave a dry laugh. Then, after a moment, she looked down at the bar with a touch of melancholy and said, "It was one of my father's favourites. You know. Mathematicians and their classical music. 'The geometry in the humming of the strings and the music in the spacing of the spheres,' he always used to say." She sipped, shrugged the moment off and, throwing the nostalgic moment aside, continued in a lighter pitch, "Anyway. When I saw that it was being performed by the new bright young thing in the world of British classical music, it brought back some lovely memories. So, I thought. Why not?" On the 'why not' she raised her glass.

170

"Why not, indeed?" Jackson concurred and they toasted again. Then he cautiously asked, "And the new bright young thing in the world of British classical music?"

Julia gave a wry smile and declared, "Lives just above one of my former favourite spots in Chelsea and, it seems," with a flourish, she gestured to her eyepatch, "was finding the challenge of the piece just a mite frustrating last time I went there to enjoy a quiet moment alone." For a brief moment a hardness overwhelmed Julia's countenance and it looked, to Jackson, as if her anger had finally bubbled to the surface. But the sharp, aggrieved micro-expression dissipated as quickly as it had appeared, her soft smile returned and she buoyantly continued, "Let's hope his replacement isn't quite as quick to fly off the handle. We're quite near the front and I really don't want to lose two eyes in the same month."

"Absolutely," Jackson concurred, matching her upbeat cadence, "As the man once said, that would just be careless. And, for now–"

Julia sat forward and, interrupting both Jackson's sentence and his movement, grabbed the champagne bottle firmly by its neck and said, "Let's make sure this soldier is well and truly dead!"

Jackson sat back and regarded Julia with a wide, captivated grin as she drained the bottle into their glasses, tossed the empty, nose first, into the ice bucket and raised her glass for a final, jovial salute.

***

The audience around them fell silent and still as the lights dimmed. Jackson sat back and, taking a moment to himself to reflect on the day, closed his eyes.

He pictured, remembered, the confused look on Sandra's face when he'd asked her if she'd remembered when his father died. Of course she remembered. She had tried for months to convince Jackson to go to New York and visit him. She had never understood Jackson's reluctance to do so. His anger when she persisted. His venomous feelings towards a man who had, as far as she could tell, given Jackson everything anyone could dream of in life and more.

"Yes, but for how long?" had always been Jackson's cryptic reply. Sandra had always put that down to Jackson just being Jackson. Pretentiously mysterious and frustratingly evasive. It never crossed her mind, until that moment, until he sat at her bedside and told her the truth, that he had been bitterly, all be it obliquely, literal.

By the time Jackson had finished telling her the deep secret he had kept from her, from Max, from everyone else in his miserable little world, Sandra felt cold. Numb. Physically evacuated and mentally eviscerated.

"You should have told me," Sandra said with a robotic, almost metallic register that Jackson had never heard. As if all emotion had, in an instant, been stripped from her soul and psyche. Jackson sat back, looking at her as she refused to look at him. Instead, she just stared forward. Beaten. Small. Her face flaccid and devoid of all expression.

For a moment, he thought he should respond. But just as he was about to, Sandra added, "You stole from me with those lies. You robbed me. Took the one opportunity no man has the right to ever take from a woman. With lies." She spoke the words thoughtfully, plaintively and, to Jackson's deepening shame, with neither accusation nor judgement. Just resigned dejection and bitter acknowledgement.

So he just stood, kissed her gently on her forehead, and quietly, ruefully, left.

Jackson still had the image of Sandra's conquered, flattened expression in his mind as the opening applause began. At the same time, there was the welcome, warm sensation of Julia's hand taking his. Julia, with whom he knew he would have to be honest. Who he knew he could never, who he vowed he would never, hurt the way he had hurt Sandra.

The music began. Already, only three beats into the piece, even Jackson's untrained ear could hear the complexity. As if to confirm his thought, Julia's hand gripped his even tighter. He smiled, squeezing hers.

Then she squeezed back. Harder than was comfortable. Jackson opened his eyes and, softly, looked at her. But she was looking away from him. She stared at the stage, her face as flaccid, drained and vacant as Sandra's had been earlier. She appeared entirely frozen, except for her hand tightening around Jackson's. Her fingers now, painfully, pressing into his tendons.

Jackson followed her gaze, and saw the Violinist. Bright, brilliant, young – and free. His oily, lank hair hanging down over his hooded eyes and cruelly twisted lips while he played beautifully, elegantly and remorselessly.

Jackson, panicked and confused, looked back to Julia. Her chest heaved in quick, irregular jerks.

"I can't breathe," she gasped, "I can't breathe."

Jackson stood, taking her by the arm and shoulder. To the sound of the perfect music from the stage, accompanied by pugnacious tuts, shushes and grunts from the audience, he eased Julia out to the aisle and towards the safety of the exit.

***

"I thought he was in jail," Julia angrily sobbed. Then bared her clenched teeth and, with a guttural, angry rasp demanded, "Why isn't he in jail? Why isn't he in bloody jail!" She cradled a brandy with one shaking hand and took a healthy sip. With the other, she stroked Hugo's reassuringly soft head. Hugo rested his massive chin on her lap – his large, concerned eyes rolled up towards her.

"I don't know," Jackson softly replied, leaning forward and placing his hand on top of hers, and Hugo's head, "But hopefully we're about to find out." He gestured past her as Max, wearing a thunderous expression, marched in from the lobby to join them in the Fumoir Bar.

Jackson shifted onto the sofa and sat next to Julia, holding her hand in both of his, while Max sat down opposite them.

173

Frankie approached, placed a large whisky before Jackson and turned to Max.

"I'm fine," Max quietly said. He waited for Frankie to move away before leaning forward and announcing, "They released him nearly a fortnight ago."

"Jesus," Jackson exhaled, "Bail?"

Max shook his head. "The CPS said there wasn't enough evidence to prosecute."

"Not enough evidence?" Julia fumed, gripping Jackson's arm with one hand, throwing the other up to her face and hissing, "What the hell do they call this!"

"He claims he was out. That he'd left the door open and there was a break in. The place was ransacked."

"That's nonsense!" Jackson bellowed, "I mean, I saw him! I saw the monster standing there! Right there! In the window!"

"Yes, Jackson," Max softly explained, "That's the problem. You saw him. And only you." Max sat back, shifted awkwardly and, with an uncomfortable crack in his voice, continued, "The CPS deemed your witness statement, the only witness statement, to be unreliable." Max opened his folio case, removed a sheet of paper and slid it across the table. "Their report."

Jackson's countenance lost all expression. It became a wax impression of a face with glass, fixed eyes staring at Max.

Julia angled the document towards her and read the text. 'Witness described suspect as, "A greasy-haired, rat-faced, skinny streak of piss".' Further down the page, 'Witness met the investigating officers wearing a dressing gown, drinking wine and appeared inebriated'. Followed by, 'The next day the witness appeared at Savile Row for a photo ID parade and, although he correctly identified the suspect, did so with the words, "That's the bastard".'

Julia scanned the document again and kept flicking her focus back and forth between three words: 'Inebriated', 'bastard' and, at the bottom of the page in the summary

174

section, 'unreliable'.

With a deliberate, mechanical motion, Julia spread her fingertips across the document and pushed it back towards Max, while slowly drawing her other arm away from Jackson. The rest of her body remained still.

Finally, in a meek voice, Jackson said, "They should have let her know."

"Jesus!" Julia snarled, "Jesus Christ. Don't speak. Don't you speak. Don't you dare speak." She remained motionless for a moment. Then she bent forward and winced, as if with a severe stomach pain, and said, "I'm going to be sick." She stood and Jackson moved to help her. She shoved him aside and marched out of the bar, turning towards the bathroom.

Jackson turned to Max, who looked back at him with a bleak combination of sympathy and damnation.

"They just couldn't take you seriously, Jackson," Max said, "I mean, look at you. Who could?"

Jackson responded with an unconvincing, low base chuckle. He heaved a deep, resigned sigh, picked up his glass and bitterly replied, "Who, indeed?" Then he finished the rest of his whisky, leaned back and gave Max a weak, defeated smile and an infantile shrug.

Over Max's shoulder Jackson caught the red flash of Julia's dress moving past the frosted doors, marching through the lobby towards the main exit. "Dammit," he whispered, rising from his seat to follow.

Julia stormed through the revolving door towards the nearby taxi rank.

"Taxi, ma'am?" a smiling, liveried doorman asked.

"I'll get it myself," she snapped.

"Julia," Jackson called after her.

"Jesus Christ," Julia spat under her breath, picking up her pace.

"Julia, please."

"Idiot," Julia muttered, still under her breath and to herself, "Idiot, idiot, IDIOT!" The last 'idiot' she screamed. A raw, guttural screech as she stopped in her tracks and rounded on Jackson, forcing him to an abrupt halt just inches behind her. "IDIOT!" she repeated. An even louder, primal shriek. Her face burning red with fury, nose to nose with his.

"I know, Julia. I am an idiot. A complete and utter idiot."

"No, me! I'm the idiot! You? You're just... Well. You're just exactly what everybody says you are. What that report says you are. What my brother, my dear, sweet brother, said you were from day one. Selfish! Arrogant! A menace! A liability! Unreliable! Inebriated! Bastard! Complete, total and utter bastard! I'm the idiot for trying to see through it all to find something more. God, what was I thinking?"

"Julia, please."

Ignoring him, Julia turned and continued marching towards the taxi. Jackson stood still, ready to surrender and watch her go.

Then, as she neared the cab, Julia stopped. She turned, went back to Jackson and, firmly planted to her spot, calmly said, "I mean. Who do you think you are? Hey? That you can just throw yourself into other people's lives with such reckless abandon without ever even considering the impact. The consequences. Do you have any idea of the effect you have? Do you care? Of course you don't care. Just look at the way you talk about other people. You don't even use our names. You just reduce us all to some sort of basic, generic label. The Lawyer. The Non-Lawyer. The Diminutive One. The Virtuous One. What's your dehumanising little epithet for me when I'm not around? The Cyclops?"

"Come on, Julia. That's not fair."

"You're bloody right it's not fair! Nothing about this is fair! You know, I really thought I saw something different in you. Something that, maybe, others had missed. A warmth. A kindness. A generosity of heart underneath all that bluster and bravado. But I was wrong, wasn't I? You're not kind underneath. There is no generosity beneath your surface. There's nothing of any real substance. Just some sort of twisted, angry rage. And what right do you have to such rage?

176

How have you earned your anger? You, who had everything handed to you the moment you were born just to piss it all away for shits and giggles. Sauntering through life as if it's a summer parade and you're the guest of honour. I mean, when have you ever taken any responsibility for anything? When have you given a damn about anyone other than yourself? Or anything other than your own petty little amusements?"

Julia stepped back. She took a breath and, with a lowered, more considered tone continued, "And you have the audacity to describe others as monsters. The great Jackson Grimes," she rasped, "Everybody should know Jackson Grimes. Well, you're right about that one, *old boy.*" She coolly removed the silk eyepatch and held it out to Jackson and with a dry, cracked voice, said, "Everybody should about you. Because you're worse than a monster. You're just nothing. You're a vacuum. You're a dessicated husk."

Jackson looked down at the ground. Avoiding her face. Avoiding the eyepatch. He buried his hands deep in his pockets and, blocking everything else around him, stared only at the pavement.

"And you're a waste of my time," Julia quietly and calmly finished. With a resigned sigh she dropped the eyepatch onto the ground and walked away.

Jackson stayed motionless. He stared vacantly at the ground, hazily seeing the red and white of the eyepatch lying on the blackened concrete between his feet. Vaguely listening to Julia's footfalls receding. The taxi door opening. Slamming. The deep, throbbing engine starting. Revving. Pulling into traffic. Moving away. Disappearing into the loud, angry, frenzied soundscape of London's night-time streets.

Chapter 17

Is there anything more poisonous than a secret? The bigger the secret, the more noxious. Festering over the years. By the time you're ready to divulge the truth, it's too late. Procrastination and fear have stripped you of the option. The decades of silence. Of covering up. Of little, white lies, designed to disguise, evolving into great tapestries of deceit. All have conspired against you. Cornered you. Left you alone to face your wretched, bitter truth alone. Staring into the abyss and wishing the fucker would stare back, just so that you'd have the company. But it never does. Another great lie.

Perhaps, that's as it should be. Perhaps, some secrets ought to be kept purely to one's self. And, perhaps, some journeys must be made alone. After all, who are any of us to impose our misfortunes onto others?

This afternoon I was subjected to a reality show about estate agents. Useless, smug bastards. Almost as bad as hedge-fund managers, insurance brokers and politicians. All of them parasites, inserting themselves into other people's business, their only agendas being that, no matter what the outcome, they'll come out on top. When I get to hell, I'm expecting to meet a lot of them.

Won't be long now...

***

Jackson smeared thick shaving foam across his beard. With his other hand, he leaned heavily on the sink, allowing the porcelain fixture to bare the weight of his fatigued upper body. His breathing was laboured. His vision was blurred. He stopped, as usual, to glare at his reflection with a corrective squint. From the mirror came a harsh stare from a tired old man with bloodshot eyes and a dried, cracked complexion. He picked up his safety razor and raised it to his face, allowing it to hover a few inches from his chin.

"Everybody hates…" he began the mantra but, as if exhausted with the sentiment, allowed it to peter away. He tossed the razor back onto the shelf, picked up a hand towel, wiped the foam from his stubble and lumbered towards the living room. Taking, as he left the bathroom, a fleeting glance at the straight razor, with the mother of pearl handle that matched the one he'd just discarded, waiting patiently on the ledge of the bath – alongside a bottle of Chateau Margeaux, the same vintage as himself. *Not a great year for Bordeaux*, he thought, *but a worse one for people*.

Crossing the living room, he pulled the robe's cord tightly around him before, with a heavy thump, sitting in the chair at the desk. He took the calendar, placed it flat on the surface and drew another thick, purposeful line diagonally through another spent day. The twenty-fourth. Only one blank square left before the twenty-sixth. Marked with that large, unavoidable 'X'.

"One day to go, old boy," Jackson rasped, looking over at Hugo, whose ears pricked up as he stared back. "Let's spend it wisely, yes?"

***

"Good morning, Mr Grimes. Will you be having your usual?"

"Oh, God. Do I have a usual?"

"Same order every day for nearly a week. I'd call that a usual."

"How dull and predictable. Go on, then. And some black pudding with a bowl of water for the dog, please." Jackson sat under a brand new awning, although the heat was nowhere near as extreme as in recent weeks. Normal September service had resumed, with a slate grey sky and a few brown leaves dancing around the table legs in a light, cool breeze.

As the waiter walked away Jackson shifted his seat around, giving himself a view of the adjacent building. He glared at the fifth floor window. Firmly closed, as it had been every day that week. Jackson checked his watch. Five minutes to twelve. He knew he'd be sitting there for, almost precisely, two hours and five minutes.

"Your food will be along shortly," the waiter politely informed Jackson, as he placed what Jackson knew to be a stiff Bloody Mary before him.

"No rush," Jackson replied.

The waiter courteously smiled as he uncorked a bottle of Veuve Clicquot and poured a glass.

One Eggs Benedict, another Bloody Mary and a further bottle of champagne later, the time approached two o'clock. Jackson removed his wallet, thick with cash, peeled off a few notes and placed them under one of the empty glasses. A fifty percent tip, as was his standard. He sat back and watched the door to the building.

At two on the dot the Violinist emerged, his instrument strapped to his back and a gold crash helmet dangling from his hand. He held his head held low as he lethargically shuffled towards a white, classic Vespa.

Instead of following, as he had the first couple of days, Jackson moved at his own, unrushed pace. While the Violinist rode his scooter towards the white, pillar-fronted townhouses of Pimlico, Jackson sauntered onto the King's Road and hailed a black cab. As the Violinist throttled across Vauxhall Bridge and past the concrete, brutalist facades Lambeth, Jackson and Hugo journeyed to the same destination on the more soulful side of the river.

They all arrived at the same time. Jackson eyed, with a curiosity still not lost over the last few days, the Violinist as he stopped at the one of the least reputable fast food stalls along the South Bank. A strange area, Jackson had always thought, even at the best of times. One of London's main cultural centres set in a collection of some of the ugliest, bleakest buildings in the city.

In the midst of the stark, grey terrain, the Violinist wolfed down his fat-soaked burger and chips before shuffling towards the Royal Festival Hall. Jackson, with Hugo at his

180

side, watched until he was through the door. Then, once more, Jackson checked his watch. Three o'clock. Four and a half hours until curtain up.

Jackson bent down on one knee, gave Hugo a close, warm hug and said, "Come on then, old boy. Nice walk for you, hey?"

Hugo gave a lick of agreement and the duo made their way to the, once wobbly, Millennium Footbridge. As they crossed the Thames, Jackson glanced over at the London Eye, slowly rotating and affording the throngs of tourists half an hour of the finest views of the entire metropolis. Then he looked down at the water, swelled and running fast as the high tide began its shift from slack water to heading out. He eyed the various pleasure boats, water taxies and permanently moored craft. Some homes, others business. A fine city, he thought. How privileged he had been to have spent so much of his life here.

The duo walked on, back to Mayfair. Back home for Hugo. Back to change, shower and finally shave for Jackson, before his last night out.

***

"You must be a big fan."

"What?"

"You must be a big fan. This is your third night in a row, isn't it?"

"Is it?"

"At least," the young, chirpy waitress said, then smiled as she handed Jackson his whisky and asked, "Anything for the intermission?"

"More whisky."

"Double?"

"At least," Jackson replied with a hollow cackle. The waitress laughed politely and moved on to the next customer. Jackson knocked back the drink, returned the glass to the bar and headed to the auditorium.

It was, in fact, the fourth night in a row he'd been there. As on the previous nights he sat alone, as high and as far to one side as possible. He was in an unoccupied area he'd always heard people refer to as 'The Gods', which made no sense to him. Up there he couldn't even see most of the stage, let alone its centre. It didn't strike him as much of a vantage point for omnipotence.

Jackson sat. He listened. He brooded. He mulled. During the intermission, he went back to the bar. The double whisky waited. He drank. He managed to procure a second before returning to his seat in time for the Violinist to appear for his big solo. Again, Jackson listened. He brooded. He mulled.

He seethed. He fumed.

***

After the show, once more, Jackson had no need to tail the Violinist, who had followed the same, post-concert routine every night. Where the Violinist putt-putted on his little scooter, Jackson again taxied, alighting at the Soho pub the Violinist ritualistically visited for last call every night.

On the first evening, Jackson had been almost offended to find that the pub the Violinist frequented was the place that he and Max referred to as The Pub That Dare Not Speak Its Name. The watering hole they had made their Sunday haunt for all of their twenties and most of their thirties. Even then, it was considered one of Soho's last proper boozers. How it had survived this long without being taken over by some cooperation to be sterilised, homogenized and eventually euthanised was a modern day miracle. Rickety, red barstools worn down to the stuffing. Wood panelled walls and a long, oak trimmed bar – once varnished, now worn bare through decades of erosion from spilt drinks and leaning drinkers. Faded photographs of regulars, former regulars and irregulars hanging at a variety of jaunty angles. Some famous, others infamous, all notorious. Jackson knew his mug shot was up there somewhere, but nostalgia was not the purpose of his visit.

That first night, he was just there to watch. To spy. To surveil. Which he did, from outside, while smoking Lucky Strikes and sipping whisky. This time as a chaser to a heavy, dark London porter.

From there, he followed the Violinist to his final venue. A dingy basement club buried in darkest region of Soho's underbelly. Another place Jackson had known in his youth, which had remained just as grubby and debauched as it had been then.

On the second night, the Violinist followed the exact same routine. Upon arriving at the same pub, Jackson's pub, he was this time was greeted warmly by the landlord. Jackson's old regular was now the Violinist's. The musician's photograph, Jackson then noticed, was also hanging on the wall. After his initial umbrage, Jackson was hardly surprised. This once bohemian corner of London had, in recent years, been stripped of almost all other idiosyncratic establishments. Where else would a musician, even a psychopathic one, frequent?

Again, he followed his target to the last venue. The sweat-steamed basement with the tiny, cattle crush smoking area in the building's architectural well.

They both followed the same routine on the third night. But on this night, the fourth night, the last night, Jackson changed his game. He skipped The Pub That Dare Not Speak Its Name and went straight to the basement club. There, he took the seat at the bar he had seen the Violinist thrice use, while keeping his jacket on the neighbouring stool.

Shortly after eleven o'clock, as Jackson had anticipated, the Violinist arrived. As the musician rounded the end of the bar, Jackson slipped his jacket from the stool. The Violinist took the bait, sat beside Jackson and ordered a large vodka and Red Bull. At the same time, Jackson ordered another double whisky.

While the bartender prepared the drinks, Jackson turned to the Violinist and opened with, "I saw you play tonight.

Superb."

The musician replied with a meek smile and a docile nod. The bartender placed their drinks before them and, as his dupe reached for his wallet, Jackson raised a hand.

"No, no. Please. Allow me," he insisted, "It's the least I can do." Jackson produced his cash supply from his inside pocket and took a crisp twenty, which he handed to the bartender saying, "This boy is a genius, you know."

"I do know," croaked the once handsome and chiselled, now haggard and gaunt, bartender, "One of our regular little stars, he is." The bartender winked at the Violinist and, when he gestured to keep the change, blew Jackson a kiss.

"You know, I owe you a debt of gratitude," Jackson said, once the bartender had moved on.

"Yeah? How's that?" the Violinist asked in a jittery, nervous voice, then gulped his drink.

"Well, I'll tell you," Jackson took a moment, looked the musician in the eye and began...

***

...Jackson, stiff and tense, sat bolt upright in the hard, oak armchair. As if hoping that proper posture would impress the man he had come to see and, somehow, increase the chances of a positive outcome. Momentarily, the door opened and he appeared. Tall, thin and, in spite of his sixty years plus, impressively athletic. He wore a tightly fitted three-piece suit, frameless glasses and sported a perfectly groomed, snow-white beard.

"I'm so sorry to have kept you," he said in a clipped, rushed voice that firmly expressed the importance of his work and the value of his time, while sitting and placing a weighty folder on the mahogany, leather-topped desk. "On your way to Venice, I hear?"

"Thinking about it," Jackson replied, "I might swing by Paris first. There's a charming little bistro near the George Cinq that prepares a spectacular Chateaubriand."

"Lovely. Haven't been to either for years. But my wife and I are planning a lengthy trip next year. So, maybe."

"Maybe," Jackson mimicked.

"Now," the man with the white beard said, shifting gears and opening the folder.

"Yes. Just before we get to that," Jackson interrupted, leaning forward, "I have to ask you one question."

The man looked back at Jackson, his pale blue eyes peering over his lenses with a weary expression, as if he knew exactly what was coming. "Go on," he flatly invited.

Jackson grinned as he asked, "Is your name really Doctor H Kissinger?"

The doctor gave a thin smile and gently nodded.

Jackson beamed, his eyes wide. "Henry?" he asked, his inflection full of hope.

"Close," the doctor tiredly replied, "Heinrich."

"Oh, my God. That is fantastic," Jackson sat back, slapped his thigh and roared with laughter. "I mean, that is truly wonderful. No matter what happens today, it will be worth coming here to meet you just for that."

As Jackson's laughter subsided, Doctor Kissinger removed his glasses and placed them on the desk. When Jackson finally fell silent, the doctor leaned forward and with a soft, kind voice said, "Mr Grimes. I really do wish that were to be true. But I'm afraid the news I have for you today is quite serious."

Jackson nodded, sat back and, with a relaxed attitude, threw out his arms and shrugged. He already knew everything the good doctor was about to tell him. He knew that, sooner or later, this day was inevitable. He'd known since he was eighteen.

On that birthday, finally free to make his own decisions, and in spite of his mother's tearful begging, Jackson went to the family doctor and demanded a test. A fortnight later, the result came through. Positive. The flip of the coin had come up tails. His mother wept with grief and remorse. His father cried with shame and guilt.

Huntington's. Known to doctors as 'the quintessential family disease'. Considered by Jackson to be the cruellest family curse.

Cruel because, at first, it forces you into hope. Desperate hope as, while you await a diagnosis, it coerces you into the mindset of a gambler playing even odds with unimaginably high stakes. Fifty-fifty to win a normal life. Fifty-fifty to lose and be damned by a genetic legacy. When a parent with Huntington's has a child the chances of that child either having the disease or not are the same as the child being a boy or a girl. That was the detail that always chilled Jackson to the bone.

Cruel because of its unpredictability and devastating progression. Years, decades of waiting for the symptoms to emerge. Waking every morning and wondering if that will be the day it begins. Waiting for that first slight shake. That first fumble. That first mild tremor when the nerve cells in the brain begin to waste away, setting the course for those mild tremors to slowly develop into uncontrollable spasms. The degeneration gradually stripping away cognitive abilities and physical capabilities. Years of decline until the helpless victim, unable to move, speak, swallow or even think rationally, dies from suffocation.

Cruel because of the choices it forces its victims to make. Whether, if at risk, to test oneself or not. Whether to test an unborn child or not. Whether to abort if positive. Whether to even risk having children at all. Better, perhaps, to ensure an end the dark legacy once and for all by removing the option altogether. As Jackson did when, the week after receiving his deferred death sentence, he underwent the only elective surgery he would ever face. Another secret he would bury deep and allow to metastasize until he eventually confessed to Sandra, as she lay in that hospital bed. Finally, truly breaking her.

Jackson often wondered if his parents would have ever told him, were it not for the fact that his father became symptomatic when Jackson was still in high school. Taking away at least one of their options, it forced them to come clean. Yes, they had known that the day would finally come. Jackson's grandmother had been damned by the same scourge and his father had been tested. He knew of his affliction before Jackson's conception. But Jackson's arrival on this earth had not been planned. And a good Brooklyn Heights Catholic family could never consider intervening in one of God's greatest miracles. Whatever was meant to be, was meant to be.

They had flipped the coin and Jackson had lost the toss. The eighteen year old Jackson, as he traversed the subway back from his Manhattan doctor to the home that had deceived him for his entire life, made himself three promises. Firstly, he would never flip that coin. Secondly, he would never tell anybody of his burden. This was his and his alone. And thirdly, when the time came, when the hourglass turned and the sands began to run, he would make his own exit from this world. On his terms. On his schedule. And, by Christ, he'd make damn sure to go out with style, splendour and ceremony...

***

..."Well, it's my fiftieth birthday tomorrow, so. As good an age as any to shuffle on, I say. And, hey, I really have spent the last year living it up in true style, splendour and ceremony." Jackson gestured for another round of drinks.

"Why are you telling me all this?" whined the, now agitated and nervous, Violinist.

Jackson leaned against the bar and slowly replied, "Well, I'm glad you asked because, you see... here's the thing. I very nearly forgot all about that over the last few weeks. I was able to put it all out of my mind. Happily ignore what I'd really come back to do. Forget about the loose ends I needed to tie up. I very nearly betrayed myself..." Jackson gulped down his drink in one sip, slammed the glass on the bar and gestured for another. Then, with a furious glare, he rounded

187

on the Violinist and quietly hissed, "And all because you had your little tantrum and chucked your violin out of the window ruining the life of the most beautiful—"

"Oh, Christ."

"Yeah, I'm not much of a fan of his, either. But I have recently become a great enthusiast of an idea that a lot of his followers sign up to. And that is confession. Good for the soul, the God squad say."

"Jesus, get away from me!" the Violinist squealed. He leapt from his seat and, pushing Jackson away, ran out of the door.

"I don't think you're his type, sweetheart," the bartender said, placing Jackson's drink on the bar. Then, as Jackson put down another note, added with a wink, "But I might be tempted."

Jackson ignored the quip as he knocked back the whisky and gave chase.

By the time Jackson reached the alley, the Violinist was already astride his scooter. The helmet dangled from his hand as he frantically and repeatedly depressing the kick-starter, causing the machine to let out various cries and splutters of torment.

"I think you might've flooded the engine there, old boy," Jackson growled as he lumbered into the dark, rubbish strewn side street.

"Christ, get away from me!" the panic-stricken Violinist yelled.

Jackson stopped a few feet before him, raised his palms and said, "Now, calm down. I really do only want to talk to you."

"About what?" the musician snapped like a frightened terrier.

"I told you. In the bar. The benefits of confession."

"You're drunk! Leave me alone!"

"I am, indeed, drunk. But that doesn't change the fact that you need to come clean."

"Why! Why should I?"

"Because you did a terrible, stupid thing and you need to make good. Because she deserves better. And because if you don't then, I can tell you, it'll eat at your soul. It'll rot you from the inside until there's nothing left. It will desiccate you."

"What will? What are you talking about?"

"Guilt," Jackson replied, with a low tone of finality, "Guilt."

The Violinist stared at Jackson for a long, silent moment. Both remained still. Then, his wide, confused eyes glistening in the dark, the musician shrieked, "You're a bloody lunatic!" He lunged forward, swinging the helmet in a wide arc.

"Fucking hell!" Jackson reeled back, just in time. He felt the rush of air as the helmet swung past his chin. "Well, that was completely out of order! My God, you really are a violent little shit, aren't you?" Jackson exclaimed, while regaining his balance.

Then he watched as the Violinist, pulled by the momentum of the swinging helmet, stumbled backwards. He tumbled, tripped and fell over his Vespa which, in turn, collapsed on top of him.

Jackson stood motionless, peering at the wreckage of the brief but drawn-out moment. He was unable to see anything except the scooter, lying on its side, with the musician's legs protruding from beneath.

"Shit," Jackson muttered. He took a tentative step forward and called out, "You okay under there?"

The only reply came in the form of a sustained, high-pitched mewl.

"Shit," Jackson repeated. Then he moved forward for a better view.

The Violinist lay trapped under the scooter, with the helmet still in his hand. Although, Jackson noticed, at a rather peculiar angle.

Again, the musician moaned. This time while opening his eyes and looking up at Jackson with a mournful, pleading gaze.

"Oh, for fuck's sake," Jackson sighed, "All right then. But don't try any of that nonsense again, okay?" Jackson moved forward and, taking the Vespa with both hands, lifted the machine and released its owner. "You okay now? Can you walk?"

The Violinist winced, clearly in agony, but managed to rise to his haunches. Then his feet. He gingerly removed the helmet from one hand with the other. He looked at the hand in which he had originally held it, with which he had attempted to deal Jackson the blow, and his face contorted into a twisted expression of pain, terror and fury.

Jackson felt momentarily bemused, then he looked at the musician's hand – and couldn't help cracking a wry smile as he deliberately, almost victoriously, proclaimed, "That, I believe, is what medics refer to as a compound fracture."

The Violinist continued to stare at his bloodied hand. His twisted wrist. The gaping, raw wound from which a sharp, jagged, white bone protruded. Then he looked back up at Jackson.

"Probably not the ideal injury for a man of your profession, I'm guessing?" Jackson cheerily jibed.

"You!" the Violinist furiously screamed, "You! What have you done?" Propelled by pure anger, he lunged forward and charged Jackson, ramming him square in the chest and knocking him over.

Jackson laughed as he toppled backwards, his head landing on the flagstones with a sharp crack.

"What have you done?" the musician again demanded. He raised the helmet with his good hand and brought it down, with all his might, onto Jackson's nose.

Again, Jackson, now dazed and on the edge of consciousness, laughed.

"What have you done!" the crazed musician repeated. Then he raised the helmet and, once more, hammered down upon Jackson's bloodied face.

Jackson's cackles, although feverish and weak, persevered.

Furious, the musician raised his weapon a third time but, just as he was about to strike, another voice intervened.

"Hey! What's going on in there?"

The Violinist looked up and out of the alley, towards the road, with wide eyes and the frightened grimace of a hunted animal. He dropped the helmet and, flashing one last glare at Jackson, ran.

"Are you alright, mate?"

As Jackson felt his awareness slipping, the owner of the voice that had saved him appeared, accompanied by the pungent stench of stale urine and fetid filth. A stranger with a thick, grimy beard and soiled, matted hair hanging over exhausted, life-wary eyes.

"Ambulance," Jackson struggled to murmur, "Ambulance."

"Ambulance. I'll call an ambulance," the stranger said with a hoarse, choked voice. Then he paused and looked past Jackson to the ground. Jackson managed to tilt his head and saw, lying beside him, his wallet. Thick with cash. Notes poking out from the leather.

Jackson stiffly reached a shaking hand towards the wallet. The stranger moved to intervene, then hesitated. Jackson grabbed the wallet and brought it up to his chest. With weak, shaking hands he removed the billfold. He pushed the money into the stranger's hard, blackened fingers.

With the weakest of smiles, Jackson whispered, "Ambulance," while drifting into unconsciousness. "Ambulance. Julia. Julia."

Chapter 18

Jackson struggled to open his eyes as his ocular muscles fought against the harsh, fluorescent lights. The pain caused by the torturous strips of brilliance was compounded by a glaring, white background.

Once the hostile ceiling came into some sort of focus, he flicked his eyes from side to side. A nurse stood over him to the right. Another figure sat to his left, just out of his field of vision.

He clacked his arid, sticky tongue and then squawked through a tight, dry throat, "Jesus."

"Hmm. I very much doubt the Good Lord has much to say to you, either," the seated visitor chided.

Jackson could feel the sides of his mouth begin to curl upwards.

"Idiot," Julia added with a snap.

"You're not an idiot," Jackson wheezed, picturing her anguished, screaming face outside the hotel.

"No, not me. You. You're the bloody idiot."

Jackson chuckled, attempting a nod of agreement. He shifted his weight onto his elbows and, beginning to wake up, tried to sit.

"Here," Julia said, "There's a button."

Jackson felt a momentary shiver, then relaxed as the back of his bed began to rise. While it brought him up to a seated position he looked around and gathered his bearings. A large, fully occupied general ward. The supportive back of the bed came to a rest at a forty-five degree angle, allowing him to turn and face Julia. He smiled. She did not.

"What the hell were you thinking?" Julia demanded.

Jackson elected to treat the question as rhetorical. He stiffly shrugged, turned to the nurse and asked, "What are you doing over there?"

"Removing your saline drip, Mr Grimes. You needed fluids."

"It seems your drinking binge, excessive even for you, has done you nearly as much damage as the nutter you went after," Julia lectured with censorious authority, "I mean, what were you thinking? Why did you do that?"

"The drinking or the stalking?"

"Either! Both! And, what do you mean 'stalking'? Oh, Christ, I don't want to know. Well, maybe later. God, you are an idiot." She shook her head and attempted to maintain a hard, composed exterior but, finally, cracked a warm half-smile, "I don't know," she sighed, "What am I going to do with you?"

"Entirely up to you," Jackson grinned.

Julia rolled her good eye to the ceiling. The other, Jackson noticed, was covered with her old hospital issue patch. He saw his jacket hanging on the back of her chair and gestured towards the side pocket.

"If you're looking for your cigarettes then good luck trying to light up in here. And if you're looking for your wallet it's in the breast pocket but somebody has relieved you of all the cash. I did warn you about that one. All your cards and IDs are there, though, which reminds me. Happy birthday."

"Thank you," Jackson croaked, "And, nobody cleaned me out. It was payment for services rendered."

"What services?"

"Saving my life, I suspect." Again, he pointed to the pocket.

Julia reached in and, when she removed her hand, found clasped in her fingertips the silk eyepatch. She stared down at it for an extended moment, remaining still and pensive. Then she looked back to Jackson, maintaining the same fixed, thoughtful bearing for an even longer spell. Finally, she softly smiled, leaned forward and took both of Jackson's hands in hers.

"Okay, then," she said. She kissed him gently and moved to bring her hands up, to replace the patch, but Jackson tightened his grip.

"Wait," Jackson exclaimed. He gave her a weak, small smile and, in a smaller voice, said, "First, let me talk. There are things you should know. Things others should have, but you definitely need to."

Apprehensively, Julia brought her hands back to rest, holding his – and listened while, for the next hour, Jackson divulged all.

He told her about his family curse. The legacy he had inherited. The price he had paid and forced others, particularly Sandra, to pay over the decades. For his secrecy. For his pride. For his stubbornness and his fear. He told her of the three promises he had made to himself. How he had spent thirty-one years living with their ideals and a further year with the reality. Preparing for his grand exit. Living every day to excess and making damn sure he was going to go out with style, splendour and ceremony. Until the day he met her. Until the moment the violin struck.

After he finished, they sat together in silence for several, long minutes. Julia stared at him with a look that Jackson tried, in vain, to read. Anger. Disappointment. Pity. Perhaps a combination of all.

Finally, she quietly said, "You should get dressed now. They need the bed and you're in far better condition than you look, and certainly than you deserve. Max is waiting down in the car, along with that antisocial dog of yours."

"How do you mean, antisocial?" Jackson queried.

"Let's just say that when I went to retrieve him from your suite he disgraced himself. So, now I've got a bruised coccyx and you owe me a new pair of shoes."

"Oh, Christ, no."

"Oh, Christ, yes," Julia replied. She then took a deep, thoughtful sigh, leaned over and, with softness in her eyes and tenderness in her voice, said, "Here's what I think. You get dealt the cards you get dealt and play them as best you can. So, what do you say, instead of throwing in your hand and giving up, you try to summon up a bit of that bravado of yours and see how long you can stay in the game?"

Jackson took a beat to think. Then, regarding Julia with a wicked squint, he replied, "Julia. Are you asking me to be your bridge partner?"

Julia cocked an eyebrow and tilted her head from side to side. "Maybe," she replied, "Or, maybe, to put it in the sort of language that a Neanderthal such as yourself might understand," she smiled and, with a flicker of menace, lent close to his ear and dryly whispered, "I am simply suggesting that rather than committing one of the most cowardly and selfish acts imaginable, you face your demons like the rest of us, however frightening they may be, and man the fuck up." She sat back and regarded him, just for a moment, with an accusatory glare.

"Oh, sweetheart. That's a bit harsh."

"Again, more than you deserve," she retorted with a light, sweet tone, and kissed him gently on his temple. She then gave him a wicked, crooked smile and added, "You know, there is one silver lining in your dark, dreadful cloud."

"And what would that be?"

"Well, even though you sometimes act like a total bastard, at least you know you're not an actual one."

Jackson gave a wide, impressed grin and cooed, "Oh, I do like you."

"Oh, I know you do," Julia retorted. Then, with sudden purpose, she stood. "Come on, you really do need to get dressed," she insisted, "As I said, there are people in this building who, although they may not look it, are in far worse states of repair than you."

"Yes, what do you mean by that?"

"Ah, that's right. You haven't seen a mirror yet. Well, you can look at yourself in Max's car. We'll all be down there waiting for you."

Jackson nodded and stiffly began to rise as Julia headed for the exit, when a thought stuck him. "Wait," he called after her. Julia paused and in a light, boyish voice, Jackson asked, "The Maybach?"

"Isn't it fantastic? He's got champagne, too," Julia brightly replied, chortling as she left.

Once dressed and in a seated position, Jackson began to feel a sense of humanity return to his being. Even so, his entire face throbbed, all of his joints ached and the back of his head felt like it had been beaten with a sledgehammer. After succeeding in his toughest challenge, tying his shoelaces, he stood. With a tired groan and a painful wince, he reached for his jacket.

"You made it," came a friendly Australian voice. Jackson stiffly turned to face the owner, a man in the neighbouring bed with a cast running from the end of his foot to the top of his hip. His arm, impaled with an array of pins and held together by a pair of steel halos, hung from a cat's cradle of wires over his chest. "I can't wait to be able to do that. I'm stuck with all this for at least another twelve weeks. And then I reckon it'll be a good six months before I'm properly mobile."

Jackson regarded the man, a good ten years his junior, with a sympathetic smile and replied, "Yes, you do look to be in a bad way, old boy. May I ask?"

"Yeah, sailing accident, wasn't it. Bloody shame of it is, we hadn't even started the trip properly. Big race, too. I'm supposed to be half way down the East Coast of America by now, I am."

"Awful. Oh, well. Perhaps after you... Wait." Jackson halted, suddenly regarding the invalid with a twinge of recognition. "Your accident," he asked, "It didn't happen to occur anywhere near Westminster Bridge, did it?"

"Yeah, it did! Some idiot waved at me and, like another idiot, I waved back. Fell off my perch and got sucked under the boat. May as well've been bloody keelhauled! How'd'ya know that, anyway?"

Jackson's eyes popped. "Oh, I can't remember, really," he floundered and, as best he could, hurried up his pace.

"Read about it in the papers, did ya? It made a column or

two."

"Yes, that must have been it," Jackson hastily replied, finally getting his second arm through its jacket sleeve, "Anyway, must go. Got a car waiting downstairs, and all that. But... well... sorry for your condition, old boy. And... best of luck with your further nautical pursuits, yes?"

"Cheers, mate!" the broken yachtsman called out as Jackson turned on his heels and limped onwards.

***

On the journey back to the Claridge's Max, once again, found himself relegated to the front seat while Julia, Hugo and Jackson shared the infinitely more comfortable rear cabin. Jackson inspected his bruised, battered and bandaged face in a vanity mirror while Max, as Jackson had expected, berated him for almost the entire journey, on several counts.

Firstly, for crowning his usual reckless and irresponsible behaviour by heedlessly confronting the psychopathic musician. Who, Max informed him, thanks to a witness of good standing and reliability, would in all likelihood now be arrested and prosecuted – if not for his original crime then, almost certainly, for his attack on Jackson. Jackson then put forth the proposition that this, surely, made his courageous endeavour entirely worthwhile. Max and Julia, in unison, strongly disagreed, both with Jackson's characterisation of his actions and their worth.

Secondly, Max let loose about this ridiculous business of Jackson still living in one of the most expensive hotels in London, therefore on the planet, and, in no uncertain terms, informed him that it needed to stop.

Finally, Max rebuked him for not organising anything for their joint birthday which, Jackson knew full well, was an annual event they had enjoyed together for nearly three decades and, these days, the only time of the year when Max would allow himself to have any proper fun. He thought it particularly unfair that Jackson had not arranged even the most modest of parties for this year since, at least for Jackson, it was such a milestone.

For a fleeting moment, Jackson considered telling Max that, up until very recently, he'd planned for this year's birthday arrangements to be, for him, a strictly private affair. But, as he looked across Hugo to Julia, he decided that his revelations to Max would have to wait just a little bit longer. One confession in a day was quite enough. Instead, he apologised profusely and, begging Max's permission, suggested that he might spend a calming day with Julia followed by a quiet, candlelit dinner. He then suggested that Max might want to return home and, perhaps, share a similar experience with his wife and children.

"After all, old boy," Jackson concluded as the car came to rest outside Claridge's, "Don't you think it's time we both grew up?"

Max turned in his seat, leaned into the back and remonstratively replied, "Are you fucking joking?" He then insisted that the least Jackson could do was treat them all to birthday champagne in the Fumoir Bar and, without waiting for a response, exited the car to go on ahead – taking Hugo with him and, less than tactfully, allowing Jackson and Julia some time alone.

The couple sat in awkward silence for a few minutes until, finally, Julia gave a nervous, slightly mischievous smile.

"I suppose," she said, somewhat coyly, "It might be opportune for us to have that candlelit dinner up in your suite."

Jackson returned her smile and, putting his arm around her, replied, "I suppose it might."

They inched closer and, as they had done on the Blue Bridge, they kissed. Tenderly, softly and slowly. Until, as their embrace become closer, Jackson abruptly pulled back.

"Or," he exclaimed, "I might have a better idea."

Julia stared at him, her mouth agape, for at least thirty seconds. "To reiterate your fixer," she finally replied, "Are you fucking joking?"

"Three things I never joke about, Julia. Food, drink and Venice. Which is my idea. Let's go to Venice. Hear me out," Jackson shifted around to face her and Julia, utterly nonplussed, stared at him as he excitedly spieled, "It's, what, just past eleven o'clock, now. We go in, have a drink or two with Maxwell, maybe a spot of lunch. Then we swing by your place, pick up your passport. Unless you have it on you. Do you happen to have it on you?"

"No, Jackson. I do not happen to have my passport, or any other international travel documents, on me. It is at home. In my grown-up house. In a grown-up safe."

"Pity. I always carry mine, just in case."

"What a shocker."

"Still, it shouldn't take long. Then we get the afternoon flight to Marco Polo Airport, water taxi straight to the Gritti and, hey presto! We're sitting on our private balcony, looking over the lagoon at sunset, sipping Aperol Spritzes. Sounds good?"

Julia continued her stare, unblinking and still.

Jackson sensed an impending rejection and, with an air of capitulation, continued, "Well, I suppose–"

"Yes," Julia interrupted.

"What?" Jackson asked, slightly taken aback.

"Yes," she repeated with a bright smile, "It sounds wonderful."

Jackson sat back and gently replied, "It really does, doesn't it?"

Julia concurred with a Cheshire cat grin, nodding slowly and purposefully.

"Well. That's excellent, then," Jackson said, then he stiffened in his seat. "Of course," he looked past Julia, through the window and, in a lower pitch, added, "That does leave one minor obstacle."

"What would that be?" Julia asked.

Jackson stared at the facade of Claridge's and, with a heavy sense of trepidation, announced, "I am now going to have to go in there and pay the mother of all fucking hotel bills."

***

The first bottle of champagne they drank to toast Jackson's and Max's birthdays. The second bottle Jackson ordered in order to soften the blow from the impending bill and, more to the point, Max's expected reaction to said bill.

Max was as thrilled to hear that Jackson had decided to vacate the most expensive hotel in London as he was horrified at the news that he and Julia were going straight to the most expensive hotel in Venice. Jackson promised that it would only be for the weekend. Perhaps, a long weekend. It was only when Julia assured Max they'd be back on Monday since she, like most normal people, she had various commitments such as running a business and making a living, that Max returned to his usual calm and jovial demeanour.

The third bottle they consumed because they had time before the inevitable checkout.

George, with a look of pure joy, slapped the document onto the marble surface and gleefully declared, "Your bill, Mr Grimes."

"Thank you, George."

"Christ, that's thick," Max exclaimed.

"Indeed," Jackson agreed, removing a black credit card from his wallet and holding it up, "Now, you're sure this will work?"

"Jesus, Jackson, I bloody hope so. Otherwise you really are up the creek! You are going to have to go back to work. Soon. You do know that?"

"Maxwell, old boy, nothing would give me greater pleasure."

"Well, I'm afraid… What?"

"Well, I can't just loaf around for ever, can I?"

Max eyed Jackson with a touch of suspicion, then smiled

200

and said, "Okay. That's great. I'll make some calls, then."

"Please do. Anything in management. Consultancy. Even private events. But, for God's sake, nothing on television."

"I very much doubt that will be an option."

"I was once a television celebrity, you know," Jackson boasted to Julia, "In house mixologist, they called me." Then, as he looked down to sign the bill, he quietly added, "Well, for about six and a half minutes."

"Six minutes and eight seconds, to be precise," Julia cheerfully corrected, "I've seen the YouTube clip."

"Christ, that's not still up, is it?"

"Four and a half million hits and counting."

"I fucking hate the internet. Hang on." Jackson looked past Julia as Marco appeared with the wheelie-bag that he had arrived with and another, larger suitcase containing his recent purchases. "Marco, could you be a star and take those to the Maybach out front, please?"

"Come again?" Max interjected.

"You don't mind giving us a lift to the airport, do you? And, perhaps you could look after that larger case for a couple of days?"

"Christ, Jackson, you are a difficult sod."

"Only women are difficult, Max. Men are obstinate."

"And yet, here you stand managing to be both," Julia brightly offered.

"Okay. Come on, then. Let's get a move on." Max ushered them along and marched towards the exit.

As they stepped outside, Jackson broke away from Julia and, approaching Max, said, "Oh, I nearly forgot, old boy. We need to go by Julia's place to fetch her – Fuck!" Jackson directed the abrupt expletive at a seemingly overzealous pedestrian who had butted between him and Max, colliding into Jackson and almost knocking him over. "Oh, fuck," Jackson repeated, his voice softer. He grimaced at a sharp, fierce pain thrashing his abdomen.

"Jackson?" Max asked, looking back at him with mild

confusion, which melted into sheer horror.

"What the fuck?" Jackson winced, feeling the searing agony rapidly dissipate and give way to an icy chill. He looked down at a red patch on his white shirt. Spreading. Glistening. Dripping. Running fast through his fingers and over his hands as he pressed them into the warm, sodden centre. Suddenly weak, he dropped to his knees.

"Jackson!" Julia screamed. She and Max rushed to catch him as he slumped onto his back, grabbing his shoulders and softening his fall.

Jackson looked over at the person who had downed him. Through the straggly, lank hair he saw the cruel sneer and the hooded eyes of the bitter musician. One arm bandaged, splinted and strapped to his chest. The other hanging low with, Jackson couldn't help noticing, a first class, Japanese fillet knife dangling from its bony fingers. A long, curved blade of shining, tempered steel, drizzled with blood.

Jackson locked gazes with his attacker. The Violinist maintained a cold, remorseless glower. Jackson a horrified, frightened stare – but only for a moment. Until, as he realised what was happening, he offered the Violinist a hard, defiant smile.

"Jackson!" Julia shrieked, "Jackson, please!"

Jackson turned to Julia, her face now close to his. His smile morphed into one of warmth and tenderness.

"It's all right," Julia tried to assure him, while her voice quavered and tears ran from her good eye, "It'll be alright, Jackson. Max has called for help. Max has called for help."

Jackson gave a soft laugh. He looked up at Julia with eyes that were gentle, devoted and adoring as he mumbled, attempting to speak. Then he coughed and spluttered as blood made its way up his throat and filled his mouth. Warm, metallic and bitter. He saw bright, red spots spray and spatter onto Julia's face. He winced with frustration and tried to get out an apology but all he heard, all he felt, was more gurgling. More gagging. All he tasted was more iron.

"Jackson, please stay still," Julia sobbed.

Jackson struggled on. Desperately trying to speak. Julia held him up, just a few inches. Just enough so that, through his hacking, suffocating rasps, he managed to utter three words. Three words only Julia heard. Three, final words that only Julia would ever know.

Chapter 19

The minutes, hours and days following Jackson's murder were chaotic, gruelling and devastating.

Chaotic in the immediate aftermath when Julia, stricken with grief but fired with rage, saw the killer hiding in the crowd of onlookers and with a guttural, anguished scream flung herself at him. She pulled him to the ground. She wrapped her fingers tightly around his thin, sinewy neck and pressed both thumbs deep into his larynx. She pressed one knee into his chest and the other onto his damaged arm. Julia managed to crack his ribs, re-break his wrist and shatter his vocal cords before Max, Marco and George succeeded in pulling her away. George then sat upon the killer until the police arrived.

Gruelling in the hours that followed because of the waiting. Julia, with Jackson's blood on her face and his assassin's skin under her fingernails, waited to be interviewed, swabbed and released. Detained in the back of an ambulance with Max, they desperately tried to comfort each other while staring at Jackson's body. A still, lonely lump under a black, rubber sheet, also waiting for inspection. Waiting for the forensic specialist to poke around only to tell everybody what they already knew. Waiting for peace.

After the police finished their questioning and the ambulances had left, the coroner conveyed Jackson to his way station and Max finally took Julia home. There she cried in her brother's arms for hours. Then she wept alone in the bathroom, furiously washing her hands in scalding, almost boiling, water. Scrubbing the tips of her fingers and deep under the nails until they became raw, blistered and bloody. Making sure all trace of the assassin's skin was eradicated. Every last flake. Each remaining cell. Except the few scales that waited on the end of a cotton bud in a police laboratory.

She then ran a hot, steaming bath in which to soak, mourn, and cry some more, while staring into the mirror at her own scarred face. Naked but for the dark, red spots and streaks of Jackson's dried blood. Julia stretched out the night by, periodically, letting out the cooling water and refilling with hot. Until the glow of harsh, morning sunlight began to illuminate the frosted bathroom window and she could no longer put off her final act of cleansing. Julia took a damp cloth, looked back to the mirror and wiped from her face her last, sanguinary vestiges of Jackson Grimes.

Then she slept, in preparation for the days to follow.

***

Max took on the arduous task of arranging his friend's final journey. Although, as could only be expected, much of the ceremony and eulogising came from within the casket.

After leaving Julia at her home Max returned to his own abode, accompanied by Hugo and Jackson's luggage. Upon opening the larger of the suitcases he found an overstuffed, Claridge's emblazoned envelope with 'Max' scrawled across the front. Within he found the epistle Jackson had, while in various states of repair, been composing since his recent return, with the intention of leaving for Max before his originally planned grand exit. Max read about Jackson's family curse. His shame. His fears. His promises. His intentions. His eulogy.

My Dear Max,

I shall, in further pages, enlighten you as to the reasons behind my ultimate, selfish act and tell you of my sorrowful woes that, to date, I have shared with nobody. Not even you or Sandra for which, for what it's worth, I am truly sorry and now regret. My only defence is that I have always said that people should mind their own bloody business and that includes me.

For now, suffice it to say that the time has come for me to get my affairs in order and, as always, that means leaning on you. I'm sure you will look after me in death as well as you did in life. And sorry about that one, by the way. I'll get you back in the next round.

Truth be told, old boy, I can't say I'm too broken up about moving on. It's a dark, miserable world out there. The only ray of sunshine I've seen in recent years is, as I write this, lying in a hospital bed with, I'm guessing, a fractured skull or worse. Which reminds me, my first request for the service: no fucking violins.

As far as the eulogy bit goes, I know you'll just rattle on forever if left to your own devices, so just say this. Jackson Grimes was born...

***

"...Christopher Jackson Grimes, exactly fifty years prior to the day he died. He arrived in the wee hours of a Sunday morning, just to start off life by being an inconvenient pain in everybody's arse. A path he would pursue with vehement zeal for the next five decades.

"A disaster of a man, a failure of a husband, a catastrophe in general, his only saving grace was that he could stir a damn fine Martini, mix a half decent Bloody Mary, and could sell either to even the most temperate of souls. Which, of course, is another way of saying he drove everybody he ever met to drink.

"He leaves behind as little as he could, aside from some first class cocktail recipes and a generous bar float for some vintage champagne which, assuming the man reading this has done his usual bang up job, shall be waiting for all in attendance once the grim formalities have been completed.

"Adieu, bon voyage and, please, charge your glasses and raise them high for the deceased."

Max folded the pages, a sensibly redacted version of Jackson's original, more vibrant words, into his breast pocket. He descended the podium and stepped aside, watching the pall-bearers push Jackson's casket, a dark, solid oak affair with ostentatious brass fittings, up the centre of the aisle.

The turnout was, Max thought, quite impressive. Although probably not enough to satisfy Jackson who, as stated in his unredacted testament, would not have been satisfied with anything less than a state funeral complete with a Red Arrows fly past and forty gun salute.

The first heads to bow towards Jackson, at the back of the chapel, were those of George, Frankie and Marco. Along with a few other faces who Jackson had come to know, and who had come to know Jackson, over the last month. Including Dave, owner of the stall outside Gray's Antiques Centre and watcher of Hugo, and several Mayfair bartenders.

As the coffin moved through the centre of the chapel many of Jackson's former friends and colleagues, most of whom neither he nor Max had seen for years, also tipped their heads. Max scanned them with curiosity. Recognising several but not sure from where or when. Knowing, once they were outside in the Garden of Remembrance, sipping the vintage Veuve Clicquot and Dom Pérignon, he would have to bluff.

Finally, as it neared the curtains, the coffin passed the front row. Julia, with her brother and Dee for support, stood on one side. Sandra, struggling to hold Hugo down, was accompanied by Deborah, Max's glamorous and statuesque wife. Max attempted to stand neutral in the centre as the curtains opened, and Jackson was delivered into the flames of the crematorium.

Once outside, and having spent the required amount of time thanking strangers and long-lost friends for their presence, Max moved to speak with Julia. As he approached, he passed and greeted a tall, elegant man donning a snugly tailored suit and sporting a perfectly groomed, snow white beard. Julia watched and felt a momentary chill. Then Max glanced across to her and they shared a brief, stifled smile. Both remembering Jackson's unabashed hilarity when, over his and Max's impromptu birthday drinks, he told them the good doctor's name – although, at the time, Max was unaware of the context.

Max finally reached Julia and complemented her on the fashion in which she had chosen to affix Jackson's silk eyepatch. A thick, black ribbon, excessively long with a large, looped bow at the back. He then regaled Julia with the tale of how he and Jackson had met. That infamous Circle Line party when the rich-kid, Brooklyn-boy bartender met the dirt poor, grammar school Croydon chap and the seeds of a lifelong partnership, friendship and brotherhood were sown.

While they laughed, a commotion from the other side of the garden erupted with Sandra shouting, "Hugo, NO!"

Both turned to see that Hugo was charging across the garden. Bounding towards Julia.

"Oh, no you don't," Julia exclaimed, "Not this time!" She dropped to one knee, threw out her hands and, instead of falling back, caught him in her arms and swung him around. "Hugo, you big oafish menace!" she cheerily cried, "When are you going to learn some bloody manners?" She gave him a firm pat and a tight hug. He reciprocated with a large, wet lick.

While the two embraced, Julia looked up and saw Sandra, clutching an urn, strolling towards them. Julia stood as she arrived and for a long, silent moment, the two looked each other up and down. Max watched and, awkwardly, guzzled down his champagne – then craftily swiped another from a passing waiter.

Julia offered Sandra a small, reticent smile. Sandra returned a guarded, polite nod, then looked down at Hugo. The dog now sat comfortably and calmly at Julia's feet.

"I suspect he'd rather be with you, now. If you'll have him," Sandra finally said.

Julia looked down at Hugo who, as if understanding Sandra's words, looked back up with pleading, soppy eyes. Julia returned her focus to Sandra and was about to reply when Sandra handed her the lead.

"Lovely as he is," Sandra continued, "I was never that well suited to him." She looked back down at Hugo and dolefully smiled. Then she returned her attention to Julia and, with a warm timbre and a hint of acceptance, added, "Either of them, really." With that she plonked the urn into Julia's arms, turned on her heels and crossed the garden to rejoin Deborah.

As Julia, momentarily stunned, watched Sandra walk away, Max leaned in and asked, "What are you going to do with him?"

"What?" Julia asked, snapping her attention back to Max. "Oh," she smiled down at her new charge and firmly replied, "Well, I suppose the first thing will have to be to stop him knocking people over and pissing in their shoes." Both laughed and Hugo gave a single, whooping bark.

"Actually, I meant him," Max wistfully clarified, gesturing towards the urn.

"Ah, him," Julia replied, looking down at the aluminium urn in her hands, "I don't know."

The urn was simple with an unpolished, matt finish. *Uninspired and inappropriately dull*, Julia thought, *clearly the one thing Jackson had overlooked to mention in his instructions.*

Julia pondered for a further moment before, with a crooked, mischievous smile, looking back to Max and saying, "Something with a bit of panache."

Epilogue

Julia delicately ran her fingertips down a long, curved strip of metal – half an inch wide, gunmetal grey and polished to a lustrous sheen. She inspected it, as she had already inspected several of its counterparts, with care and scrutiny. After a few more minutes, on another such strip, she found her treasure. Three words, laser etched into the surface. *Christopher Jackson Grimes.*

Jackson's name was one of ten on the swathe, which looped back to the centre of the piece. There it joined thirty-six more similar, but not identical, bands. They all met at the mid-point of a stand which held a massive, perfectly symmetrical hourglass in which the ashes of Jackson, along with three hundred and sixty-four others, merged and mingled. They had been sharing the space for a little under six months so half of the ashes were resting in the lower bulb while the other half, less those that were falling, waited above to join them.

Julia wondering how much of Jackson had arrived, how much was waiting to descend and how much, if any of him, was in transit. Cascading, as she watched, through the tiny, mid-point aperture.

She stepped back from the piece: Mitchell Mitchelson's second such endeavour, confusingly titled *Three Sixty-Five, Two*. This version had been firmly bolted to a concrete block at sea level. The sea in question was the Adriatic. The sculpture stood under a purpose built shelter in the Giardini della Biennale.

Julia spent a few meditative minutes studying the work, watching the ashes gently fall while reminiscing on that fateful month she had spent getting to know Jackson Grimes, as well as anybody could get to know Jackson Grimes, a little over one and a half years before. She felt a sudden chill and shivered as an icy March breeze caught her neck and she tightened the ornately printed pashmina she had acquired before leaving London. Pure white silk emblazoned with red roses on green, thorny branches. All chaotically entwined around each other. Not a match but a suitable companion for the silk eyepatch – today fastened with a dark green ribbon.

The wind bit again and she felt a light, purposeful knocking at her knee, accompanied by an impatient whine. She looked down and Hugo, doe-eyed and restless, met her gaze.

"Oh, all right then, you big lummox," she huffed, shaking her head. Hugo hopped to his feet and let out a subdued woof of excited approval. Julia picked up a light, canvas holdall, casually slung it across her shoulder and, with a confident bounce in both of their strides, the duo made their way out of the garden, turned up the shoreline and marched towards San Marco Square.

As they skipped along, Julia fitfully scanned the Venetian lagoon. Growling water busses and wailing motorboats of all types and sizes chaotically sliced the choppy, deep blue water as they raced around each other. From small, wooden pleasure craft to hardy, bruised and dented working vessels. One of which, Julia wryly noted, was branded as a Domino's Pizza Delivery boat.

They made their way along the water's edge and Julia fleetingly eyed the famous landmarks, knowing she'd have plenty of time to take it all in later, as she reflected on the last eighteen months. Her burgeoning friendship with Max who had become, as he had been to Jackson, her confidant, ally and, when needed, fixer. Most notably when she and Julian were finally faced the death of their mother followed by the inevitable commandeering of the family home. An ordeal throughout which Max helped her retain her business and at least a token of their capital. She thought of how Max then embraced her brother with such kindness, becoming a mentor of sorts. Even convincing Julian to step up and temporarily look after Julia's business for the next twelve months while she set out on what she had decided to call her 'two decades overdue gap year'.

Approaching San Marco's Square, Julia began to take more notice of the surroundings. The Doge's Palace, the dungeon's of which she planned to visit to see if she could find the graffiti Jackson noted in the first edition of Jan Morris's *Venice* he had gifted her.

May God protect me from the man I trust, I shall protect myself from the man I do not.

Passing the gondolas, stepping over obstinate pigeons and splashing through the remnants of a high-tide flood, Julia made her way through the square. She flashed a look at the ornate Cafe Florian, where she looked forward to spending her mornings taking the strongest coffee they could possibly prepare.

Through the square, she glanced down a side street, at the end of which she knew Harry's Bar to be located. Home of the Bellini – although Jackson, never a fan of the sweet, maintained that their Bullshots were equally iconic.

"They use chicken consume instead of beef, you see," Jackson had expounded during that final, impromptu celebration with Max in the Fumoir Bar, "Which, of course, means that rather than a Bullshot, it should really be called a–"

"Don't say it!" Max firmly interrupted. Acutely aware, as they launched into a third bottle of Dom Pérignon, that Jackson had started to perform for the entire bar – including a wide-eyed honeymoon couple from Vermont.

Julia grinned at the memory, flashing another glance down the street and wondering if they'd allow Hugo in so that he could sample their equally famous beef carpaccio.

A little further on they turned a corner back towards the water's edge and approached their destination: the Gritti Palace. Once home for a medieval Doge and still fit for any king. With neither of them breaking pace, Julia and Hugo marched through grandiose doors and into the opulent lobby. High ceilings and polished marble floors punctuated with bright Persian rugs. The strong scent of beeswax furniture polish wafted from a variety of antique desks, cabinets and tables.

With long, purposeful strides, Julia approached the front desk, behind which stood an impeccably liveried, stiffly postured concierge, whose stern face already showed signs of five o'clock shadow at barely a little after noon. Both came to a halt and Hugo, obediently, sat at Julia's heel.

Julia casually allowed her bag to drop to the floor, leaned against the desk and, regarding the increasingly apprehensive concierge with a wry, crooked smile, breezily announced, "We're checking in."

Lightning Source UK Ltd.
Milton Keynes UK
UKHW011807240120
357574UK00002B/76

9 781789 556926